Th
la
p

●

﹀

Cath Weeks has been writing since she was a child, and won a national writing competition aged nineteen which spurred her on. She lives in Bath with her husband and two sons. *Blind* is her first novel.

BLIND

Twyla Ridley — resourceful, optimistic — has just had her first child. It's what she and her husband, Dylan, have always wished for. However, Charlie is blind. For the first time in her adult life, Twyla feels truly tested. She cherishes her son, showering him with love and boundless affection — but there's a part of her that aches for him to see. So Twyla throws herself into motherhood with a very private agenda, because maybe, if she strives hard enough, she'll be able to find a way to fix him. But is it a risk worth taking?

CATH WEEKS

BLIND

CHARNWOOD
Leicester

First published in Great Britain in 2016 by
Piatkus
An imprint of Little, Brown Book Group
London

First Charnwood Edition
published 2017
by arrangement with
Little, Brown Book Group
London

A catalogue record for this book is available
from the British Library.

ISBN 978–1–4448–3181–8

Published by
F. A. Thorpe (Publishing)
Anstey, Leicestershire
Set by Words & Graphics Ltd.
Anstey, Leicestershire
Printed and bound in Great Britain by
T. J. International Ltd., Padstow, Cornwall

This book is printed on acid-free paper

For Mum

Love looks not with the eyes, but with the
    mind,
And therefore is a winged Cupid painted
    blind.

William Shakespeare

Prologue

How to describe a mother's devotion to her child?

Some would speak of unconditional love. Others might reach for words such as overbearing, neurotic.

Few could describe it accurately. For however that love presented itself from day to day, whether through nagging or nonchalance, tears or hysteria, that wasn't the half of it.

The other half was deep within — a vast, unmined energy.

Sometimes it rose when a child veered too close to a road. But ordinarily it lay dormant, lurking.

It was why nails were chewed, corks were popped, cupboards reorganised, hoovers activated at dawn, hours of sleep lost never to be found again.

Men didn't entirely understand it; nor did children. Even the mother was unhinged by it, unaware of its strength. The only way to fully appreciate it was to lay it out on the table for everyone to see — to wear it permanently on the outside, like an armadillo's armour. Yet who could live like that?

Twyla wouldn't recommend it.

Once unearthed, her maternal feelings hadn't spurted upwards with the *hallelujah!* of striking oil, but had glugged fatefully like an oil spill, prompting universal condemnation.

Yet how to explain all this to the man from the *Daily Herald* who was waiting for her to speak into his handheld recording device?

'Perhaps you could start by telling me how you felt at the beginning, Twyla,' he said.

She smiled.

In some ways, it was easier then, she told him. They were naive, finding things out for the first time.

'Hindsight's a wonderful thing, eh?' he said.

'Perhaps not.' She shook her head. 'Knowing what was going to happen would probably have made it worse.'

She shivered suddenly. It was a cold afternoon. Beyond the window, the sun was pale and transparent, like rice paper.

'Does that mean that you wouldn't do it all again, Twyla? I'm sure everyone's curious to know the answer.'

She opened her mouth to reply. He sat forward, pushing the recording device closer to her.

As she spoke, she imagined thousands of *Herald* readers drawing near, holding their breath, the air growing brittle with suspense.

1

The moment Twyla looked into her baby's eyes, she feared something was wrong.

Her newborn was lying in her arms, his body inert yet purring with potential. His arrival heralded an awakening, an addition in the grandest sense that both thrilled and daunted her.

She tucked the blanket delicately underneath her baby's chin. The midwives had asked whether she wanted him delivered on to her chest or cleaned first. It felt like a test. They turned to look at her and she had hesitated, seeing in an instant that in this new world her decisions would be weighed and judged. Was she a natural mother who would accept her baby howsoever he came to her?

She couldn't have known the importance of this question, how important this question would become. Yet still she stumbled over it.

'Could you clean him, please?' she asked in a voice that was thin in confidence.

And now he was in her arms, encased in waffle blankets, his skin shrivelled from having sojourned in fluid for so long, and yet so pure and soft.

'He's perfect,' Dylan said.

Dylan hadn't stopped crying yet — silent, bold tears that it pleased her to see. How lucky she was that her husband was here, that he was of a generation of men that wanted to witness their children's births.

'He's going to be a heartbreaker,' the midwife said. 'And wise . . . This one's been here before.'

So many contradictions. Wise, yet newborn. Wrinkled, yet smooth. Tears, yet joy. Ecstasy, yet fear.

What was that fear?

Was there something wrong with their baby?

Twyla glanced at the midwife to see if she looked concerned, but she had joined her colleagues at the sink where they were snapping off rubber gloves, slamming pedal bins, chatting. It was the first birth in the hospital on Christmas Day and the air was light with the triumph of an easy delivery.

The whole thing had taken only twenty minutes — twenty spine-breakingly painful minutes. Twyla's snow-capped boots were still by the bed where she had kicked them off.

It had been such a panicky rush. One minute they were turning out the bedside lamp, next they were circling the hallway looking for car keys. They hadn't even unzipped her hospital bag or used its contents. Had she really imagined that she would give birth accompanied by harp music, Dylan spraying her brow with cooling mist?

She turned to look out the window, suddenly conscious of life beyond. It was a white Christmas, although the world outside was black at ten past midnight. Somewhere down the corridor 'Fairytale of New York' was playing.

It was Christmas Day.

The notion hit her. It was Christmas and she was a mum.

She wanted to cry uncontrollably. And at that moment she wanted her mother more than she could ever remember having wanted her before.

But her mother wasn't here, couldn't be here, and Twyla couldn't cry — not in front of everyone.

She touched her son's cheek gently. He was the priority, not her. And it was this adjustment, she realised, that was the hardest one of all: the pushing away of the self in surrender to another, breaking the habit of thirty-four years in doing so.

Her attention was drawn to her aching body. She shifted position, trying to get comfortable on the hard surface of the delivery bed. She didn't want to look below to see what was happening south of her hips, but it felt to be burning and numb at once. There had been a tear — a tiny rip that the midwives had stitched up with the cheerfulness and deftness of mending a quilt.

'Would you like to have a go at feeding?' the midwife asked. Her tender tone was enough to make Twyla want to cry again, to picture her mother stood there instead with her summer-leaf green eyes.

'OK . . . ' Twyla said, timorously.

'You'll be fine,' the midwife said, motioning for Twyla to unbutton her nightshirt. 'I'll help you.'

'Thank you,' Twyla said, feeling her shoulders drop in submission.

'Now, if you'll excuse me . . . ' the midwife

said. She was fiddling with Twyla's breast, pushing it towards the baby's mouth. But he wasn't interested. 'Hmmm. Not hungry,' she declared.

'Oh,' said Twyla. 'Is that normal?'

'Absolutely.' The midwife smiled. 'We'll try again in a minute.'

Dylan returned and crouched before Twyla, his hand on her knee. 'There's a bath through there,' he said. 'Would you like me to run you one?'

She reached forward to touch a tear on his cheek that had got stuck, like a congealed blob of paint on an easel. It dispersed immediately, that drop of salty euphoria.

They were interrupted by a knock on the door. A tall man in a leather jacket was stood in the doorway, looking apologetic. '*Daily Herald*,' he said. 'Mind if I take a quick snap? The *Herald* always runs a piece on the first baby born on Christmas Day.'

'Gosh,' Twyla said. 'What do you think, Dylan?'

Neither of them looked camera-worthy, yet it hadn't occurred to her that their son would be a feature, that he might be singled out. She rather liked the idea. Dylan seemed to too. He nodded his consent.

They sat together on the bed, starchily, fatigued. Twyla tried to smile, but the anaesthetic was wearing off and her stitches were starting to smite.

'Lovely,' the photographer said, as the lens flashed. 'Just one more . . . Great . . . Thanks very much . . . So what's the little lad's name?'

Twyla and Dylan looked at each other blankly.

They had argued about names on the car ride over, wheels spinning on the snow in the race to not give birth in their old Honda. Dylan disliked the idea of two first names for a boy. She had to explain again about how it was in keeping with tradition in Louisiana. 'Louisiana?' Dylan had said, as a lump of snow landed on the windscreen. 'We live in Bath!'

He nudged her now. 'Go on then,' he said.

'Are you sure?' she said, searching his face for unspoken truths. She didn't want this to be something that he might resent at a later date.

'Go for it,' he said.

She blushed with pleasure. 'Thank you,' she said.

She turned to the photographer. 'Charlie Ross,' she told him. 'No hyphen.'

Those who saw the front page of the *Herald* the next day would be struck by the image of the attractive couple showing off their perfect Christmas baby.

No one would have guessed what Twyla was thinking. They couldn't see the fear that was taking root inside her, its secrecy being the very thing that would cause it to expand. For there was no fertiliser or plant food in the world that could promote growth like unaired anxiety.

★　★　★

The maternity ward was hot and noisy. Christmas meant nothing to Mother Nature.

Babies were arriving in cots on wheels and leaving with dark-eyed parents, as the hospital wheel turned and processed them.

Twyla was watching Charlie who was asleep, his chest shifting rapidly. He still wasn't interested in feeding, but the midwife said that it was normal and that she should try to relax.

There was a young mum in the bed opposite watching television, a tube of Pringles on her chest. Twyla eyed her curiously, coveting her blasé manner. For Twyla in contrast was exhausted, in pain and only just realising what it meant to lack family.

Family was everywhere on the ward — a flow of coats that appeared with crystal snow drops on shoulders and helium balloons on strings.

Wow, he looks just like Uncle Dave . . . Oh, bless, she's got curls like Angie, look . . .

Twyla listened to the conversations around her with a growing sense of loneliness and isolation. It would have been nice to have someone here to tell them that Charlie's hair was from his grandfather in Louisiana or his great-aunt in Basingstoke. Which was why she had sent Dylan out into the corridor to call his mother again. But Eileen was at church for Christmas Mass and wasn't answering her phone. She wouldn't make it in time to visit them on the ward.

Her own mother would have run barefoot over snakes to get here.

She gazed at her mobile phone. There was one other relative she could call — *should* call. Yet her father didn't even know she was expecting a baby.

She was too tired to execute the conversation well. She would say something stupid and make things worse.

'Knock knock.' A paediatrician wearing a Santa hat pretended to knock on her cubicle curtain. 'Just here for baby's check-up,' he said. 'Any concerns?' He began to unbutton Charlie's Babygro.

'Well . . . ' she said, the fear beginning to stir and rise within her. 'There is this one thing . . . '

'Hmm?' he said, cycling Charlie's legs.

'It's his eyes,' she said. 'I'm not sure about the colour.'

'Oh, right?' he said. He woke Charlie, picked him up and held his finger out in front of Charlie, who began to cry.

Twyla felt a twist of guilt at the sound — for waking him, doubting him.

'Don't worry,' the doctor said, laying Charlie back into the cot. 'He's perfect.' He turned away. 'Happy Christmas!' he added.

★   ★   ★

Perfect.

What did that mean exactly?

The paediatrician said Charlie was perfect. Dylan said so too, and the midwives. And now they were back home and Dylan's mum and sister had just held Charlie for the first time and declared him perfect too.

Everyone was using the word 'perfect' because they thought it was what Twyla and Dylan most wanted to hear.

Not so long ago — some seventy years before — the priority during childbirth would have been survival. It was literally a matter of life and death. Yet now the focus was slightly different. Few expectant parents wondered what would happen if the mother or child died; most speculated about what they would do if there was something wrong with their baby.

Twyla gazed at Charlie as he lay in her arms, feeding on formula milk from a bottle. His dark hair lay in spikes on his forehead. His nose was speckled with white dots that were accentuated when he wrinkled his nose to feed. He made a clicking noise at the back of his throat as he sucked, a sound that she found enchanting and rhythmic. She drew closer to inhale his intoxicating aroma of sugary milk. There was nothing like that scent, nothing that any baby manual could describe.

Click, click, click.

Charlie's gulps were the only sound in the lounge, save for the buffeting of the gas fire. The tinsel was fluttering gently above the mantel-piece. It was Christmas Day evening. They hadn't opened their gifts yet, which were sat unattended under the tree, like neglected guests.

She could hear Dylan outside in the street seeing his mother and sister off, their voices muffled by the snowfall; car doors closing.

And then all was still.

She yawned. Charlie was still refusing to breastfeed. The midwife was coming to help them tomorrow and in the meantime she was to keep trying.

It was disheartening. Everyone knew that *breast was best*. But for those mothers who couldn't breastfeed, this high bar was just something else to fall short of.

From the moment they had tried for a baby, Twyla was aware of the emphasis on doing things the right way. Increasing zinc levels might improve sperm quality; eating fish could result in a healthier newborn; Mozart played to the foetus could render it more intelligent; hearing parents' voices in the womb improved the bonding process.

A rational person knew how to pick and choose advice, knew when to close the book and go to bed.

Yet if disaster could be averted, if there were preventative measures, solutions and know-hows, where did the blame fall when things did go wrong?

Charlie had finished his bottle. She propped him on her shoulder, rubbing his back. Close to her like this, she felt as though they were one. 'I love you,' she said to him for the first time.

It felt wonderful. He gurgled as if in response.

Dear sweet Charlie Ross. Such a tiny being, yet an enormous part of her life now.

She held him before her to smile at him. He blinked back at her.

The fear rose so quickly that it tightened her throat.

His eyes were cloudy blue, and utterly blank.

* * *

On day four, Twyla's milk arrived. One of her friends had warned her about it.

11

She rose furtively that morning, tiptoeing around the bedroom lest the bogeyman was activated by movement and would spring out from hiding and attack her.

Instead, it caught her out by surprise at breakfast.

She was just putting Charlie down to nap in his Moses basket, when she felt overwhelmed by misery. It gripped her so hard that she began to cry. Her shirt was unbuttoned where she had been trying to feed Charlie again, her breast hanging there redundantly, and the sight of it made her cry even more.

Dylan came hurrying into the room, a bottle in one hand, a dripping washing-up sponge in the other. 'What's going on?' he said, staring at her with worry, and some alarm, she noted.

Had she ever cried in front of him — whopping unrestricted tears? Probably not. Why not? What was wrong with her?

'Ohwww,' she moaned. 'I'm a wreck. A big fat failure . . . I can't even . . . feed my son . . . Ohwww.'

Dylan wasn't looking at her any more. He was looking at her breasts, both of which were now hanging loose.

'My God,' he said. 'They're enormous! When did they get like that?' Dylan gazed at Charlie as though he were somehow responsible, but Charlie was fast asleep after his long feed.

She glanced down at herself. Dylan was right. Her breasts were gigantic and burning hot. Her milk was in.

The realisation halted her tears, as logic ruled.

There was a reason for this. It was what her friend had warned her about. But then she remembered that Charlie still wouldn't latch on, so the health visitor was bringing her an expressing machine today to milk her like a cow, and she began to cry again.

'Come here,' said Dylan, pulling her towards him. 'It's all right.'

He held her for what felt like a long time, but it probably wasn't. The clock hand didn't appear to have moved, was as stuck and hopeless and out of its depth as she was.

She stopped crying and gazed out the window at the grey sky, drawing her shirt around her in a belated bid for modesty.

It had been snowing continually. The thick layer of snow only added to the sense of heaviness and yet it was soothing at the same time, fitting in nicely with the ocean of white baby garments that had flooded their home. White for births, christenings and weddings. After that nothing was apparently pure any more and the tradition faded, becoming greyer and darker, until arriving at black for funerals.

Now there was a nice thought for a winter's day. She sighed forlornly.

The health visitor had somehow made it through the snow to see them yesterday. She listened earnestly to Twyla's concerns about Charlie's eyes and had promised to refer them urgently to a specialist. When she asked Dylan whether he shared Twyla's worries, he wholeheartedly agreed, even though he said later in private that he wasn't one hundred per cent sure what Twyla meant.

13

Yet the deed was done and Twyla's fear had sunk back down to the pit of her stomach, temporarily appeased.

'You're exhausted,' said Dylan. 'Why don't you take a nap?'

'But the health visitor's — '

'I'll wake you,' he said.

He kissed her — a brief hot-lipped kiss. He looked tired too and there were milk stains on his shirt. Yet he smelled so good. Even though they had no time to wash or preen, he still smelled good.

'What would I do without you?' she said, beginning to cry again.

'Nothing,' he said. 'Because that'll never happen.'

★ ★ ★

He meant it. He would never leave Twyla, and now he had another person in his life never to leave: Charlie, who was slumbering in the Moses basket while Dylan washed up breakfast.

He had just checked on Twyla to see whether she was actually in bed and not folding laundry or cleaning the bathroom. She had a tremendous amount of energy, but right now she needed to rest.

He was pleased to see that she was lying on the bed. He made her get under the covers and drew the curtains. 'I don't want to see you for at least two hours,' he told her. And now everything was quiet up there.

Seeing her like that earlier — sobbing,

vulnerable — had made him feel oddly powerful. Not because he was a sadist, but because it brought out the protector in him. Since there were no beasts to slay or even much bacon to bring home in the dawn of feminism, there were few opportunities to fend for one's family. Yet now his time had come. He took the charge readily, determined to be good at it. He would look after his wife and child, no matter how crumbly he might be feeling.

And he was feeling pretty crumbly. He had done a double-take at himself in the mirror this morning. Was that really him — that black-eyed apparition? But he had glimpsed something else there too: excitement and pride, the two emotions he had felt constantly since Charlie's arrival.

He still couldn't get over it — that they had made such a perfect boy; a human being who breathed and sucked, and filled nappies. OK, so it wasn't much as of yet . . . but it would be.

He had been holding a soapy plate for a minute or so, caught in a reverie. He put the plate down and thought again of Twyla's emotional outburst.

He hadn't just felt powerful, but a bit scared too. Why was that?

He paused again, a mug dripping in his hand.

Because he hadn't ever seen her break down like that before.

It was her hormones. He would watch her carefully, would get her through this. He wasn't very good with women's stuff though. It was a shame that she didn't have any female relatives.

Yet she had lots of friends. People like Twyla always did. There was a vitality about her that others found enticing, himself included.

Her positivity was the first thing he had noticed about her, aside from her green eyes that reminded him of carbonated water. She was light of touch and loved to laugh. She wasn't a classic beauty — was too freckly for that and her smile a little wonky, yet no one noticed because her warmth smoothed it all out, like an iron on a crease.

It was that warmth and energy that charged him. They had been married for four years and almost every day he woke up next to her feeling electric with hope.

So her outburst had wobbled him slightly. But it was just that: a wobble, nothing more.

He finished the dishes. And then bent down to look at his son.

He wasn't sure what Twyla meant about Charlie's eyes. They looked fine to him. The health visitor said that eye conditions were rare, but that Twyla had a right to seek opinion if it was worrying her. Besides, if there was something amiss it was better to know now than later. Not that there would be anything wrong.

'Because you're perfect, aren't you, my little friend?' he said.

He placed his hand on Charlie's, noting how oversized and hairy his limbs looked by comparison, how one day Charlie's hand would be the same size as his.

He glowed with pride. His very own boy.

Lying on his side, Charlie looked just like

himself: dark-haired, sharp cheekboned. But if he was lucky, he would have his mother's ace of hearts: her optimism.

'Yep, you're about as perfect as can be,' he said, leaning forward to kiss the tip of Charlie's nose.

★   ★   ★

It was so hot in the waiting room. Her stomach flipped queasily. She reached for Dylan, who squeezed her hand reassuringly, but his leg was bouncing up and down. 'Is it me,' she said, 'or is it boiling in here?'

'It's you,' Dylan said with a smile.

She leant forward to ease the blanket away from Charlie's mouth. He was asleep in his pram, blowing milky bubbles on his lips. At nineteen days old, he was officially a formula milk kid. She hadn't managed to breastfeed him, yet it didn't feel so important now. And in this she had learnt an invaluable lesson: that nothing in parenting stayed the same for long. They were now tackling flaky scalp and colic.

She looked about the waiting room. There was an energy hanging in the air that was jaded at best. The walls were toilet-gel blue and adorned with posters about disability helplines. *Feeling alone? Don't know which way to turn?*

There was one other family in the room, a couple with a teenage boy who was blinking constantly. Every now and then the boy rubbed his eyes and his mum pulled his hand away from his face, evidently having done this so many times she could continue to read a magazine whilst doing so.

A door opened and a young woman appeared. 'Charlie Ross Ridley?' she called.

'Here,' Twyla said.

'I'm a student,' the woman said. 'I'll be observing your consultation today.'

'That's fine,' said Twyla, who felt that she would have agreed to anything.

Dylan pushed Charlie's pram into the consulting room. They sat down, Twyla trying to still her trembling hands.

The consultant was sat at a counter reading paperwork.

'So you're worried about the appearance of your baby's eyes,' he said, matter-of-factly, swivelling round to address them.

'Yes,' Twyla said.

The consultant extracted Charlie from the pram. Charlie woke and began to fidget, but he wasn't much of a crier and, when he realised that it wasn't Twyla holding him, he moved his head from side to side as though his neck itched.

A silence fell over the room, a silence that seemed to expand and smother them, making her ears pound and her hands perspire.

The consultant was shining a torch into Charlie's eyes. Twyla reached for Dylan's hand and found that his skin was equally as damp. He smiled and winked at her.

Just as the silence drew to deafening levels, the consultant brought Charlie back to her, handing him over without a word.

She held Charlie, suspecting that he could feel

her heart beating through his cardigan. There were beads of sweat on Charlie's nose. The whole family was overheating.

The consultant was writing something down, as though they weren't there in the room — waiting for his verdict, his reassurance.

When Twyla could bear it no longer, he turned to face them.

'You did the right thing,' he said. 'Serious eye conditions are very rare and unexpected. Not everyone would have picked up on it.' He gave a taut smile. 'You have good instincts.'

The student shifted in her seat behind them. Twyla gave a little jump, having forgotten there was anyone else in the room. The jolt made Charlie whimper. 'Hush, sweetheart,' she whispered, jigging him. 'It's all right.'

'A newborn's eyesight is fuzzy at best. It's early days and the eye is a complicated organ. There are a myriad of possible diagnoses and variables. But . . . ' He took off his glasses. 'I've been doing this job for a long time.' He squeezed the top of his nose, before replacing his glasses again.

Twyla was watching his mouth, following the movement, the formation of the words as though struggling to hear him.

Dylan heard the words much sooner. She could tell by the way he was hanging his head in devastation.

She felt faint. Suddenly the heat in the room was unbearable.

The consultant was talking about consultations and testing and a comprehensive healthcare programme and specialists and treatments.

She wasn't listening to what he was saying. She was staring at his lips, wondering when they were going to stop moving, when she could go home — whether it was too late to start again.

She wanted to start again. She wanted to put a stop to whatever she had started and go back to their old life. But the new life was forcing its way forward with startling speed, declaring its ugly self.

She wanted to hold her hands up, to stop the words. But it was too late. They had reached her and now she knew.

I'm terribly sorry to tell you this . . . but your son is blind.

2

The morning after the diagnosis Twyla woke up happy, as she had done almost every day of her life, and then suddenly her heart plummeted with force, like a broken lift, as reality dawned: the shocking news, the consultant's words.

This used to happen as a teenager in love, she recalled. She would wake happy, only to remember that she had just been dumped. Life had evened out since then, had become less tempestuous and she hadn't experienced that sensation for a long time. But now it was back — the instability, the storms — and she wondered whether it would be thus when she woke up forever more.

Charlie was blind.

She stared at the ceiling, feeling her throat swell with sorrow.

Dylan was still asleep. She didn't want to wake him, lest he should experience the same thing as her. Maybe he was having a nice dream. Maybe he was on a boat in the Caribbean, or walking through a forest, the sunshine streaming on to his shoulders.

She stepped into her slippers and moved noiselessly round to Charlie's Moses basket that was in the middle of his cot for security. She sat down on the carpet with her hands on the cot rails and watched Charlie sleeping.

Oh, Charlie. How could he be blind? It wasn't

right. It wasn't fair.

Why him? Why them?

Yet it had to be somebody. The consultant had told them as much. He said it was shocking and a million-to-one tragedy, yet whilst it was tempting to think *why Charlie?* that they might look at it differently: *why* not *Charlie?*

The consultant had been kind, compassionate. He sat with them for a long while, giving them lots of information that she wasn't able to absorb. Dylan scribbled some things down on the back of a throat cancer pamphlet that he grabbed from a display stand.

Cloudy corneas.
Both of them.
Anterior segment development disorder.
Rare.

He underlined this last word.

What the consultant said about *why not Charlie* was one of the few things he said that she remembered. In a funny way it had helped. If it had to be someone, in a line-up of a million bonny babies, would she really beg them to single out another child in place of Charlie?

It had to be someone. And Charlie it was.

But oh . . . Charlie.

He looked so peaceful in his white sleepsuit, so ignorant of the fate awaiting him. Yet what was that fate precisely? She had no idea.

All she could do was live that morning through and start again that afternoon. She was too tired to do otherwise. It was all about colic and feeding and dry scalps and bath time. How could she cope with adding anything else to the mix?

She thought of the first time she bathed Charlie at home. She had lowered Charlie into the tub with trepidation, in awe of his miniature downy limbs, frightened of breaking him, of how he might react to the water. Yet he hadn't reacted, aside from poking out his tongue. Even so, she was relieved to bundle him into a towel and get him on to dry land again.

Was that part of his condition? Was his lack of vision what made him slow to react, less inclined to fuss or cry? Or would he have been placid anyway?

She didn't know.

She began to cry, sat there beside Charlie's cot in the early morning light.

Everything felt like a terrible waste, a sick joke; everything from the misguided hopes of pregnancy down to her son's very name.

When she had chosen 'Charlie Ross', she hadn't pictured a blind boy. She had named him after the hearty boys of Louisiana whom she had played with as a child — boys like Tommy Joe and Lee James who swung from tyres and fired catapults. Charlie Ross was supposed to have a shock of hair, a lizard on his palm and marbles in his pockets.

He wasn't supposed to be . . . blind.

The pain grew too large to contain in neat tears. She might well have screamed had it not been for her sleeping child. Instead, she rocked and moaned, gulping in air, certain that her heart was going to swell and burst.

But then Dylan slipped his arms around her waist from behind, his head nestled into her neck.

He was crying too, one of his tears trickling down the inside of her nightshirt.

Neither of them spoke. There were no words for this. *Why not Charlie?* didn't cut it. There was no consolation, no magic way of looking at it, no optimism big enough to counteract the grief.

It was right there in front of them, within their sleeping baby. He contained it within him — the problem that was going to become the biggest part of their day, that would skittle the colic, nappy rash and dry scalp to the ground, like a giant gnarly hand.

There was no getting around it.

This was their life now. And somehow they had to find a way to live it.

★ ★ ★

It was mostly the shock. Not only because of what the consultant had told them, but of waking up the next day to Twyla like that, rocking on the floor as though her life were ending.

And in a way it was. He could almost hear it — the click, as their old life snapped shut and the next one slotted into place.

It was the fourteenth of January. They had received this awful news at the beginning of a new year. It felt like the meanest of timings. And yet this wasn't planned by a spiteful hand, wasn't a diary date intended to inflict optimum damage.

If he could have done something to stop it, to protect his family in his role as defender, he would have. But this was bigger than him — bigger than every man on earth combined.

He couldn't fight it. He had to find another way.

After breakfast, he offered to take Charlie out for a walk in the snow. Somehow the snow was still out there, lingering on pavements, on the hilly horizon. He could sense the snow as soon as he opened the windows of a morning and felt winter on his face. The city had quietened down. Traffic was slow. Children were playing en masse outside, their laughter amplified around the neighbourhood.

He couldn't remember the last time he had heard the sound of children playing. And now here they all were — those lusty lungs of childhood fun, taunting him at a time when he was trying to come to terms with his son's devastating condition.

Was it devastating?

The shock was making it seem so. Once they had absorbed the news it would fall more neatly into place. The trick was to make it fall just right, at the start.

So he offered to take Charlie out and for Twyla to join them. There was little point cowering at home. And besides, the sun was out.

They were a pitiful sight he supposed, traipsing the snowy street, wellington boots crunching. Twyla was tense beside him, her hands thrust into her pockets, her mind somewhere else. He had to know where.

'What are you thinking about?' he asked.

The pram wheel was stuck in a ridge of snow. He gave it a little push and it gave way.

'Nothing much,' she said. Her voice sounded a long way away. He felt a ripple of alarm at the base of his spine.

She stopped to check on Charlie. Dylan watched as she leant in towards their son, her face the picture of love and yet with something new there too — a dread that was pressing heavily on her.

'Everything's going to be all right,' he said.

She gave a little nod. Her bottom lip was trembling. It could have just been the cold. The watery sun was trying its best to offer them some warmth. He could feel it squeezing rays from the exhilaratingly blue sky, wringing moisture from the trees.

'How can you be so sure?' she said.

She had stopped again and was gazing up at him. There was only a small height difference between them, but that morning it felt exaggerated. She seemed childlike in her wellingtons and red coat. She reminded him of someone, but he couldn't think who. There was a faint frown between her eyes — a frown that was gone as quickly as it had arrived.

She turned away. He grabbed her hand and pulled her back to face him. 'Because I know,' he said.

'I want to believe you,' she said. 'But I don't know how to do this . . . And you're due back at work next week. How — ?'

'Forget work,' he said. 'I'll tell them I need some more time.' He touched her cheek, the action rather clumsy in his huge padded gloves. 'I've been there long enough and I've never asked for anything.'

They continued to walk. There were no lights on in the houses that they passed. Everything was shut up, dark, abandoned.

'Would it help if my mum moved in for a while?' he asked.

Twyla shook her head. 'I don't think so.'

'Oh,' he said. 'Then how about Bindy?'

'No. I don't think so,' she said again.

When they reached the recreation field, they stood looking across the way at the view of the city that had opened up before them, like a crevice in the earth. It was deathly silent. A snowman was nearby, grimacing with pebble teeth, his carrot nose blackened with decay.

'The reason I know it's going to be OK,' Dylan said, parking the pram and taking Twyla's hands to face her, 'is because . . . '

She looked at him anxiously. He longed to kiss her then. He felt a rush of euphoria as he imagined everything working out. But he had to concentrate. He wasn't great with words when there was emotion attached to them. They sat in broken syllables in his mind, like a botched Scrabble game.

'Because of Felicity,' he said.

'Felicity?' she said. There was the frown, and then it disappeared again. 'Your sister? But . . . '

He knew what she was thinking: that Felicity

was dead. How could a dead person be of reassurance to them?

She reached for his hand. 'Tell me,' she said.

'It's nothing,' he said. 'Just that she was worse off than Charlie.' He looked away, at the snowman's crooked smile. 'I think we can do this, that's all.'

She bit her lip. 'I hadn't thought about Felicity,' she said, her head cocked to one side.

'This isn't the worst thing in the world,' he said.

'No. It's not,' she said, taking a deep breath and looking about her as though waking up to the beauty of the winter scene.

They paused a moment longer to admire the view of their city, which was slumbering under snow. And then they turned back for home.

★ ★ ★

Dylan extended his paternity leave by only a few days before returning to work. He wanted to stay home longer, but she assured him that she would be OK. He was only down the hill and could be home in ten minutes if she needed him.

He acquiesced, and she saw him off with a cheerful kiss. But after closing the door, she stood with her back against it, feeling raw with loneliness. Their neat family trio had dispersed. It was hard not to be sad about that, even though Dylan would be back later.

She smoothed the front of her shirt, lifted her chin resolutely and went into the lounge where Charlie was waiting for his morning bottle.

As she fed him, feeling his toes stiffen with pleasure inside his diddy socks, listening to the *click click click* of his sucking, she felt her mood lifting. 'We can do this, Charlie Ross,' she told him. 'Yes, we can.'

It was Dylan's mention of Felicity that altered things for her, only five days ago but seemingly longer. The days were stretchy, formless, like a string of chewing gum being pulled from a shoe. There was so much time spent holding bottles, gazing into space wearily, that vast landscapes of contemplation could be covered in a day.

Mostly the landscape was inward and backward — into the soul, back to the past, as time hovered between feeds and sleeps, as days ended and began again.

The urge to look backwards was why Dylan had mentioned Felicity. Just hearing her name spoken out loud was rare and significant. And at that moment she knew that Dylan heard them too: the murmurs of the deceased and of those still alive yet frozen by time, preserved in the cryptic pickling juices of the mind.

During the six years she had known Dylan, the only other time he had spoken of Felicity was to briefly relay her history. His family was equally as taciturn on the subject.

Yet this little sprinkle of Felicity had worked its poignant, potent magic, and a change had been made.

For Twyla now realised that Dylan had been through a similar situation before. He knew the private agonies of disability — the behind-the-door tensions and hardships. His confidence in their ability to get through this was enough to give her the glimpse of hope that she needed.

And now she was here on her first day alone with Charlie, and so far so good. The snow had gone, washing the streets, and everything was new. It was the eighteenth of January. She had put a cross on the calendar to mark the spot — the day when they began.

She looked down at Charlie, tucking her index finger into his palm, feeling his fingers grip hers. It was a potent reflex mechanism that babies soon acquired: the instinct to grip. It was the most human thing she could think of, the purest indication of a desire to survive. It was the clinging hand on a cliff edge, the grip of ownership, of money, of power. And Charlie was in possession of this small, undervalued skill.

And that in itself spoke volumes. There would be other things in due course — his first smile, his first steps; achievements that would pile up, like gold sovereigns in a treasure chest.

She had a treasure chest of sorts as a child — a shoebox where she stashed trophies and certificates. She was the type of child who jotted down PO box numbers at the end of television shows, and sent off for memberships and commemorative mugs. She loathed swimming yet endured the stench of chlorine and the hazard of swallowing flies in an outdoor pool for years in order to collect badges for her swimsuit. She couldn't sew very well and sometimes the badges came off and she had to fish them out of the pool before they clogged the drains.

Why hadn't anyone sewn the badges on for her?

That was the sort of question that becoming a parent provoked, the reason the head was turned backwards in assessment of one's own parents, so that one could do it so much better oneself . . .

Twyla intended to be the best possible mother to Charlie Ross.

If you aim for nothing, you'll hit it every time. She had read this on a car bumper once and had never forgotten it. If you followed the rules, you were safe. If you did things properly, you got results. If you aimed high and worked hard, you succeeded. She believed this absolutely.

Thus she had followed the rules implicitly throughout pregnancy. Yet Charlie was blind.

All her sacrifices — refusing wine, getting rid of the microwave, picking over menus, taking up yoga, even swimming again . . . felt rather pointless now.

She shook her head and stood up, tapping Charlie's back to wind him.

Yet in truth, when it came to maladies in modern times, the question wasn't how you had acquired the problem or what you had done to deserve it, but what you were going to do about it now that you did have it. For if you looked hard enough you would find that there was something you could do, even in the most hopeless situations. Few things were to be endured.

And it was this that made it so difficult for Twyla. Because even if she taught herself not to care what other people thought, she knew it would still bother her that her baby would be considered flawed, as someone to be pitied.

In a time when there was a solution for everything from baldness to flat breasts, where did that leave the permanently, inoperably afflicted?

Twyla left the lounge and began the routine of going up and down the stairs to wind Charlie, using the motion to jolt him. She held him close, his hot cheek pressed against her ear, his breath rattling into her hair.

Take Charlie's colic. The mere mention of the word had provoked a torrent of advice from the well-meaning health visitor. Twyla could try a fast-flow teat, or Simeticone drops or lactase drops for his milk; she could switch to a hypo-allergenic milk formula, or take Charlie for chiropractic or massage therapy.

Even crying was no longer allowed. A crying baby was no longer communicating naturally, but suffering from an ailment and was as sure a sign as any of incompetent parenting.

And you could forget being out of shape.

It was a brave mother who bared her post-birth stomach at the beach for all to see. Surely the woman could purchase a kaftan, or a girdle-fitted swimsuit, an abdominal exerciser, gym membership, or a tummy tuck? Anything but *that*.

It was shameful not to help oneself when there was so much information out there, so many solutions to be had.

Perfection, tweaking, self-improvement — call

32

it what you liked, but to Twyla it had never looked so evil . . . and so enticing.

Charlie gave a little belch and Twyla returned to the lounge where she strapped him into his chair and knelt down before him, softly bouncing his seat. It was time for his nap and today he needed little inducement.

As he fell asleep, she thought of the one other thing the consultant said that had stuck in her mind.

He had used the word casually, speculatively, but it hung there in the air for some time before her.

Cure.

She liked the look of it, the shape of it. It twirled before her, like a tantalising ornament, before disappearing.

But that morning in the cool silence of her first day alone with Charlie, it crept forward.

As Charlie gave in to sleep, she opened her laptop.

It was only when he began to twitch beside her, to kick his legs and open his mouth to root around for milk that she came back to the present. She felt guilt-ridden. Where had she just been?

She was lost in another place, temporarily assuaged.

She slammed the laptop shut and vowed never to look at those websites again.

3

He would rather not have done interviews today, but the appointments had been scheduled whilst he was on paternity leave. The first interview was in ten minutes. He opened his diary to find the candidate's name: Molly Carpenter.

He yawned discreetly. It was hard leaving Twyla and Charlie today. He had been back at work a week and it wasn't getting any easier. He wanted to be home with his family. There was a magnetic pull surrounding their house that summoned his thoughts, gathered his spirit to them. Something really big was happening there, and instead he was here.

Being with Twyla and Charlie made him feel purposeful. When he came away from them he felt like a cardboard cut-out being moved about a graphic design office. Here's Dylan by the coffee machine. Here he is exchanging quips with a colleague.

The sound of laughter distracted him from his musings. He looked up to see Molly Carpenter at reception filling out her name tag.

She was wearing a suit jacket and skirt. Her hair was wavy, nondescript brown, and when she turned to glance about the room he saw that her nose turned up at the end and that she had a dimple on her chin. She wasn't unattractive. What was the word for her?

Humdrum. No — homely.

He straightened his tie and made his way over to greet her. 'Dylan Ridley,' he said. 'Head of Design.'

'Pleased to meet you,' she said, extending her hand, blushing ever so slightly.

He saw her through to the interview room, sat down and began to read her application form.

They were only a few minutes into the interview when his phone beeped. Molly was telling him about her extensive experience in graphic design. She was twenty-eight and over-qualified for his junior role. Her voice was slightly nasal, as though pinched on the tip by invisible fingers.

He placed his mobile on his lap and glanced down at it, reading the text.

Charlie burped right after his milk. No stairs involved!!!!

He smiled to himself.

'I have a real passion for design,' Molly was saying.

'Good,' he said. 'You've got the job.'

'I have?' she said, looking astonished.

'Yes,' he said. 'Congratulations.' He shook her hand. 'Can you start Monday?'

'Yes,' she said, laughing. 'I can. Thank you. That's great!'

* * *

Just before four o'clock, Dylan turned the key in the front door and crept into the house. He would surprise them.

He stopped in the lounge doorway. Charlie was asleep in his basket. Twyla was lying out on the couch, her hands tucked neatly underneath her head like a child might do. She looked pale, worn out.

He picked up a throw and laid it carefully over her. He paused a moment, watching the frown that flickered on her forehead, like a dodgy transmission on a television set. He wondered what it was that was troubling her dreams. It wasn't hard to guess.

Then he turned to survey his son, who was peachy-cheeked by comparison and devilishly cute in red.

He would let them sleep in peace. He went upstairs to the bedroom, where he pulled off his tie, stepped out of his suit. Off with the cardboard, back to himself.

As he left the room, he saw something gleaming on the bed-cover. It was Twyla's bola necklace, which she rarely took off, although sometimes did before showering. He went through to the bathroom. Sure enough the tub was wet.

He didn't know why these details mattered, they just did. Perhaps it told him that she wasn't taking her treasured necklace off for any other reason than practicality.

These little household clues were a glimpse into her mental state. He had taken to looking for them daily since returning to work, just to make sure that she was doing as well as she said she was.

When he tiptoed back downstairs, Twyla was standing at the foot of the stairs. 'Hello, my love,' he said.

She looked confused. 'Why are you home early?'

They went through to the kitchen, where he pulled her towards him, kissing her. She tasted sweet — of cherry lip balm.

'I'll be home at this time every day,' he said. 'It's all arranged. Just until everything's settled.'

'Oh,' she said. 'But . . . '

'It doesn't mean you can't do it on your own. It's just that I want to be a part of this too.'

She hesitated and then smiled. 'That's lovely,' she said. 'Thank you.'

He remembered that he was still holding her necklace. 'I found this,' he said. He unravelled the chain and put the necklace back on her where it belonged, the bola charm chiming enigmatically.

He placed his hands on her shoulders. 'Twyla . . . ' he said. 'I think you should call your dad.'

'Yes,' she said, turning away. 'You're right. I will.'

★ ★ ★

She rang her father the following morning. He didn't answer so she left a message, informing him of Charlie's arrival.

It was a wet Tuesday that would have been mournful had she not been making an effort to steer things otherwise. She made camomile tea, put *Soothing Classics for Babies* on the stereo, and folded Charlie's socks and Babygros. He was asleep in his basket beside her, his lips pursed as though whistling to Debussy.

When the phone rang, she reached for it absently. 'Hello?'

'Twyla?'

She sat back on the floor with a bump. 'Stephen,' she said.

'*Dad*,' he corrected. 'Just picked up your phone message . . . So you're a mother now. You have a son.' He always spoke this way, as though phoning to report to her about her own life.

'Yes I do, Stephen . . . Dad.'

'I had no idea you were expecting.' He paused, allowing her to absorb the deeper implications of this statement. *That I was going to be a grandparent.*

'I'm sorry.' She picked up a pair of Charlie's socks and tucked them into each other. She enjoyed sorting his clothes — the wholesome fragrance of laundered cotton. 'I did put Charlie's name in your Christmas card, although I know I posted it rather late . . . '

'I assumed you were referring to a dog.'

'A dog?' Twyla said. 'I've never had a pet in my life.'

'Huh,' he said, sounding in that one word distinctly American.

After decades of analysing housewives on his therapist's couch, his Louisiana accent had gone, but he didn't sound English either. He would be going along nicely and then would say something like 'I done told you twice'. Twyla liked it and over the years had made a sport of spotting his errors, but she sensed that Stephen didn't like it — that he would sooner die than regress.

There was a silence.

'How's business?' he said, at last.

'Good.' She thought of her neglected workshop in the back garden. She hadn't been out there for weeks — couldn't imagine when she might do so. Spiders would have set up home underneath the counter.

'Still making the uh . . . ?'

'Bola necklaces,' she said. 'Yes. They sell very well. Dylan converted our shed into a workshop for me.'

'Good,' he said, then paused. 'Charlie Ross is, what, one month old?'

'Thirty-two days,' she said, embarrassed by the level of detail that she insisted on, was consumed by in her housebound role as mother to a newborn.

'And he's well?'

How to answer?

She put the socks down and looked out the window. The rain was lashing down in pestering nudges against the glass. *Go on! Tell him the truth!*

'He's great,' she said.

'Excellent,' he said.

She tried to picture her father at the other end of the line. When had they last met — three years ago? Four? Would he look the same? Was he ageing well, or was his conscience carving his face into lines and furrows?

He would be wearing an expensive suit, of that

she was certain. His hair would still be mostly blond — an extravagant amount of hair at a time of life when others were on rations. He was tightly laced, but knew how to loosen his tie in a way that many women would find attractive. To the casual observer, he was a man without regret or even a past, for he kept his secrets well hidden.

'Perhaps we can visit you?' he said. 'Juliet and I?'

She might have known that was coming. She hadn't met Juliet and didn't want to do so now, not while everything was so up in the air. She couldn't bear the thought of her father lording over her, patronising her about her ill fortune.

They had argued at their last meeting. It was over the stupidest of things. He had driven down from London to take her out to lunch and she was flattered by his efforts. Yet it wasn't to spend time with her, but to gain her consent before he married Juliet. She told him that she didn't care who he married, he had taken offence and they hadn't spoken much since.

It seemed ridiculous now. What did it matter who he married? At the time, it had felt as though she were making a last stand for her mother, to protect her memory. But her mother was long gone, not even buried in this land but deep in faraway soil.

No wedding invitation had arrived. Had she allowed herself to ponder this, she might have considered that it wasn't because she wasn't invited but because no ceremony had taken place.

'I'll set up something soon,' Twyla said. 'Leave it with me.'

She knew he would be disappointed, that it was the sort of response that one gave a distant relative or unwanted guest. Yet she couldn't risk it. There was a gap between them that she wasn't fit enough to leap. Maybe someday, but not this week or the next.

★ ★ ★

At their follow-up appointment, the second specialist agreed with the first. The diagnosis hadn't ever really been in doubt. Charlie was six and a half weeks old, was putting on weight and had kicked the colic and the flaky scalp into touch. And now it felt like there was just this one big problem — an insurmountable obstruction.

Both Charlie's corneas were cloudy. He had an anterior segment development disorder that was very rare. Its cause in Charlie's case was unknown. There was no reason to believe that the condition would recur with any future offspring of theirs. It was just terribly bad luck.

Dylan was surprisingly upbeat. He led the questioning, his voice slightly higher than normal. It was as though the situation were energising him, giving him a cause to fight for and believe in. He was trying his best to be positive, something that didn't come naturally to him.

It came naturally to her. Yet it wouldn't come now that she needed it. Her optimism had been cut off, like a water supply and just like when the water did come back on, it came in clumsy spurts — discoloured, sporadic.

Yet it would eventually run clear. She kept telling herself that. It had to, because her family was depending on her.

She watched the specialist's lips moving, just as she had at the first consultation — not able to absorb the information, hoping that Dylan could.

At the end of the appointment as the consultant saw them out, he drew level with Twyla and met her gaze. 'Any day now,' he said sympathetically, 'Charlie will smile.'

She nodded in response, before muttering goodbye.

'Well, that went as well as can be expected, hey?' Dylan said, pushing the pram down the corridor.

She was thinking about what the consultant had said about Charlie's first smile. When she didn't reply, Dylan stopped.

'What's wrong?' he asked.

'Nothing,' she said.

'You sure?'

'Yep,' she said.

It didn't sound totally convincing, but she was working on it. Any day now, Charlie would smile and she would be ready for it when he did.

★ ★ ★

Paul had always imagined that the people in his photographs, his subjects, were linked to him in some way. The Aborigines were on to something

42

in believing that the spirit was stolen when a photograph was taken. It was true that he captured, stole something when he snapped his subjects. Why else use the phrase 'take a photograph'? What were you taking if not something during the process? They often visited him at night, the subjects of his pictures, hoarding around his bed, like aggrieved ghosts. He swatted them away and rolled over, delirious with insomnia.

He didn't sleep well; no more than two or three hours a night. Photography was one of a dozen vocations suggested to him. Certainly nothing that required precision, or life and death decision-making, said the lady at the careers advice centre.

He had just come back from Australia and his mind was filled with red dust and empty space. It had felt like a good idea at the time to chuck in his job as a lawyer and travel the Outback and photograph what he saw. The careers adviser seemed to think there was some merit in the snaps that he had spread out on the table for assessment. Either that or she wanted to hurry things along since it was lunchtime.

'Have you thought about doing this professionally?' she asked.

'Well, uh . . . ' He rubbed the stubble on his chin, ticking himself off for not having shaved. He had meant to.

'I think you're very talented,' she said.

'Really?'

She smiled at him and there was a look there that he recognised. He had seen it on the faces of the bar girls in Cairns and the coffee shop waitresses in Melbourne.

'I've a friend at the *Daily Herald*,' she said. 'She's the features editor. She might be able to give you a bit of freelance work.' She opened her drawer, pulled out a business card and handed it to him. 'Interested?'

There was the look again.

He thanked her, tucked the card in his pocket and left.

The features editor at the *Herald* proved to be a good shout. She hooked him up with some work and he made enough money to rent a small flat in the centre of Bath.

And it was because of that flirty careers adviser that he met *her*.

It was Christmas Eve and he rolled out of bed having barely put his head on the pillow because he was supposed to be at the hospital to photograph the first baby of the day.

What a job. No one else would do it but an insomniac.

As he waited on the maternity wing, trying to ignore the screams of childbirth, he thought about what he had been doing this time last year — of how hot it was in Adelaide, sat in a pub on Christmas Day, eating roast turkey with the ceiling fans whirling and Cliff's 'Mistletoe and Wine' on the radio. The loneliness was unbearable. Almost enough to make him call his ex-wife. But instead he drank another pint of Guinness and spent the night with a skinny girl from Manchester who cried because she was missing her mam.

He was summoned back to the present at the

hospital by the noise of something he was supposed to be tending to. It was a baby crying. He hurried into the delivery room because the first baby of Christmas Day had been born — a baby with two names.

It was not what he was expecting.

He stood staring at the mother, at her long blond hair gathered over one shoulder, at the perspiration around her hairline, at the freckles annihilating her arms.

There was something luminous, magnetic about her.

He momentarily forgot his task and her circumstances.

'*Daily Herald*,' he said, with a start. 'Mind if I take a quick snap?'

'What do you think, Dylan?' she said.

So there was a Dylan.

He assessed the rather good-looking man at her side, feeling irrationally, ridiculously envious of him.

'So what's the little lad's name?' he asked.

'Charlie Ross,' she said. 'No hyphen.'

And that was the moment when his theory was proven — that he was linked with the people whom he photographed. He felt it so strongly with her, as though he had met her before and knew everything about her.

He left in the early hours of Christmas Day, trudging through the snow back to his little flat.

It was a joyless place, he thought for the first time, looking about the room critically. He didn't even have a tree; not a smidgen of tinsel or a gold pine cone about the place.

4

Twyla's mother-in-law, Eileen, usually came over after Mass on Sundays. She would bring a basket of Tupperware pots containing home-made food so that Twyla didn't have to cook, and they would all sit down for lunch together. It was a ritual that Twyla looked forward to. She didn't mind Eileen's company, although Dylan's sister, Bindy, could sometimes be hard work.

She watched Bindy now, as they ate stew at the dining table. Bindy was dark-skinned and dark-eyed like Dylan, but had a more pulled-down face than his. Not that she wasn't attractive, but she wore a permanent look of melancholy as though her features were snagged by an invisible wire.

Eileen, immaculate in a green cardigan and brown trousers, like a chocolate lime, kept turning to look admiringly at Charlie in his bouncy chair. 'He's such a precious little thing!' she said, in her soft Irish accent.

Charlie was a month and a half old. Twyla had stopped measuring his age in days or weeks. Things were beginning to expand, inching past paltry details into denser things as his limbs grew sturdier. Gone were the stringy chewing gum days; in were the chunky days that seemed solid enough but were in fact brittle and dusty, like sticks of chalk.

So she was thinking when she saw something

out the corner of her eye and dropped her fork with a clatter, causing her guests to jump.

'Oh, my word!' said Eileen, putting her hand to her chest. 'What on — ?'

Twyla dashed to Charlie. 'Oh, my goodness . . . Oh my goodness!' she said.

Dylan scraped back his chair. 'What is it?' he said.

She was struggling to undo the plastic clips on Charlie's chair in her fervour. 'He smiled, Dylan!' she said. 'He smiled!'

She plucked Charlie up and held him before her, his legs dangling. The smile came again and she wanted to cry with happiness and pride. Dylan was laughing too. And then all four of them were gathered around, laughing and tickling Charlie's toes to try to get him to do it again.

The consultant had been right to proffer this milestone to Twyla as a point of reassurance. Charlie had just smiled for the first time and it felt wonderful — this great, little leap forward.

And she thought that perhaps the moment had come, that everything was going to be all right now.

But to her disappointment, she still felt it — the very private pain of something being wrong.

★ ★ ★

At the end of February, as Charlie turned two months old, another flurry of snow fell and Twyla invited a friend and her toddler daughter over for afternoon tea. Twyla set out pink wafers and a pot of tea. Yet the moment the mother and child entered the room, she felt a crushing sensation of resentment that she tried immediately to quell.

She settled Charlie in his chair at her feet for his nap. And then sat with her hands gripped on her lap, trying to smile at the little girl and to make conversation with the mother.

And she was doing very well, until the child climbed on to her mother's lap and begged her to read a book.

She and Charlie would never be able to share a book in the same way. Such a simple act that millions took for granted every day.

'Charlie's blind,' Twyla found herself saying.

Her friend lowered the book and tapped her daughter's legs for her to get down from her lap. 'Hey?' she said, wide-eyed.

'He's blind,' Twyla said.

'Oh, my God!' said her friend, staring in mortification at Charlie. 'I'm so sorry . . . You must be devastated!'

They didn't stay long after that. The child had a toddler gym session, the mother a hair appointment, as though they were hurrying back to normal life, away from Twyla.

Although it wasn't like that. Twyla's friend was gracious. Yet she knew that it would be a long time before she heard from her again. The gap between them would be too big, their lives too different now.

Twyla swept the wafer crumbs away and decided that what she and Charlie needed was a walk. Dylan would be home soon. They would go out and buy his favourite supper: steak and red onions.

As they walked, thin snowflakes fell around them. Twyla looked up at the sky and saw the throng of grey dots toppling down, like dislodged insects.

She sang a tune to Charlie. The afternoon was so quiet it could have been just the two of them alive. These were the moments that she cherished, that lingered at the end of each day, long after she closed her eyes.

But the moment she entered the supermarket, she had a bad feeling about it.

She got the steak and the red onions, and was queuing up when it happened. The checkout girl was picking her teeth, bored; a mother was stood behind Twyla with four children who were coughing and sneezing. Twyla kept her back to them, trying to shield Charlie from the onslaught of germs. But one of the children had run forward and was pointing at Charlie.

'Look!' the boy said. 'He looks like an alien. A — lee — an. A — lee — an!'

'Hush now!' the mother said. She was flapping her arms, trying to deter her other children from darting forward to see the baby alien.

But Twyla had gone.

The steak and red onions remained in the wire basket on the floor by the checkout.

She couldn't remember the journey home. The snow had stopped, had come to nothing. The pavements were speckled with damp; the air was static, frozen.

At home, she secured Charlie into his cot, bending to kiss his forehead reverently, pausing to watch him settle into sleep, before returning downstairs to the lounge and closing the door behind her.

'No! No!' She knelt down and pummelled the carpet with her fists in an anger that quickly subsided to anguish.

There was a noise behind her.

'Twyla?'

She stood up, straightened her top, looked at Dylan shamefacedly. 'Someone called Charlie an alien,' she said, beginning to cry.

She knew it sounded ridiculous, like telling tales on someone in the school yard. In this case, the offender was a five-year-old child who knew no better. Yet it still hurt.

He tossed his keys down, came forward and held her, stroking her hair. 'It's all OK,' he said.

He made her a cup of tea and they sat together as daylight faded. When Charlie woke from his nap, they placed him in his chair by their sides, with the gas fire puffing before them.

Charlie wasn't an alien, Twyla thought, gazing at him, feeling her heart lurch in defence and with love. He was their precious little boy.

'I'm not finding this easy either,' Dylan said. 'Not by any stretch of the imagination. But we need to concentrate on what really matters.'

'I know,' she said. 'And I'm really working on it because it's got to work out — all this has to be all right.'

His face brightened. 'You'll get there,' he said.

'Yes,' she said. 'I will.'

In the last week of April, as Charlie turned four months old, they received the results of an ophthalmologist's report that scared Dylan half to death.

The sun was really straining that day, trying to warm the glass on the windowpanes, trying to warm the blood in their veins. Before he even reached for Twyla's hand, he knew it would be cold too.

Normally he didn't find these appointments too bad, but today they were getting the results of a report that would determine whether a corneal transplant was a possible solution for Charlie.

The report wasn't something they had pursued, but was par for the course. And who wouldn't welcome it? Even the most accepting parent would embrace the possibility of curing their child's affliction.

He glanced at Twyla. Her arms were folded and her legs were twisted around each other, corkscrew-like. The specialist was building up with small talk to the crux of the matter.

'As you know, Mr and Mrs Ridley, we've been running tests to determine whether transplant is an option for Charlie. And whilst it is a solution for many with corneal disorders, in Charlie's case it's not.'

That was how he said it, just like that.

Dylan turned open-mouthed to obtain Twyla's reaction and was surprised to see that she was staring ahead of her as though listening to the shipping forecast.

'Charlie's inoperably blind,' the specialist said, with the emotional depth of a Petri dish.

Dylan was watching Twyla out of the corner of his eye. She was still motionless.

And it was this that frightened him far more than the consultant's shocking bedside manner and the ghastly prognosis he was delivering.

Far more daunting to Dylan was the notion that this would be the thing that would shatter his wife's spirit.

But then she came to life. 'Well, thank you,' Twyla said, standing up, 'Dr . . . uh — ' she leant forward to read his name tag ' — Maggs. You've been most helpful.' She kicked the brake off Charlie's pram and made for the door.

Outside in the corridor, they waited for the lift. 'We're going to do this, Dylan,' she said, smiling exuberantly.

She looked just like she had on their wedding day. She had turned to him as they left the town hall, as their friends threw confetti and cheered and the sun came out from its hiding place, and she had smiled at him. And he had suddenly felt the urge to lift her hand up high as though they had just won Wimbledon.

'That's my girl,' he said now, kissing her on the cheek.

It was only as the lift lunged down, as silence enveloped them and they returned to their private thoughts, that he wondered what she had meant by that — what it was exactly that they were going to do.

But he dismissed the thought. She was happy and that could only be a good thing.

Twyla had told the social worker about the mother and daughter afternoon tea incident, and the social worker had promptly handed her a flyer for a support group.

The Parents of Blind Children Support Network was a small group of mums who met with their visually impaired children in the back room of a community centre. It was a bus ride away on the other side of town, but was worth a try.

It was a long while since Twyla had travelled by bus. The experience was comforting, lulling, reminiscent of childhood. She gripped the handle of Charlie's pram, closed her eyes and listened to the rumbling of the engine, her legs vibrating.

She used to take the bus to school in London once upon a time — the number ninety-three from Putney to prep school in Wimbledon, back in the days of sewing badges on to swimsuits and sending off for commemorative mugs. Her nanny travelled with her, taking up too much of the seat, reading *Woman's Own* or *Take a Break*, snorting in response to the articles. Twyla would gaze out the window at the fog, or watch people getting on the bus and imagine that she knew what they were thinking and who they were. In truth, she didn't know anyone. She shuttled to her school and back again, and the two worlds weren't connected in the slightest.

She had a peculiar relationship with her nanny. The nanny never paid any attention to her, sometimes coming across Twyla in the kitchen with a surprised look as though she hadn't expected a hungry child to be sat there. Twyla treated the nanny with mutual indifference, not caring whether she showed up or not — whether Twyla was squashed up on the bus, or whether she got more space to spread out on her own.

Her early years in London were smudgy, indistinct. She could remember the blue checks on her plaid school skirt, and the elderly neighbour who shouted obscenities at passers-by, and that one year it snowed so hard the number ninety-three got stuck.

It had taken her a while to realise that the fog outside the bus window wasn't the fog of London town that they had sung about in kindergarten in Louisiana, but one of her own making. Grief veiled her eyes — a damp mist that tinged everything she looked at, and quelled any desire that she might have had to connect with others. What was the point in liking people if they up and died?

She was vaguely aware that she had lost the wrong parent, that she had lost the one whom she had known inside out and had kept the bare one. It was like putting the contents of the pantry out into recycling and restocking it with empty bottles and jagged open tin cans. Whenever you went to fill yourself, to cure the terrible hunger pangs of grief, there was nothing there. Old Mother Hubbard didn't know the half of it.

Yet Twyla remained optimistic. She knew even

then that each day she made a choice to be happy or sad, and that the latter wasn't an option. She sang as she moved about the house, slamming drawers, bouncing balls, blowing bubbles in the hallway. The nanny didn't give her any rules and Twyla wasn't about to make them up of her own accord, so she ate peanut butter from the jar with her finger and drank milk straight from the bottle. And sometimes, if she was feeling devilish, she left the fridge door open.

She heard the nanny complaining to her father about her at night. Twyla would sit on the stairs with her knees against her chest and her nightie pulled down over her legs and rock herself from side to side, feeling like a heavy sack of potatoes.

'She's weird,' she heard the nanny say.

'Weird?' her father said wearily.

'She's not interested in anything or anyone.'

Her father laughed. 'She lost her mom and just crossed an ocean. What d'you expect?'

Back then he had an American accent. She had one too. She loved to hear his *y'alls* and *where y'ats?* And she had loved him. It was just that the sensation took a while to arrive, as though she were using a sonar system like a bat and had to wait for the echo to reach her. Sometimes she couldn't bear that he was an empty can so she hurled herself rashly over the sharp edges and jumped right in, hugging him hard. But it was no use. He always did the same thing: peeled her off, tapped her head and said, 'OK, sweedie.'

She hardly ever saw him. He was working long

hours in the role they left America for. He was director of a private health care division that spanned south London. It was a good job, he said, and would provide well for them, but it would swallow a lot of his time. He hadn't lied about that bit. The thing he had lied about was that there would still be time for them on the weekends.

She wasn't doing well at prep school in Wimbledon. So Stephen's colleague recommended a private school in Reading that was achieving impressive results.

And so they moved to Richmond, Twyla boarded at school, and the nanny and the number ninety-three bus were no more.

There was a hiss as the bus came to a halt. Twyla checked that Charlie was still asleep and looked about her. They weren't even halfway to the community centre yet.

The bus jerked into motion again. Twyla yawned, her mind settling on the day her father packed her off to Leighford Park in Reading.

He had intended to drive her himself on her first day, but was due at a conference in Brussels that afternoon. Instead, he ordered her a taxi. Her new form tutor would be there to greet her at the other end.

'You ready for this, sweedie?' he asked, leaning into the black cab.

'Sure,' she said.

The next time they met it was Christmas and she no longer said 'sure' but 'of course' and she was no longer 'sweedie' to him.

The fog lifted finally when she discovered boys

56

at Leighford Park. One boy with caramel eyes and Old Spice toiletries kissed her for so long that she said she would run away to Hawaii with him and live on tropical fruit. They didn't run away, but they did smoke Camel Lights until their faces turned green.

It was the Old Spice boy who taught her about love, who answered her question about the point of liking people only for them to die. He taught her that it was all worth it. And then in sixth form he dumped her for a girl with bigger breasts.

She smiled to herself. The bus had stopped. The passengers were spilling out into the street, dispersing into the sunshine. They were outside the community centre.

★ ★ ★

One of the best things about the support group was Ofelia, an Argentinian single mum whose youngest child had glaucoma. Ofelia referred to the support group as 'Blindoes'.

'The trick is,' Ofelia told her within minutes of their having met, 'to forget about normal. *This* is normal,' she said, circling the air with her finger. '*This* is where it's at. You get it, hey?'

'I hope so,' Twyla replied.

The other best thing about the group was the chatter. Twyla had never heard so much noise amongst so few women. It took her a moment to work it out, to realise what the noise was all about. The mothers were talking not only to each other, but to their blind children

— constantly, incessantly.

It made her realise that up till now she had been curiously tongue-tied, that she had assumed a sad state of silence around Charlie, broken only by the occasional song. So that afternoon at home she began to talk.

'I'm going to give you the rattle, Charlie,' she said. 'Here it comes . . . It's plastic and it's got a picture of a giraffe on it. Giraffes are funny animals. They live in Africa and have long necks and splodges on their skin, like custard . . . What's custard? Well . . . '

The support group had done something remarkable for her after only one visit. They had shown her how to help Charlie see the world.

She scooped Charlie up and took him to the window. 'We live in Bath. You can see the city down there through the trees. Bath's very pretty. The buildings are made from beautiful cream-coloured stone . . . '

As she spoke, she realised that if she could do this one thing to improve Charlie's life then surely there were hundreds of other things that she could do.

And so that May, as the sun warmed the air and the cherry blossom tree in their garden flowered, she built Charlie Ross a sensory garden. It wasn't much — a small fountain, wind chimes, bells on sticks, pungent herbs in pots that released their fragrance when brushed past, but Charlie kicked his chubby legs in approval.

Encouraged by these improvements, one night, finding herself unable to get back to sleep after Charlie's feed, Twyla opened her laptop and visited the websites that she had vowed to never look at again. They drew her in, compelled her to visit their fascinating corners, like exploring the chambers of a beating heart.

She read for hours, not heeding the advancing hand of the clock, oblivious to everything around her.

Finally, she crept to bed and lay with her back to Dylan.

Charlie was in his cot at her side, his face glowing in the rays of the full moon that was soaking through the curtains like a celestial spotlight.

She could improve Charlie's life in a myriad of ways. But what if she could take it a step further?

What if they could cure him?

Curing Charlie prompted lots of slippery questions about life that would make people squirm, overheat, divide.

She gazed at Dylan, at his sleeping form. What would he think about it? He had grown up with a disabled sister. How much would Felicity have a bearing on this? And he no longer went to church, but was still Catholic.

Yet what did his being Catholic have to do with it? Why was this a religious argument, or even an argument at all?

There were so many things that could afflict a baby at birth: jaundice, a broken collarbone, muscle weakness, unusual breathing, skin conditions, a lazy eye — all of which caused parents anxiety, but were remediable. No one thought anything about giving a child physiotherapy or antibiotic skin cream.

Why was blindness any different? Was it because healing the blind was biblical, and curing a baby born with flat head syndrome or a dislocated hip wasn't?

Was there a chart on which afflictions were graded, whereby you could alter the small but not the mighty?

This felt mighty. And Twyla, lying there in the dark, felt small.

She couldn't begin to answer any of these questions without Dylan.

And so she remained pondering and fretting, her mind whirring, until sleep at last stepped forward and rescued her.

The next day was a Saturday. Twyla took her coffee out to the garden to watch the sun rise, as she often did.

She pulled her cardigan around her and gazed up at the cloudless sky. The sunrise made her feel more alive than anything else in her day, even her moments of pleasure with Charlie. Because such moments were always curdled with something else: the niggling desire to improve the quality.

If only Charlie could see, it would all be better.

When a dragonfly skimmed the water, when a hot air balloon drifted across a cloudless sky, when a rainbow wobbled through the trees, she longed for Charlie to share the experience with her. And on such occasions, she found herself unwilling to describe what she saw because if it was that exquisite, that breathtaking, then maybe Charlie was better off not knowing.

To protect him, she lied to him — lied by omission about the details that he missed.

Her yearning to cure him both expanded her with hope and crushed her with guilt, for she knew that the worm in the apple was her failure to accept Charlie just as he was.

She couldn't help it. She loved her son with an intensity that could power the national grid and yet still she ached to improve him.

It was instinctive, unconscious — the desire to adjust something to make it better; the brushstroke to finish the masterpiece.

Except for the sunrise, which wasn't to be touched or meddled with.

And so it was there in the solace of the garden, with the birds twittering their chorus and the buddleia bush blooming above her, that she felt most at peace.

The sun's rays suddenly became strong enough to activate the solar fountain. The water started to trickle down and she took this as a sign that she was to go ahead with the path she had chosen.

★   ★   ★

Dylan flicked back the curtain, saw Twyla sitting outside in the garden and went downstairs to join her.

He sipped his coffee, gazing up at the back of the house. The gutters needed clearing and the fascia boards needed a lick of paint.

'Dylan . . . ' Twyla was sat with her knees drawn up to her chest. 'What would you say if we could cure Charlie?'

'But we can't,' he said.

'We can't do cornea transplants, no,' she said. 'Not with human tissue.' She dropped her legs down with a thump. 'But what about artificial transplants?'

He looked at her in surprise. 'You what?'

'They're being developed in Sweden and the States,' she said. 'Keratoprosthesis surgery.'

He laughed lightly. 'We're not sending Charlie abroad for dodgy surgery.' He tapped her leg, as though settling the matter.

'It's not dodgy,' she said. 'And it's not abroad. There's a research centre in London that's doing clinical trials. I can show you all the information.'

He put his coffee mug down and took her hand. She was trembling, like a deer gazing into the barrel of the hunter's gun.

'What is it that you want to do?' he asked.

She blinked slowly, stalling to find the right words.

'To find out if Charlie's eligible,' she said. 'And if he is then maybe we could help raise some money towards their research . . . So that they can operate on him.'

Dylan inhaled sharply. 'Oh, God,' he said. He gazed up at the fascia boards again, wishing that was the only thing to occupy his mind. Instead of this.

She touched his arm, spoke softly. 'But, Dylan — what if we do this for him and it means he can see?'

He thought about that for a moment, held a

glossy image in his mind of Charlie playing catch, before clicking on to the image of Charlie riding a bike. It reminded him of his View-Master toy that he had treasured as a child — how he had spent hours gazing into it to see 3D images of *The Jungle Book*, pressing the lever to rotate the picture reel to the next slide. How he had longed to climb into that enchanted colour-soaked world. And how Charlie would be forever deprived of the simple pleasure of sight.

What if Twyla was right about this? What if his own desire to keep everything as it was, to paint the fascia boards, to go about life with his head down and tucked in, wasn't the right way for them — for Charlie?

'OK,' he said. 'Show me the information.'

She didn't jump up or punch the air or hug him. She knew this was more delicate than that. She merely nodded. 'Thank you,' she said.

5

Christmas, and Charlie's first birthday, passed without snow or fuss. They had a small family gathering to celebrate both occasions. Twyla might have organised for her father to visit, but his early Christmas card informed her that he was going to Sweden over the holidays.

In the new year, they settled into a routine of outings and appointments. Dylan had gone back to full hours at work and was given a pay rise for Christmas. Charlie had sprouted four teeth, had learnt to crawl with his head on the floor, and had formed an attachment to a blue elephant with enormous ears that he chewed at night.

They saw healthcare professionals several times a week, the appointments adding a rhythm to their days, a safety net of attention and advice. Their life had become a medical carousel with Charlie as the central pole. Around him bobbed three types of eye specialists, an eye clinic liaison officer, a paediatrician, an occupational thera-pist, a physiotherapist, a social worker and a health visitor.

Twyla continued with the support group, and made friends with parents of blind children online. In the main, things felt good. She was finding it easier to accept Charlie's blindness — now that she had found a way of potentially removing it.

Nothing was certain, but they had visited the

eye centre in London, the Royal Square, in the autumn and Charlie was deemed a potential candidate for artificial corneal transplant surgery. So she had set about doing some fund-raising for the centre.

The money wouldn't assure anything. They would still have to find the thirty thousand pounds for the operation, if they even got that far. But the fund-raising gave her something positive to focus on. She set up a donations page online, consulted with a fund-raising body, contacted charities and rich benefactors. And by January she had managed to put twenty-five thousand pounds into the account.

That January, Twyla and Charlie began to visit the public gardens in the centre of town. The gardens had an old-fashioned feel with deckchairs, a bandstand and prize-winning floral displays. Set beside the weir where the river crashed down relentlessly, the park was the perfect place for Charlie to listen to and experience nature.

At just over one, Charlie's hair was blond now, like hers — *cut from the same piece of cloth*, as Eileen was fond of saying. He had a toothy smile, but didn't often show his teeth for he was a serious boy, prone to holding himself still to absorb what was going on. He wasn't talking yet, but the speech therapist said that was to be expected and that words would eventually come.

The public gardens were their sanctuary, the place where they got off the carousel. She talked less there too and Charlie seemed OK with that. They would lay their blanket underneath the elm tree and Charlie would sit with his hand lightly on hers, gazing up at the sky as though he were an ancient philosopher.

Sometimes, as they packed the blanket away and made to leave, she heard her bola necklace chiming from beyond the layers of her winter clothes, and felt a pang of regret. She hadn't been out to her workshop since Charlie was born, hadn't so much as checked on her tools or stock levels.

It wasn't just because there was too much else to do. She missed her work and Dylan kept suggesting that it might do her good. But going out to the workshed felt like a step backwards somehow, at a time when the future was the priority. And so she left the door latched and the air grew stale and the spiders relaxed and the dust thickened.

★ ★ ★

'I've no idea how you do it,' said Bindy, plucking an apple from the fruit bowl. 'You're like Wonder Woman. We should get you a leotard and some red boots.'

Eileen, who was drying up the dishes, laughed.

Twyla smiled tightly.

Bindy was always pleasant, yet there was often something spiky in her voice. Maybe it was Twyla's imagination. She hadn't slept well last night, had a dilemma pressing on her that she had asked her in-laws over to talk through. Dylan said he would support her whatever she decided — a lenience which on this occasion wasn't very helpful.

Bindy took a bite out of the apple and leant languidly on the kitchen counter.

She was a funny thing, Twyla thought. She was capable of so much more than her job as a dentists' receptionist, where she had worked for over twenty years. Apparently she hadn't wanted children, although there was a husband once — a rich banker who set her up in a huge house post-divorce. She seemed perpetually, insatiably bored. And sometimes in her company, Twyla actually found herself shuddering.

'I don't really do that much,' said Twyla in response to Bindy's remark. 'Just what every other mum does. I'm sure you'd do the same.'

'Hmm,' said Bindy, dropping the barely eaten apple with a flick of her wrist into the bin.

'So I spoke to Father O'Brien about you, my dear,' said Eileen, reaching into the cupboard to put a glass away, her jeans legs rising. She always wore her trousers too short, and put everything away in the wrong place. 'He's more than happy to help with some fund-raisers.'

'That's very kind,' said Twyla, watching Eileen putting a plate into the saucepan cupboard. 'But leave that now. Let's go and sit down.'

They went through to the lounge. It was early morning and the frost was still on the windows, the patterns feathery and faint as though fossilised. Twyla put the gas fire on, the blue flames rising with a sudden whoosh.

'Do you reckon diamanté nails are too much?' Bindy said, stretching her manicured nails out to show her mother.

'I think *you're* too much,' Eileen replied.

Sometimes it seemed as though Eileen's God had played a huge trick on her with Bindy. The two women couldn't have been less alike, and yet there was something unspoken, indefinable between them that united them.

'So . . . ' Eileen said, picking up her cup of tea. 'What time will Charlie be awake?'

She only really came for Charlie.

'Soon,' said Twyla, sitting down.

'Well, that's grand,' said Eileen.

She was a rather funny person too: acutely aware of social standing and reputation, yet a fan of home-made simplicity and values. Her Cork accent originated from the town of Bandon, where the motto was 'With the help of God small things grow'. Eileen had carried this saying with her her whole life, cross-stitching it on to cushions and wall hangings around her home.

'So about the local press,' Twyla said. She felt Bindy's dark eyes immediately turn to look at her. 'The *Daily Herald* wants to run a feature on me about the fund-raising campaign. It'll be written sympathetically, to help drum up support . . . But I'm not sure whether to do it.'

'Oh?' said Eileen. 'And what does Dylan say?'

'That he'll support me whatever I decide.'

'I see,' said Eileen, a flicker of a smile appearing on her lips. 'And what do you think, dear?'

Twyla paused before replying. 'That it could help,' she said.

'Then go for it,' said Bindy. 'Where's the harm?'

'Well, I'm glad you both agree,' said Twyla.

'Agree?' said Eileen. 'I'm not sure that I've expressed an opinion.'

A silence fell.

Bindy laughed. 'Oh, just do it, Twyla,' she said, gesturing with her hand dismissively. 'Who knows where it could lead?'

And it was then that Twyla realised exactly what the problem was with Bindy: she always backed Twyla too readily, agreed with her so unilaterally, it couldn't possibly be the truth.

Eileen emitted a little snort. 'That's exactly what I'm afraid of,' she said.

★   ★   ★

'Afraid?' said Dylan into the phone, scrolling through his work emails. 'What's she afraid will happen?'

'I don't know,' Twyla said. 'Maybe you could ask her?'

He clicked off the email and gave her his full attention. 'No,' he said. 'We're doing this, if it's what you've decided.'

She sighed.

Molly Carpenter stood up and was walking towards the coffee machine. She was wearing a cream blouse that billowed as she moved. He watched as one of the lads joined her and was sharing a joke with her. Her nose wrinkled when she laughed.

Was she attractive? Dylan thought. Yes. Probably. More so when you got to know her than at first glance. She wasn't the sort to inspire a trucker's beep.

'I want this to be your decision too,' Twyla was saying.

'And it is,' he replied. 'I agree with you.'

'But you know why we're doing this, don't you?' she said. 'The article could really boost the campaign. It could be the thing that helps Charlie to see.'

He looked at the photograph of Twyla on his desk. Next to it was a picture of Charlie on his first birthday, his expression saying, *Which way should I look, Daddy?* The photograph of Twyla was older, taken not long after they met. She was wearing a top that showed her shoulders and her hair was ablaze in sunshine. It was his favourite picture of her — the one that visitors to his desk drew closer to admire.

'I'm with you all the way,' he said in a hushed voice, steeped in intimacy.

Molly was hovering nearby, blowing on to her plastic cup of coffee. He motioned for her to wait.

'I've got to go,' he said into the phone. 'We'll speak more tonight. I love you,' he added, before hanging up. 'Molly,' he said, swivelling his chair to address her. 'How can I help?'

'Could I take next Friday off?' she asked.

''Course,' he said. 'Doing something nice?'

There went that blush that often appeared when she spoke to him. He put it down to coyness around a superior — a gaucheness that was as touching as it was rare.

'My boyfriend's taking me to Paris,' she replied.

'Sounds good,' he said.

He watched her return to her desk. Somehow he hadn't imagined that she would have a boyfriend who would take her to Paris.

He glanced at his watch. He just had time for another call. He picked up the phone and dialled. 'Mum,' he said.

'Oh, hello, Dylan,' she said. 'Nice to hear — '

'Please go easy on Twyla,' he said.

'Whatever do you mean?'

'Let her do this — the article, the fund-raising.'

She gave a high-pitched chuckle. 'But of course!'

'This is her way of dealing with things.'

'To be sure,' she said.

He was about to end the call, when he added something. 'It doesn't mean that I've forgotten anything, Mum,' he said. 'I just need to explore this with Twyla — to explore what might be . . . Do you understand?'

She was silent, but he knew she was there, quiet, listening.

'Well, I've got to go,' he said. 'I'll see you Sunday.' And he hung up.

★   ★   ★

Christmas in Stockholm was predictably cold. Stephen was too old for skiing, so they kept their feet on the ground and their coats drawn close to their chests. They strolled along the harbour beside the frozen sea and when the cold began to bite they retreated indoors for Swedish apple cake.

71

If it wasn't then whilst relishing the cinnamon spiced apple cake laden with vanilla custard that he first began to feel an unfamiliar anguish inside, then it was during the procession on St Lucia's Day, when hundreds of little blonde girls in white dresses floated before them carrying electric candles in the snow at dusk.

The vision was so evocative and his distress so strong he thought that his legs might buckle.

'What, Stephen?' Juliet asked him with concern.

'Spot of heartburn,' he told her. 'It's nothing.'

Considering it was nothing, it was very hard to shake. And by the time they were sat by the log burner in their home in Highgate sipping Swedish *glögg* and opening the stack of Christmas cards, he knew precisely what it was. It was indeed heartburn, in a manner of speaking.

The vanilla custard of the apple cake in Stockholm had taken him somewhere far away the moment he had tasted it, the instant the glorious flavour met his tongue. He was no longer in a cold climate wearing woollen outerwear, but somewhere where the sun was warm and his clothing light.

It had tasted just like something he used to eat on the front step of a house with a little girl he no longer knew, in a time that no longer existed.

And as for the fair-headed girls in white dresses?

They were her, every one of them.

He had clutched Juliet's arm and pulled her

away from the procession. 'Let's go in here,' he said, diving into the first shop they came to. Juliet trotted along to keep up with him, her tiny feet taking two steps to his one. She was small and sweet in Stockholm, in fur-lined boots and cashmere sweaters.

He stood inside the overheated store, gazing about him. It was an antique toy shop. The light was dim and all around were clockwork monkeys, jack-in-the-boxes, doll's houses.

He reached out to touch the hair of a rocking horse that was stood next to him.

'What are we doing in here?' said Juliet.

'Hush,' he said, holding up his hand. Juliet tutted and turned away to watch the procession from the window. Out of the corner of his eye he could see the white dresses of the girls passing with their lights, like a silent glow-worm snaking through the city.

He approached a display cabinet, not knowing what he was looking for, why he was drawn there. A lady was sat reading behind the counter.

'Could I take a closer look at that, please?' Stephen said, pointing into the cabinet.

'Of course,' the lady said. 'It's a beauty.' And she turned to get the key to unlock the cabinet. 'It is for someone special?'

He nodded. 'Yes', he said. 'It is.'

★   ★   ★

He wasn't nervous until the last minute. He had distracted himself on the journey with Classic FM. But as he pulled on to Orchard Drive, he

73

turned off the engine and sat gazing uneasily up at the front of the house.

Juliet had been supportive, had offered to join him. He didn't want to shut her out, but the situation felt private. He wasn't sure of his own boundaries and didn't want to overstep by bringing in another pair of feet.

He picked up the ribboned parcel from the passenger seat. Then he put it back down. He would come back for it shortly.

He chewed his lip in contemplation. No, he would bring it now. It would give him something to do with his hands.

Odd, this nervousness and indecision. Most out of character.

He stood on the doorstep with the parcel extended in front of him, like a boy attending a birthday party.

Footsteps were approaching. 'Hello, Twyla,' he said, as the door swung open.

She looked exactly the same as when they had last met. She didn't look like a mum with a . . . he had to think . . . twelve, no, thirteen-month-old baby.

'Stephen!' she said, surprise registering on her face. 'What are you — ?'

He would let the Stephen thing go for now.

'I should have waited for an invitation,' he said. 'But I thought you might never get around to asking me.'

'Oh,' she said, putting her hand to her face. 'I'm sorry. I meant to give you a ring. I just don't know where the time's gone.'

'That's all right,' he said. He held up the

parcel. It tinkled merrily. 'A small gift for Charlie Ross.' He glanced past her down the hallway. 'Can I come in? I'm looking forward to meeting the little man.'

'I . . . uh . . . '

He could hear someone talking beyond her, from inside the house. He hadn't realised anyone was there. 'Is this an awkward time?' he asked. 'Do you have guests?'

'Only our social worker.'

'Social worker,' he said. 'Why would you need . . . ?' He tilted his head in incomprehension.

He hadn't considered that Twyla's life would be less than ideal. His own dial had been set at perfect for so long it was reluctant to budge, like a rusty kitchen timer.

He tried to think quickly what it could be, why his daughter had been so reluctant to invite him here.

'You'd better come in,' she said, holding the door open.

He followed her down the hallway. She didn't turn into the lounge like he expected, but continued to the kitchen. 'Tea?' she asked.

'Please,' he said.

In the kitchen he felt too tall, too big in his suit and loafers. She brushed past him briskly, opening drawers, reaching into the cupboards, flicking on the kettle whilst reaching for teabags and mugs.

He reached out and took her wrist gently. 'Stop,' he said. He turned her by the shoulders to face him. 'Tell me.'

She looked up at him, her bottom lip wobbling.

For a brief moment, he glimpsed her: the little girl he had lost.

And then she was gone.

She lifted up her chin. 'Charlie's blind,' she said.

* * *

Somehow his legs carried him through to the lounge to meet with the social worker with her wiry hair and to sit by the fire on that January afternoon and exchange pleasantries about the cold front coming in from the east.

He managed not to sniffle as Twyla unwrapped the parcel to reveal the exquisite kaleidoscope from the toyshop in Stockholm.

And when he saw his grandson for the first time, he didn't react at the oversized blue eyes that reminded him of moonstone.

Could he have chosen a more useless gift for a blind child?

'I'm sorry,' he said. He meant about his redundant purchase, but it could have applied to the whole situation.

'Don't be,' Twyla said. She sat down on the floor next to Charlie and took his hand. 'Grandad's bought you a lovely toy.'

Grandad.

He was Grandad.

'It's a kaleidoscope . . . Here.' She pressed it into Charlie's hands. 'Shake it. That's it.'

Charlie was rattling the kaleidoscope. 'You

look through it, like a telescope,' she said.

Stephen could feel goosebumps on his legs. The social worker was nodding supportively, making notes in her file.

'When you turn the dial here, it makes pretty patterns, Charlie,' Twyla said.

Charlie was actually holding the kaleidoscope to his eyes, looking upwards. The sight of it made Stephen want to weep. He tightened his feet and kept them curled until the sensation passed.

He didn't stay with them long. Twyla had a busy diary. He said he would be in touch again soon, and departed.

He only got as far as the outskirts of Bath before he had to pull over.

There, with schoolchildren and mothers passing by, with buses and lorries splashing through puddles, with his engine running and his pride low, he cried.

When he was done, he loosened his tie, put Classic FM on, and made his way home.

6

The article in the *Daily Herald* boosted the fund-raising campaign fourfold. By Easter, there was nearly one hundred thousand pounds in the account. Twyla let the fund-raising slip in favour of other things. She had raised far more than expected and had made herself known at the research centre. As soon as the Royal Square was ready they would be in touch.

She tried not to pester them. They wouldn't tell her much when she rang. Sometimes they told her there was still a lot of controversy surrounding the procedure. Sometimes they warned her of the risks. Often they put her on hold listening to Handel's *Water Music* and forgot to retrieve her.

Easter was unseasonably warm with an enthusiastic sun that lifted her spirits and made her feel blessed. At sixteen months old, Charlie had discarded the baby persona in favour of looking like a little boy, and Twyla in turn had shed the wariness and fear of the early days and wore motherhood far more comfortably. There was a security that came as they grew into their roles, unable to imagine life any other way. They had begun low-level house-hunting for a place to suit this new life — somewhere with a flatter garden and less traffic nearby. And she was concentrating on trying to help Charlie walk.

Charlie's muscle tone was very good. He just

didn't trust the world and his ability to navigate it alone. On the rare occasions that he did let go of their hands, as soon as he tumbled he looked at them accusingly and refused to let go again for days. They taped foam to sharp edges and propped doors open with wedges. Eileen bought Charlie a push-along trolley filled with wooden bricks, but Charlie promptly emptied the trolley out, sat in it and clacked the bricks, like maracas.

As well as trying to get him to walk, Twyla was encouraging him to talk by continuing to describe everything to him, reading to him and playing audio books. She bought a Braille instruction book and a Braille label marker, and set about labelling everything from the television to Dylan's underwear drawer.

And when she was done she dropped into bed each night, wholly exhausted.

★   ★   ★

One Tuesday after Easter, when she arrived at the support group, the mums gathered around her. The room was warm and smelt of hot socks, even though the windows were open and a breeze was wobbling the blinds, like rigging on a boat.

'What's going on?' said Twyla, setting Charlie on the play mat and locking him between her legs.

The group leader came forward. 'Now don't be cross,' she said, 'but we entered you for an award — the *Star*'s 'Inspirational Woman of the Year' — and you've won!'

'What?' said Twyla, looking about her in shock. 'How . . . ?'

'I know,' the leader said. 'It's crazy. We thought you had a good chance or we wouldn't have nominated you, but then we heard yesterday that you've won and we — '

'The *Star*,' Twyla said. 'As in the national paper?'

'It's brilliant, yes?' said Ofelia, nudging Twyla.

Twyla couldn't think straight. The mums were all starting to talk at once.

'Maybe we should have asked her first,' someone said.

'But why me?' Twyla said, feeling her face flush red. 'What have I done?'

'The fund-raising, silly,' said Ofelia. 'You don't think that hasn't inspired us — made us want to do something for our own kids, hey?' Ofelia looked at the other mums, who confirmed her words with nods and affirmations.

Twyla didn't know what to say.

She gazed at Charlie, who had wriggled out from between her feet. He was reaching out to a little girl of similar age and they were touching palms together, smiling.

She hadn't ever seen him do anything like that before. The sight transfixed her.

'You're not cross, are you?' said the leader, frowning.

'No,' Twyla said. 'But what exactly do I need to do?'

The leader smiled. 'You've done the hard bit, my sweet. There's just an award ceremony next month. But we'll all be there with you.'

'An award ceremony,' said Twyla flatly.

'In London,' said Ofelia, nudging her. 'Girls' night out in a fancy hotel? Whaddya say, hey?'

There was nothing to say, except thank you. Which she said as graciously as possible.

★   ★   ★

The award ceremony was at a hotel in Mayfair, where they were staying the night courtesy of the *Star*.

Dylan and Twyla travelled to London by train with the rest of the support group mums. They drank Prosecco in plastic glasses from the buffet bar and it was so long since Dylan had been on any sort of a jolly that he enjoyed himself.

In order for Twyla to accept the award she had to agree to an article in the *Star* and a women's magazine, plus a short interview on daytime TV. Despite the daunting prospect of television, the worse kerfuffle was over what to do with Charlie during the ceremony, since they hadn't left him for the night before. In the end it was agreed that Eileen would look after Charlie at theirs.

Dylan's feelings about the publicity were mixed, not so mixed that they were a whirlpool, but more like minestrone soup, where you got something different with every spoonful. He hadn't minded about the local press, but the award felt more hazardous because of its scope — the national exposure, the millions of viewers.

There were some guarantees, however. No personal details would be divulged and the emphasis would be on Twyla's fund-raising. The end goal remained the same: to secure the eye operation for Charlie. Thus there appeared to be more good in the venture than bad. There was a pioneering element to it, a natural sense of insecurity at entering the unknown. Anxiety was an intrinsic part of the exploration process, yet if everyone yielded to it, no one would ever take that first step into the schoolyard or through those office doors.

And yet . . . mothers weren't obvious pioneers, weren't equipped with fearless hearts, weather-all skin, assassin-trained nerves. And Twyla, despite her proclamations otherwise, was as vulnerable as the next person. He couldn't help but wonder about the toll all this was taking on her.

Yet looking at her now — drinking Prosecco with Ofelia and toasting their friendship and the support group, their children, the *Star*, the wheels of the train, the waiter in the buffet bar — it was hard to see any cause for concern.

He put his head against the window and allowed himself to think that he was lucky — that what his wife was putting into motion here was something rather special and unique.

And yet it was there: the frailness of the wrists, the tense lines framing the lips.

'Top-up?' said Ofelia, offering him the bottle.

'Why not?' said Dylan.

People who achieved things, who strived for change, didn't get through life unscathed. There was comfort in the couch, in the inert, in the same. Strivers didn't slouch, didn't sleep well. They lost weight during battle, gained it again at the celebratory feast. He knew all this to be true.

And so in the end it was pride that ruled him on the train and continued to do so as they got ready in the hotel and took their places at the awards ceremony table.

But when Twyla's name was called, she suddenly blanched and looked at Dylan for support and then about her, as though lost.

And then she quickly regained composure, stood up and made her way to the platform, her dress sparkling as the spotlight followed her. The music was 'I Believe I Can Fly' — a poignant choice.

When she reached the stage, her support group friends stood up, cheering and clapping. Dylan joined them, but was beginning to feel light-headed.

Why had she looked at him like that, as though frightened?

What was she frightened of? The award, the attention?

A coating of sweat lined his lip. He sat down and drank a glass of cold water. The audience was hushing. And for the first time he felt the scratchy sensation of doubt.

★   ★   ★

There was a moment as the applause was resounding around the room and her name was booming through loudspeakers, when she felt fear cramping her ribcage.

Somehow she made it to the stage, feeling as though her heels were stilts. The editor of the

Star handed her the award — a trophy that she would have been delighted to add to her shoe-box collection as a child, and she turned to the audience with a smile.

But as the cameras clicked lullingly, like thousands of false eyelashes fluttering, as the editor began to speak, she realised that she didn't feel right about standing up here at all.

How many people felt like that — how many monarchs and medal winners at the point of coronation, knighthood or prize-giving, reflected guiltily on the short cuts they had taken and games they had played in order to arrive where they were now standing? How many doubted their worth, as the sword touched their shoulder?

There was no sword or crown here. Just a bronze trophy of a sharp-breasted female figurine that was sticking into her palm. Her right knee was shaking independently, unwilling to stop. Her mouth was dry as though filled with sand. It was insufferably hot under the lights. She thought of a sweltering desert, of a corrupt ruler with gold teeth — of sins committed and evil bargains made — and wondered what it was exactly that she was on trial for internally.

'And so I give you, ladies and gentlemen, our wonderful Inspirational Woman of the Year: Twyla Ridley!'

She stared in shock at the microphone as it was handed to her.

The room fell silent. The ruler and his gold teeth became dust, the Saharan sun packed away.

She leant against the rostrum for support and

began to speak, the microphone brushing abrasively against her lips. She kept her speech short, humble, thankful.

When she finished, applause broke out and escalated around the room. Some people were standing. More people were standing. Hundreds of people were cheering. She thought for a moment she could see Dylan, but couldn't be sure.

She waved the trophy in the air and smiled.

$\star$ $\star$ $\star$

In the hotel room, as she prised off her heels and rubbed her feet, she was aware of Dylan sitting in a shady corner of the room, a look of quiet repose on his face.

She knew what that look meant. He wanted to talk. Yet she didn't want to — was all out of energy.

'Twyla . . . '

She went through to the bathroom and took her make-up off. She looked sallow and bleached in the harsh light. Dylan appeared by her side in the mirror. He had loosened his bow tie, which hung sexily around his neck.

She managed to evade him until the lights went out.

'Twyla . . . ' He turned on to his side to face her. The blackout curtains were drawn. It was so dark in the room she couldn't even see him. 'What happened back there?' he asked.

She didn't have to see his expression to know that he was anxious to hear her thoughts. She had led him for so long — not through manipulation or control, but with passion and enthusiasm. When someone in a partnership harboured strong opinions and the other didn't then it was fair to assume that the one with the opinion should have their way.

And yet was that fair? If Dylan didn't have a preference, wasn't that a preference in itself — the right to remain neutral, to do nothing?

'Back where?' she replied.

He reached for her, touched her shoulder. 'When you stood to get the award . . . You looked scared.'

She feigned a yawn. 'Well, wouldn't you be, with all those people looking at you?'

'It wasn't because you're having second thoughts, then?'

'No,' she said to the ceiling. 'Are you?'

The pause was too long.

'No,' he said.

'Well, night then,' she said.

'Night,' he replied, withdrawing his arm.

They remained like that for a long while, on their backs, side by side, staring into the darkness.

★ ★ ★

He was sorry to see the front page article in the *Herald* about her blind baby. They used his Christmas photograph. It was such a shame. She had looked so happy the night her son was born. Only for this to happen.

He had thought about her an awful lot, had

known that their lives would intertwine in some way and that he would see her again. So he was barely surprised when he turned on the television one morning and she was right there before him.

She was wearing a lemon-coloured blouse. She was nervous, kept flicking her hair from her face and was picking over her words carefully, but otherwise faultless.

She looked tired, he thought, and slightly thinner. She was fiddling with something — he sat forward to look — a charm on a chain around her neck. Then she let it drop back on to her blouse. He sat back as though dropped too.

She was honoured to have been given the award, she was saying.

A number appeared and a website to donate to her fund-raising campaign. He grabbed a pen and jotted down the details.

It's been a real pleasure, Twyla, the host was saying. *Best of luck, and don't forget to come back and tell us how it all works out.*

★   ★   ★

Only a week later, he was in the gardens at his usual spot when she appeared, holding her boy's hand. She was wearing a white dress that accentuated her slenderness.

He panicked. She was heading right for him. He grabbed his book and hurried away into an enclosure of trees and shrubs.

When he was confident that they couldn't see

87

him, he peered out amongst the branches. She was laying a blanket underneath the elm tree in his favourite spot.

He couldn't go back out the way he had come. He would have to force his way through the trees and out the other side.

He wrestled himself free, stumbling out on to the path, his arms covered in shrubbery. A woman was sat nearby breast-feeding her baby. She scowled at him. He darted off, wiping leaves from his shoulders, and ran up the exit steps three at a time. At the top, he stood looking back down.

He could see her. She was cradling her son in her arms and pointing up to the sky. The boy's face was turned upwards compliantly.

He observed them for a moment before realising that he was late for a photo shoot, and so hurried off on his way.

⋆ ⋆ ⋆

One early morning in July, everything stopped. They both felt it.

The media attention and the fund-raising had waned. They were just waiting for the Royal Square now. Even house-hunting hadn't come to much. There was nothing for it but to enjoy summer.

They decided to drive to the beach. Charlie was adorable in purple shorts; Dylan in good spirits whistling to the radio. The blue elephant had to come too, hanging from Charlie's mouth, soggy, beloved.

Weston-super-Mare didn't really have a beach, but an expanse of mud that in places became dangerous sinking sand. The sea was so far out that on sunny days like today it appeared like a silver snail trail on the horizon. The wind was pushy, coming in from the Bristol Channel. People were staggering along the promenade, their legs being knocked out from underneath them.

'Feel the sand, Charlie,' Twyla said, pulling his socks off. 'Can you hear the sea? It's a long way away, but you can just hear it.'

Charlie clapped his hands with glee. He was curious about the sand and tried to eat it, leaving traces of it around his mouth. They built a sandcastle. The sun was high and strong, and the wind buffeted their T-shirts causing the cotton to swell on their backs.

Dylan went to the kiosk for ice creams. Then he kicked a large softball back and forth to Charlie. 'Here it comes, Charlie boy,' he said. Charlie sat wobbling on the sand, his legs stretched out either side of him. He waited until the ball came right to him before tossing it back in the wrong direction. Dylan patiently fetched the ball and brought it back.

Twyla closed her eyes, surrendering to the fresh air and the rare chance to rest. She could still see the orange glow of sunshine on her eyelids, could feel the warmth on her face despite the wind.

They always had a lovely time at Weston. The beach wasn't much to look at, yet it always felt rather magical.

Funny that she had met Dylan here. She was on a day out with friends and they were sitting on the beach debating whether to get the next train home, when a group of lads arrived and sat at a respectable distance, flicking chips at them. When they discovered they all lived in Bath, they decided to go for drinks together.

It took her a while to realise that Dylan liked her. He was less forward than his friends, less inclined towards self-promotion. And yet he was the best-looking of the group, of probably all the men she had ever met. His reticence drew her forward longingly. It couldn't have been more seductive and effective had he planned it. Where she enthused, he nodded; where she cheered, he smiled. The balance felt right. She fell in love almost immediately.

They got married in Weston-super-Mare town hall on a spring morning two years later and celebrated in a bar around the corner. They stayed the night in a Victorian hotel and in the morning travelled jubilantly back to Bath to resume normal life.

Normal life.

Had someone told her how things were going to end up, she would never have believed them.

★ ★ ★

Twyla woke to the sound of Dylan calling her.

Her first instinct was to panic. She stood up, hands to her forehead in a sun shield. She was groggy from sleep and had stood too quickly. She could see stars.

Dylan was raising his arms in celebration. 'Twyla! Look!' he was shouting.

Charlie was walking towards her, tottering jerkily on his feet, laughing his head off at the absurdity of the sensation, of this new and fascinating thing that he was doing with his legs.

She had never heard him laugh like that, had never really heard him laugh at all. But now he was laughing and walking, just like other children.

'Mummy's here!' she called out, feeling weak-kneed with joy.

It was hard to take it in — the enormity of the moment. All she could do was hold her arms out to Charlie, who was rapidly approaching in purple shorts, his cheeks wobbling.

'That's it, Charlie!' she said. 'Mummy's here!'

By some miracle, he missed the hole that a child was digging, missed the picnic blanket that a family had spread out, and fell neatly into her arms, trembling, soaked in sweat, tasting of salt air and love.

They stayed late at the beach. Charlie kept walking between the two of them, dashing from one of them to the other, laughing so hard that he soaked through his nappy.

Finally, when Charlie had fallen asleep exhausted, they sat with their backs against the beach wall, with their arms around each other and Charlie lying on their laps — eating corn-yellow chips from paper cartons, watching the sun set.

Had she known where they were headed she

would have tried to bottle that day — to trap it in a jar with the seawater and sand so that she could shake it on grey days; a treasured snow globe of memories.

7

Stephen was born in Louisiana in 1950 and moved to New York in late childhood. Although the Thibodeauxs were wealthy and lived on the Upper East Side of Manhattan, they were never fully accepted into social circles because they were from the south and Mrs Thibodeaux often dropped the 'g' from the end of her words.

Mr Thibodeaux was an esteemed psychiatrist so it was natural that his only child, Stephen, would follow in his footsteps at Harvard. Stephen had a stiflingly formal relationship with his parents and the gulf between them widened once he moved to Massachusetts to begin his studies. Since his parents were paying for his education, he kept in touch through birthday and Christmas cards — a system which served him well and didn't seem to disappoint, because the feeling of indifference was mutual.

So it was that Stephen grew up believing that love was a matter of duty, and his relationships at Harvard mirrored this belief. His girlfriends were academics so there was lots of debate and few emotional breakthroughs. He had a vague idea that there were people out there doing things differently, but were he not so obsessed with the brain, he might have understood the heart more easily.

He was a gifted scholar and qualified as a licensed clinical psychologist with ease, but needed to expand his outlook which was limited to the lives of the rich. So when a job arose in New Orleans at a community mental health centre, he seized the challenge.

And it was whilst gobbling a hot dog from the stand outside the health centre and turning the corner of the street too quickly that he bumped into Robin, squirted mustard on her catsuit and immediately understood that love had nothing to do with duty whatsoever.

Robin suited the fashions of the seventies. She was pretty and slim, with shiny hair scooped from her face by an Alice band. She was light-spirited and delicate of touch and was attracted to anyone whom she deemed strong yet gentle. She would have hated the eighties.

What drew him to her initially was her lack of definition. She was neither girlish nor butch; neither educated nor ignorant. For a psychotherapist wishing to categorise everyone, the ambiguity was tantalising.

She, however, could take or leave him. It took him the best part of a year to get her to take him seriously. This hadn't been a problem at Harvard where his reputation preceded him, but in vibrant New Orleans he was a flop. Men were queuing to date Robin, who was rather partial to muscular poets. He had height on his side, but needed to beef up so he started lifting weights and reading Byron.

Robin, despite her literary demands, worked in a typing pool. If she deemed this beneath her, she never let on. It wasn't until they had been dating a year that he realised that her mother was one of his patients and was the reason why Robin was outside his surgery that day. Robin had been her mother's carer since early childhood. Her boss at the typing pool allowed her flexibility in return for a low wage.

He never really got to know her mother. By the time he worked out who she was, she had died.

Robin handled her grief well. She had been preparing for this day all her life, she said. And like a fool, he believed her.

*   *   *

He rapped on the front door. Twyla answered promptly, looking less rested than when he had last seen her.

'Stephen,' she said, surprised.

This time he wasn't going to let it go. 'Why not call me Dad?' he said.

'Why not phone before you visit?'

They were off to a bad start.

He softened his voice. 'Would you and Charlie care to join me for an ice cream?'

'You drove all the way from London to take us out for ice cream?'

'Sort of,' he said. He was about to add that he was passing by after a meeting at Bath university, but decided that it might dampen the gesture. When in fact he had set up the meeting to give him an excuse to visit them.

'You'd better come in,' Twyla said. 'Charlie's having a nap, but he's due to wake any minute.'

'Good,' he said. 'Thank you.'

'Coffee?' she asked.

'Please.'

As Twyla went to the kitchen, he turned into the lounge and stood looking about him, whistling softly. Something caught his eye on the coffee table. It was a newspaper clipping.

Inspirational Woman of the Year: a mother's quest to help her blind baby see.

He stared at the article in astonishment. He knew nothing of this — nothing about trying to cure Charlie. He hadn't even known for the first year of Charlie's life that he was blind.

Could she have made her indifference towards him any clearer?

He dropped the cutting absently and it fluttered to the floor. He gazed out of the window. It was July. The trees were in full bloom outside the house, blocking the view of the city.

He heard movement behind him. Twyla was picking the article up from the floor.

'You couldn't tell me about that?' he said.

'It's not a big deal.'

'But why didn't I know about it?' he said.

She stood still, biting her bottom lip.

He sat down on the sofa and pulled his fountain pen and chequebook from his suit. 'How much do you need?' he said.

'What?' she said. 'I don't need money!'

'You're fund-raising, Twyla.'

'Not any more. It's just a case of waiting now.'

'Waiting?'

'For the research centre to give us the

go-ahead.' She took a step towards him and then stopped as though an invisible obstruction barred her way. 'I can email you all the details if you like?'

'Sure,' he said, nodding. 'An email.'

So that was how it was going to be.

He stood up, straightened his jacket, ran his fingers through his hair and made for the door.

'Where are you going?' she said, hurrying after him.

He went down the hallway. Charlie had woken and was moaning softly upstairs, the sound of which saddened him.

He opened the front door and, as he stepped outside, he turned to face her. 'It's clear that you don't want me in your life,' he said.

'That's not true!'

'Unfortunately, it is.'

She looked as though she were about to cry. But then she gained control, folding her arms high on her chest.

'When will I see you next?' she said.

'When you're ready,' he said. 'I'll wait for you to get in touch with me this time.'

She glanced upstairs. Charlie was moaning more urgently now, to her agitation.

He admired her for that — for her devotion to her boy.

'I'm proud of you,' he said, trying to end things on a high.

'Why?' she said.

'For the award, for your determination . . . It's how I raised you to be — to never settle, to expect great things.'

To his surprise, she began to laugh. 'You think I'm like this because of you?' she said. 'I'm like this in spite of you.'

He stared at her, his Adam's apple feeling too large for his throat.

He swallowed loudly. 'Please, Twyla . . . '

'I must see to Charlie,' she said. 'Goodbye, Stephen.'

It was the final blow, calling him that.

She closed the front door. He gazed at the grooves in the door, reflecting on how badly this visit had gone. And then he walked slowly to his car.

One day, he would leave her company feeling differently, without this sagging sensation as though he were an old cowboy weighted down by saddlebags and water bottles.

He groaned and put his head on the steering wheel.

Why couldn't that day be now?

He lifted his head. The only way to not leave like this, was to not leave like this.

As he got back out of the car, the front door opened. And there on the step with his hair on end and an elephant hanging from his mouth was his grandson.

'Well, whaddya know?' Stephen said softly.

She had done the same thing — must have realised that it wasn't good enough to part on bad terms any more; that sometimes you had to get back in the ring and fight. And Twyla was adept at that — not at fighting, but at staying the course.

She appeared in the doorway beside Charlie

and they all met midway on the driveway.

'Charlie said he wasn't going to let you leave without that ice cream,' Twyla said.

'He said that?' said Stephen, ruffling Charlie's hair. On the two occasions he had met Charlie, he hadn't heard him say a single word.

'Yep.'

'Well then,' he said. 'We'd best get going if that's what the little man said.'

And so they set off up the road, Charlie pausing to feel around for stones on the pavement and for holes in walls, Twyla talking about the operation, and Stephen, who had learnt that suddenly relieving oneself of saddle-bags was as precarious as being overladen, since he was now feeling as light and bandy as a scarecrow.

★   ★   ★

Dylan was on his way to the Italian deli to ask whether they would cater for Charlie's christening in August. The idea had evolved on the drive back from their trip to Weston. Worn out, sand-blasted but overjoyed about Charlie's first steps, they had decided to hold a big christening party so that they could make a fuss of Charlie.

The sun was powerful today, but it had rained earlier and puddles were steaming on the pavements. There was a strong smell of moisture and warmth that reminded him of camping as a child, of sunshine burning off the dew on canvas.

As he entered the deli and saw the array of stripy pastas, he realised that he hadn't eaten yet.

And it was whilst he was perusing the menu that Molly entered the shop, blushing on spotting him. The owner was on good terms with her, calling her 'Moll-*lee*!'

'Your food will be ten minute,' the owner told them. 'But if you wait in garden,' he said, 'I bring espresso on house?'

'That sounds nice,' said Molly.

'Why not?' said Dylan.

He hadn't been out to the back garden before and had no idea what he was in for. Neither apparently did Molly. She stood gazing about her, her blush deepening. The small suntrap whiffed faintly of romance. There were statues of semi-naked figurines peeking out from the ivy. Water trickled from a fountain. Soft music teased the senses through hidden speakers.

'Here?' said Molly, pointing to the nearest table and chair. The garden was empty, exacerbating the air of intimacy.

The espressos arrived promptly. Dylan stirred his coffee, wondering what on earth they would find to talk about at such close quarters.

'Do you normally come here for lunch?' she asked, with her nasally voice. She tended to keep her lips slightly parted as though her nose were blocked.

'Not often,' he replied. 'I'm here to sort the catering for my son's christening.'

'Charlie Ross?' she said.

He nodded, with mild surprise. He couldn't recall having told her any personal details.

'I saw you in the paper,' she added.

Ah.

'It must be difficult,' she said, stirring her coffee.

He considered this. Honesty seemed best. 'Yes,' he replied.

She smiled, her nose wrinkling. 'Your wife must be really special,' she said.

Molly had a simple way with words, a way of stating things frankly. She chose her clothes like her words: unadorned, clean cut. Today she was wearing a white blouse, black trousers.

'She is pretty special, yes,' he said, feeling rather awkward about the nature of the conversation.

'Do you think you'll manage to get the operation for Charlie?' she asked.

He glanced at her. She was looking back at him enquiringly. There was nothing on her face but the apparent desire to make small talk with the boss in a confined space. She was following textbook procedure: find something that he wants to talk about — probably himself.

'I've no idea,' he said. 'Let's hope so.' He sat up straight, tugged his suit trousers at the knees. 'Molly, there's a project coming in that I'd like you to work on . . . '

She nodded politely as he talked about work. There was something old-fashioned about her, he thought; something modest, unassuming. She was the sort of girl he would have gone for years ago, back in sixth form, when all he wanted in a woman was someone to show up on time outside the Palladium Cinema and to not break up with him after he'd paid for the tickets and interval ice creams.

There was a crackle as the music stopped and the owner's voice appeared on the speaker system. 'One Brie on ciabatta for Moll-*lee*,' he said. 'And one Parma ham . . . Is ready.' The music came back on.

'I can recommend the Sicilian pastries,' Molly said, as they left the garden.

'Hey?' said Dylan.

'For the christening,' she replied.

'Ah, yes,' he said. 'Thanks.' And they went into the café to pick up their lunch.

★ ★ ★

One warm afternoon, as the bees dipped in and out of the lavender pots and the air was filled with the aroma of cut grass, Twyla finally opened the workshop and resumed work.

She took Charlie out with her and was surprised to discover that he was happy to play on the rug for hours. She wouldn't solder around him, but could get on with hammering and polishing. He seemed to enjoy the sound of her working, liked feeling the shapes of the materials that she handed him to explore. And when he wasn't interested in her work, he played with his learning table, slapping the keys to hear the ABC song.

When Charlie napped, she soldered, working on two wire mesh stacking kiln shelves. The shelves were very old. She had picked them up at a flea market years ago and had stuck with them for sentimental reasons.

Becoming a jewellery-maker hadn't been part

of her life plan. As a teenager, she evolved from badge-collecting to qualification-bagging. Yet during her law degree she began to make jewellery to reduce the stress of finals and found that it was not only satisfying but she was good at it. So she then took a course in jewellery and silversmithing, and when she won the jewellery category of a V&A competition, she started to receive enough commissions to earn a living.

She rarely advertised now and mostly only made bola necklaces. The best advertisement was the necklace that she wore herself. All the support group mums had wanted one as soon as they saw Twyla's, and now she was going to fulfil some overdue orders.

The bolas — or balls — were Mexican in origin. The charm, on a long chain, contained a musical bell intended to soothe the baby in the womb. The chain was adjustable so that once the baby was born it could play with the ball whilst feeding.

Twyla made all sorts of charms, depending on what the client wanted: pebble-shapes, hearts, orbs, etchings of flowers or stars. She used a selection of chains: silver, natural cord or printed ribbons. But most clients wanted one exactly like Twyla's.

The necklace that Twyla wore had been her mother's. It used to tinkle as her mother bent to bath Twyla in the metal tub on the porch, or as she chased Twyla round the peach trees in the back yard. The sound was so synonymous with her mother that Twyla thought she possessed magical powers that accompanied her movements with fairy chimes.

Sometimes Twyla used to sneak up to her mother when she was asleep out on the porch and shake the charm to hear the chime within. Sometimes, if she was really brave, she would pop it in her mouth, feeling the prickles of the metal against her tongue. The design wasn't like any others Twyla had seen — an intricate pattern of swirls and crosses. Admirers requested the same, but she never managed to imitate it precisely. The pattern was like an ancient language that had become extinct, never to be revived.

Charlie might shake the charm, as he often did, might suck or bite it, just as she once had, and the charm jingled. Yet that was all it gave them: an enigmatic tinkle that lingered in the ear before disappearing.

The intercom crackled as Charlie shifted about in his cot inside the house.

She stopped work to listen. He had settled again.

She picked up the small butane-powered torch and bent her neck to solder a hook to a charm.

Funny that she knew so little about her mother's life.

There was only one person whom she could ask about her — one keeper of the gate, one other human who could recall the decibel of her laugh, the smell of her violet *eau du parfum*; someone who could procure a brush with her hair entwined in its bristles or a cardigan with a handkerchief folded triangle-shaped in a pocket, like a forgotten sandwich.

Yet there were no such mementos, she was certain. All the possessions — the brushes and cardigans and traces of violet fragrance were banished long ago.

It was her father's way of coping. His loss would have been profound, devastating at thirty-two years old, and his reaction was to deal with it methodically.

As a five-year-old child, she had craved the opposite of logic and reasoning. Yet that was what she was offered as they buried her mother.

Perhaps he was too close to see it — too smothered by his own grief to notice what was happening to them. Scarcely was the last guest gone from the wake, the last coffee cup washed, the last condolence offered, than the silence enveloped them. It accompanied them as they packed up the house, and all the way in the car up to Boston.

'This will be your room,' he told her, showing her into a bedroom in a Beacon Hill brownstone overlooking the Common. It was nice enough, prestigious even. But so quiet.

She went about her business and he did the same, pausing to do a button up on her coat, or to pass her the syrup at breakfast.

Sometimes she had shyly climbed on to his lap to ask if he missed Mummy, if he knew whether she was coming back, if she could borrow Mummy's perfume to spray on her pillow to help her sleep at night. But her father just said that her mother wasn't coming back, no, and that lavender was better than violet for inducing sleep.

105

By the time they had crossed an ocean to London, things were hopeless between them.

It was such a waste of a relationship.

Without thinking, she put down the butane torch and picked up the phone.

He answered immediately.

'Hi there,' she said, rather too cheerfully. 'Where did my bola necklace come from?'

'Well, good afternoon to you too,' he said.

She pictured him taking off his glasses, chewing the end of the spectacles before replying.

'It was your mother's,' he said.

'I know that,' she said. She turned the radio down. It was a jazz piece — sporadic, slightly manic.

'But where did she get it from?' she asked.

'It was her mother's — your grandmother's,' he said. 'That's all I know.'

The music had stopped. The conversation was flatlining.

Jazz. Say something about that.

'Mum liked Miles Davis, didn't she?' she said, wincing with the effort of saying 'Mum' like that, as though they batted her name about all the time.

She could remember jazz playing at home. One of the neighbourhood boys used to dance on their lawn with skinny legs, flapping his arms like a chicken.

'No,' Stephen said.

'Really? I thought — '

'It was me.'

'Oh,' she said. 'So what did Mum like?'

It took him a while to answer. She put him on loudspeaker and waited, picking up the torch. Melting metal was her favourite part of the process — that and sanding the solder seams to make them smooth. There was a predictability in the process that appealed to her. Heat this, it'll melt; hammer this, it'll flatten; rub this, it'll shine. It brought to mind the words of the gospel songs that had drifted from chapel on Sundays.

'John Denver,' her father said finally. 'And Carly Simon.'

'Carly Simon,' said Twyla. 'Wow. I don't think I could name anything by her.'

' 'You're So Vain',' he said. ' 'Nobody Does It Better'.'

'I don't know those,' she said. 'Maybe you could sing one.'

He paused. 'You're teasing me.'

'Yes.'

'Goodbye, Twyla.'

'Goodbye, Stephen . . . Dad.'

She hung up, and tested the hook on the charm, checking it with a magnifying glass. It was good. She picked up the next hook and ball, and bent in close with the torch again.

Their relationship had been awkward in those early days, but cordial. Yet everything changed after the Cape Cod trip that they didn't take.

She had just finished school at Leighford Park. Her father showed up to collect her, surprising her with the trip. It was a great way for them to spend time together before she went to university, he said. They could meet his parents in Manhattan en route. Wouldn't she like that

— to meet her grandparents, the legendary Thibodeauxs?

She told him to get his money back. She wasn't going home with him in the car today, nor was she going to Cape Cod. She was staying in Reading for the summer. When term began, she would be going straight to Bristol university to study law. She was going to rent a house there and work to support herself.

His face had been awful. He had ground his jaw, a vein in his temple bulged. She thought that he might keel over, or grab her and stuff her into the car boot. But he just got behind the wheel and drove away.

He visited her student-let only once, picking his way over pizza boxes to find a chair to perch on in his expensive trench coat.

'Is this really necessary?' he said. 'You don't need to live like this. I can give you money.'

Her friends had scattered, as they always did when parents arrived. A bass was thumping upstairs. 'Are you well, Twyla? Are you eating? Sleeping?'

He left. It was a few days before she noticed the envelope on the coffee table. She ripped the cheque up. He tried to call her about it, but she didn't answer the phone.

After graduating, she moved to Bath. Her first rental was a squalid bedsit, which in the area translated as cramped and unstylish. Again Stephen visited, eyeing the room interrogatively as though expecting to find syringes. The conversation was even more minimalist.

'Good. You're alive,' he said.

Once more, he left a cheque and once more she destroyed it — this time more dramatically by setting fire to it on the gas stove.

As her business flourished, so her living quarters improved and her relationship with her father deteriorated. By the time she was living in a one-bedroom apartment in the centre of town he had stopped visiting, which was a shame because he would have liked the new place.

She put down the torch and picked up the phone again.

'Did you ever get your money back on Cape Cod?' she said.

He was typing. She could hear his fingers tapping the keys. 'I beg your pardon?'

'The trip we were supposed to take that summer.'

The typing stopped. 'Oh,' he said.

'Well?'

'No,' he said. 'Twyla . . . Don't — '

'Maybe we could go some time.'

'I'd like that,' he said, resuming typing.

They would never go, but it was a comforting thought.

★   ★   ★

When Charlie moaned to her over the intercom, Twyla went indoors and was just climbing the stairs when the letterbox rattled.

She bent to retrieve the mail from the doormat. 'Coming, Charlie,' she called.

The envelope was unmarked. She opened it

and read the letter within, halting halfway up the stairs.

'What . . . ?' she said.

She ran back downstairs to the front door and out into the street, looking up and down.

A neighbour's laundry was moving in a back garden — a white sheet fluttering, like an arm waving.

She returned indoors and ripped the letter and its envelope up into cream and brown pieces like cappuccino-coloured confetti, before throwing them in the bin.

'Coming, Charlie!' she called as she ran back upstairs.

But the words stayed with her for the remainder of the day, despite their fragmented state, despite her fierce desire to obliterate them.

Mrs Ridley,
     It was the Lord's desire that your son be born blind. It is not for you to say otherwise. Stop this now before it's too late.
     'Be not wise in thine own eyes: fear the Lord, and depart from evil.'
     Proverbs 3:7

8

It was quiet at work. A few staff and several big clients were on holiday. Dylan was finding it hard to concentrate. He got himself a machine coffee and took his laptop into a side room, closing the door behind him.

He had started some research yesterday that he wanted to look at again today. There was a lot of information on the Royal Square website about keratoprosthesis surgery that he had looked at many times with Twyla. But today he wanted to look again, to satisfy the doubt that had set foot in him during the award ceremony and wouldn't go away.

It was stuffy in the room. He nudged open the window, but the roar of the traffic was too much to bear so he promptly closed it again. As he read, he rolled up his shirtsleeves, loosened his tie.

The cornea, the website said, worked in much the same way as the clear glass of a watch face. During keratoprosthesis surgery, the damaged cornea was replaced with clear artificial material that the body was unlikely to reject. The keratoprosthesis itself was like a tiny telescope. It was fitted into the transplant and then stitched into the patient's actual cornea. A contact lens was then placed on to the eye for protection and cosmetic reasons.

Dylan clicked on to the link to look at the

images of transplants in place. The eyes looked like jellyfish: a black hole in the centre with lines going from the middle to the outside, like stitching. The examples of wearing coloured contact lenses on top were infinitely more pleasant. Yet the implant would never look natural, no matter what.

He shuddered and went back to the information page.

It was estimated that up to fifty per cent of patients would experience raised intraocular pressure, with about twenty-five per cent developing glaucoma after the procedure. There were also other risks, but there wasn't enough data to justify statistics: bleeding or infection inside the eye; the retina coming away; scar tissue forming and blocking vision; inflammation inside the eye; the transplant tissue melting or thinning; the eyelids could droop; the eye could be lost entirely.

There were no guarantees that the surgery would work. It could even make existing conditions worse.

In capitals, it said:

KERATOPROSTHESIS SURGERY IS AN ELECTIVE PROCEDURE.

Dylan took his tie off and sat back in his chair with his hands behind his head.

He sat like that for a while and as he did a vision came to him from so long ago that he whistled softly in surprise.

He was about six years old. He could see his long socks and high-waisted shorts; could see the amber colour of the patterned carpet that always looked like it would taste of Terry's Chocolate Orange; could see Bindy stood there in her favourite T-shirt that said 'Stay Alive in '85'; and Felicity in her wheelchair playing with a basket of plastic fruit.

'Come on, Dills,' Bindy was saying. 'Don't be a cowardy custard.'

He was too little to respond effectively to these taunts from a far more dexterous tongue, other than to declare himself otherwise. 'Me not custard!'

'Cowardy custard, cowardy custard, cowardy custard,' Bindy jeered.

Dylan stamped his foot, but dared not do more than that. Secretly, he lived in fear of his big sister who had five years on him and according to the boy next door could crush spiders in one hand, although Dylan hadn't actually seen her do that.

'Let's see if we can do it,' Bindy said.

Dylan stood still, rigid with the idea of doing something wrong.

'Poor Fee has to spend all her time in this blasted thing,' Bindy said, with a kick to the back of the wheelchair that made Felicity drop the plastic banana she was holding.

Dylan gazed at the banana before moving forward to pick it up, but Bindy held him back.

'Uh uh,' she said, wagging her finger. She turned to look at Felicity. 'Let's see if she can get it.'

Dylan didn't understand his sister — either of them. But if he felt any affinity with either of them it was to the silent one in the chair rather than the big one with her spider-crunching fists. He was never sure whether she was being mean or helpful. He only knew that it felt wrong, that his heart was thumping like it did the first time he saw the Daleks on television.

'You need to stand there with your arms out, Dills,' said Bindy. 'And I'll stand here and tip the chair up.'

Dylan didn't answer. He felt the urge to go to the toilet and clutched himself between his legs.

'Come on, stinky pants!' said Bindy. 'Quick, before Mum wakes up.'

He eyed the door. Any minute now Mummy could come through that door in her nightgown. Sometimes, if her hair was in rollers, she looked like a judge with a curled wig.

'Hurry!' said Bindy. 'Get in place! Hold out your arms!' She went behind the wheelchair and, with her teeth gritted, she began to tilt the back of it up. Felicity was tissue-thin. Dylan held out his arms.

It was a moment before he realised what had happened. Felicity had landed on him with a smack. She was heavier than she looked. His arms had folded instantly, like deckchair legs. Their chins had collided. There was blood coming from Felicity's mouth and from his nose.

'Holy moley!' Bindy was shouting. 'That wasn't supposed to happen! Get up, quick!'

He sprang to his feet, tasting the trail of blood from his nose with the tip of his tongue.

Yukky. Metal. Warm. Warm metal.

'Don't just stand there, cabbage brain! Help me get her back in!'

114

They lifted Felicity with all their might. She moaned as they moved her, as though telling them to leave her alone. She continued to moan after they got her back in the chair and Dylan realised it was because she wanted her plastic banana back. The whole basket had been scattered all over the floor.

As Dylan collected the fruit, Bindy drummed her fingers on the kitchen counter. 'So you really can't walk then, Fee, eh?' Bindy said. 'Well, we won't try that again. Duly noted.'

'Who's Julie?' Dylan said.

⋆ ⋆ ⋆

Dylan waited until Charlie was asleep before talking to Twyla. She was sitting in the lounge watching television, her legs underneath a throw. It had turned cold for summer — wet and dark.

'Do you know what elective means?' he asked.

She pressed the mute button on the remote control and turned to look at him. 'As in elective surgery?' she said.

'Yes.'

'Well, it means — '

'It's from a Latin word meaning 'to choose',' he said.

She turned the television off. It crackled before falling silent.

'I've been looking at the surgery again,' he said.

'Oh?'

'And I . . . ' He stopped. How did he feel? Doubtful? Well, she was too. Frightened. As was

115

she. Optimistic? No. That was back in Twyla's territory, something that he had tried and wasn't all that good at. He had known everything would be all right when they were trying to accept Charlie as blind. But this . . . he just didn't know about.

All he knew was that thirty years ago when they tried to get Felicity to walk it had resulted in bloodshed. Maybe that memory had stepped forward to try to tell him something.

'Elective means that the surgery isn't required in order to save a life,' he said. 'This operation is still controversial for small children because of the risks.' He took her hand and pressed it. 'Why are we doing this?'

'To restore Charlie's sight,' she said.

'But how can we restore something that was never there?'

She gazed at him not with a look of betrayal exactly, but of something else. Rejection perhaps, or immense disappointment.

'But I asked you about this over a year ago — when I first looked into this. We went through the risks and talked it through with the Royal Square and — '

'I know,' he said, feeling wretched. 'And I'm not saying no . . . I'm not sure what I'm saying.'

She rallied then. 'Then don't say anything,' she said. 'He might not even have the operation. The Royal Square might never be ready. We might miss our chance.'

He felt relieved by the opportunity to defer judgement. He reached forward and kissed her. She smelt of the lavender oil that she dropped into Charlie's bath water each night. 'I knew you'd understand,' he said.

'Oh, Dylan,' she said, trying to smile but not quite getting there. 'Of course.'

She returned to the sofa, but this time she didn't put the television on. Instead, she sat motionless, sipping tea, watching the summer rain.

★　★　★

In August, the letters began to arrive silently, tentatively. Their anonymity made them easy to destroy. She told herself that the writer's inability to put a signature to the letter was a weakness. This wasn't a hand that she should fear, an omnipotent source of condemnation. She would continue to deal with them the same way, adding coffee-coloured confetti to the bin on a weekly basis.

But then someone did send a letter with a signature. The envelope was postmarked Southampton and was from the mother of a blind son who had read Twyla's interview in the women's magazine. The interview had gone more deeply into the risks of the procedure than Twyla would have liked, but she had answered the questions frankly.

This is just plain wrong, the mother wrote. *The risks are far too great for such a young child. Why can't you let him be and accept him the way he is?*

Was it the risk that she objected to, the principle, or both? Twyla wondered. If the operation had a guaranteed outcome of success would it still be morally reprehensible? There was no return address on the letter, no means of Twyla asking this question.

The letter became confetti.

The mother was soon joined by a father of blind twins; a single mum of a teenage boy going blind; a support group; a religious sect; a concerned priest; several concerned priests. She had no idea how the public had obtained their address details. So much for data protection.

What gives you the right to play God?
How could you do that to your own child?
Shame on you.

One day the letters came in such a glut, she went out and bought a shredder to keep discreetly behind the sofa.

Fortunately, the post came whilst Dylan was at work. She couldn't tell him about the letters. He would take it as a definite sign that they were pursuing the wrong course. Things were already so precariously balanced. If they decided not to do it, well so be it. But complete strangers weren't going to decide it for them.

And so she kept shredding.

The anonymous ones — the brown envelope and cream paper ones — were the trickiest because they were delivered by a hand that she was never quick enough to spot, at a time when Dylan could have intercepted them. They came so sporadically that she found herself listening out for them, keeping one eye on the front door, checking under the doormat several times a day.

Looking for false miracles will bring doom upon your family.

Instead of a name, they always signed off with the Proverbs quotation which she now knew by rote.

No one was brave enough to approach her directly. Aside from one person, in the unlikeliest of places.

They were in the local supermarket. It was a hot day with barely any breeze outside to unstick clothes from backs. Charlie was reaching into the freezer for an ice pop and Twyla was holding him by his legs, trying to prevent him from trapping his hands in the sliding doors and from slipping out of her grip. She began to laugh and Charlie laughed too. Sometimes they got themselves in the most ridiculous positions.

'Excuse me!'

Someone was behind them, impatient to get to the freezer.

Twyla hoisted Charlie up. They would wait. There were twenty sorts of lollies for him to fondle. She wouldn't hurry him.

An elderly woman was standing before them, staring angrily at Twyla.

'It's all yours,' said Twyla, gesturing at the freezer. She set Charlie on the floor, but held him against her legs.

The woman made no move towards the freezer. She was working herself up, her aged face vibrating with the effort. Her lips were dark purple, dotted with blood spots. 'What you're doing is evil,' she said, pointing at Twyla.

'You what?' said Twyla.

'It's not the Lord's desire,' the woman said. 'Depart from evil.' Then she flapped her hand and turned away as though she didn't intend wasting any more energy on them.

Charlie gripped Twyla's hand. He might not have understood the conversation, but even toddlers knew whether someone meant them harm or not. He looked upset, his bottom lip protruding.

She bent down to look at him, pulling off his cap to give him some air. 'It's all right, Charlie,' she said, kissing him. 'Everything's all right. Come on.' She lifted him gently. 'Let's look back inside the freezer. There are rocket lollies and ones with teddy bear jelly sweets in . . . '

She dangled Charlie just like before. But this time neither of them laughed and Charlie chose the first lolly that he touched.

★　★　★

'So how many people are coming?' said Bindy, yawning. The christening was in a fortnight and Twyla had it all under control, but they were here today to discuss napkins. Bindy sensed that Twyla didn't really want their help, that she considered their idea of personalised Charlie Ross napkins trite. Naturally, Twyla was too polite to say so.

'About fifty,' said Twyla.

'Gosh!' said Eileen. 'Isn't that . . . ?' She was probably going to say something like frivolous,

120

over-generous, but then closed her mouth with a little snap of teeth.

'Many of the guests have helped with fund-raising,' Twyla said. 'It's our way of thanking them. Plus, there's your extended family . . .'

Extended family. Bindy pictured aunts and uncles with elongated limbs, a tangled mass of tentacles.

She shook her head. She should lay off the Jack Daniel's. She was drinking too much lately. It was the stress.

'Stress of what exactly?' her mother had said on the car journey over, grabbing the opportunity to list what Bindy hadn't achieved. 'You've got *no* husband, *no* mortgage, *no* children, *no* career. Doesn't sound stressful to me.'

Sometimes, Bindy thought, having a big blank space to tend to was harder than a detailed one.

'We'll see to the cake,' said Eileen, making a note in her diary.

'No need,' said Twyla. 'I'll make one.'

Bindy raised an eyebrow and spun round slowly on her heel.

This should be amusing.

'Oh?' said Eileen. Her face looked pinched, as though clipped by a giant clothes peg.

'It'll give me something to do,' Twyla said.

'Something to do?' said Eileen, looking around her as though there were jobs lined up all around the room. 'Don't you have enough to see to?'

Bindy's mother was wearing a puce cardigan that on anyone else would have made them look jaundiced but that somehow worked on her, given her orangey hair and poppy-red lipstick.

Her trousers were still too short, Bindy thought, eyeing her mother's sheep socks. She had told her time and again to leave them alone, but still Eileen attacked the hems with her sewing machine, ensuring that her trousers never scooped floor dust or picked up dirt. It was the ultimate in not connecting with anything or being defiled. Because their mother, for all her adoration of God and Charlie Ross, was someone who preferred to skim the surface.

'Honestly,' Twyla was saying. 'I'll enjoy making it. I like keeping busy and using my hands.'

'But I've already mentioned it to Mrs Jessop,' Eileen said. 'We always use Jessop's.' She looked at Bindy. 'Isn't that right, dear?'

'It's Twyla's choice,' Bindy said, turning to Twyla with a smile. 'Do what you like.'

Her mother wasn't letting it go. She was whittling on about Mrs Jessop's superior royal icing. And Twyla was doing what she always did. She would argue her case cordially and then if things didn't go her way, she would withdraw. And go do it her way anyway.

Sure enough, Twyla stood up. 'More tea?' she said, obviously seeing her opportunity to run away.

'No, thanks,' said Bindy mischievously. 'You don't want any more do you, Mum?'

Eileen shook her head.

Twyla began to twitch, looking about her for her misplaced excuse. She wasn't her usual self today, hadn't been for the past few weeks. She had dark circles under her eyes and was edgy

— starting easily. 'I'd better go see to the laundry,' she said.

Bless those cotton pants.

Bindy turned away and gazed outside. It was hot today — a warm afternoon in August. The trees were still, the bees fat and sluggish as they bumped against the windowpane.

'I really don't know what to be telling Mrs Jessop,' Eileen said in a hushed voice. 'You could have backed me up, Belinda. Honestly! Sometimes I don't know whose side you're on.'

'Side?' said Bindy. 'Isn't that a bit much?'

Her mother tutted. 'Don't split hairs. You know what I mean. Mrs Jessop — '

'Oh, enough about Mrs Jessop,' said Bindy, her eye on a figure who was walking up the street. It was a young woman wearing sunglasses. Nothing odd about that. Except that she was wearing a long black coat in a heatwave and was glancing about her nervously as though expecting to be jumped. The coat was open and swelling as she hurried, like the flapping wings of a crow.

To Bindy's surprise, the woman darted up Twyla's driveway.

Bindy waited, expecting the doorbell to go but there was nothing. The caller was hurrying back down the driveway, her coat from this angle now resembling a vampire's cloak.

Curiosity propelled Bindy away from her basking spot. She went out to the hallway and listened for Twyla.

It sounded as though she was still busy in the utility room.

123

Bindy approached the front door. There was something lying on the doormat. She stooped to pick it up, then withdrew upstairs. 'Just popping to the toilet,' she called out.

Upstairs, in the privacy of the bathroom, she tore open the unmarked brown envelope and pulled out the letter inside.

'Well, well, well,' she said.

She stood gazing at the frosted window, at the blurred objects beyond, lost in thought. Then she eased the note carefully into her back pocket, pulled her top down over it and returned downstairs.

★　★　★

Dylan paused before entering the workshop. He could hear Twyla working within, singing happily along to a tune on the radio. Such moments were so scarce, he could barely bring himself to steal them from her. Yet he had to.

He opened the door. The air smelt warm and musty. Twyla was bent over her workbench, soldering, a yellow cloth over one shoulder, her hair scooped up into a messy bun. He liked her hair like that and pictured himself kissing the back of her neck, although wasn't foolish enough to do so when she was using a blowtorch.

On seeing him, she took off her glasses and lay down her tools.

'Hello, love,' she said cheerfully. Evidently, she had had a good day, although she looked tired. He was tired too — could do with a freshen-up

124

before tackling this. His shirt was damp from the hot drive home.

'Twyla,' he said, sitting down on the wicker chair, which creaked loudly in greeting. 'There's something I have to show you.'

'Oh?' she said, swivelling round on her stool, wiping her hands on the cloth. There was a smudge of black on her chin. He bent forward to wipe it and she grabbed his hand, pulling him towards her and kissed him on the lips, laughing. 'Caught ya!' she said.

He laughed too, but then remembered his mission and fell quiet.

'What?' she said.

He thought of his sister's unexpected arrival in his office earlier as though there were an emergency. His first thought was that something had happened to Twyla or Charlie.

Bindy was apologetic about interrupting his work. She was speaking quickly, her expression animated. He thought momentarily of the wheelchair-tipping idea, of the way she had looked then too, and once more was struck by how he had never been sure of her motives — neither then nor now.

She had intercepted a hand-delivered note to their house, she said, and thought he should see it right away.

He read the letter. They were stood in the stairwell, the most private place he could find in the time provided. 'Has Twyla seen this?' he asked.

'No,' she said. 'I didn't want to upset her.'

'What about Mum?'

Bindy shook her head. She was watching him intently. He wondered why. And then he realised. He waved it at her. 'This is what you've been waiting for, isn't it?'

'What?' she said, her mouth flopping open. 'Don't be daft! Why would — ?'

'You and Mum,' he said. 'You don't approve of what we're doing.'

'Dills . . . ' said Bindy. 'Mum's just Mum. She doesn't approve of anything. You know that.'

'And what about you?'

She was so much older than back then — worn by the years, disappointed by them, lonely too perhaps — and yet exactly the same as on the wheelchair incident day: tossing her head back, defiant, nonchalant.

'What have I got to do with it?' she said, with a shrug. 'It's your choice.'

He thought then that her nonchalance was a mask, that she cared far more deeply than she would have people know. But there were other more important thoughts fighting for occupancy of his mind, namely the letter in his hand.

'I have to tell Twyla about this,' he said, more to himself than to her.

Twyla flicked the radio off. The music faded away. A branch was tapping faintly on the workshed wall behind him, like a visitor in no hurry to be let in.

'What is it?' she said.

He opened his satchel and pulled out the letter. 'Here,' he said, handing it to her, watching her warily.

She clutched the envelope mid-air and didn't move.

'It's not very nice,' he said. 'But you need to read it.'

She still didn't move.

'OK, let me help,' he said, taking the letter back from her. He leant on the work counter, began to read. ' 'Mrs Ridley, Jesus gathered his flock of' — '

'Stop,' Twyla said.

He lowered the paper, gazed at her. 'Maybe we should do this later when — '

'I know what it says,' she said. She was wearing a mauve sweatshirt that somehow made her look darker under the eyes. Her hand was resting on the silver orb she had been soldering. It tinkled as she pushed it away and it came to a stop against a chipped mug that she stored ribbons in.

'But Bindy said she didn't show it to you,' he said.

'Bindy?' she said. 'What's she got to do with this?'

He felt inexplicably guilty. He hated it when people put him on the spot. It always made him feel as though he had done something wrong. He felt the same way whenever a police car appeared behind him on the road. 'She brought it to me at work,' he said. 'She thought I should see it.'

Twyla stood up. 'But why would she do that — go to you rather than me?' She looked hurt. Her cheeks were red as though smacked. Her hair was hanging down in wisps around her face.

He reached out to tuck her hair behind her ear. 'I think she was trying to protect you.'

'Oh.'

'Although you never can tell with Bindy,' he said, smiling.

His smile changed the mood. She suddenly looked contrite. 'Dylan . . . ' she said. 'That's not the only letter.'

'Hey?' he replied. 'What do you mean?'

'We've had dozens.'

'Dozens? From the same person?'

'No. From all sorts of people. From all over the country. But all saying the same thing — that what we're doing is wrong.'

He stared at her in astonishment. 'What?'

It was so close in this room. Why didn't she work with a window open, for heaven's sake? He looked about for air, before thrusting open the door, the night breeze wafting in.

He stood with his back to the door, feeling the breeze.

'But why wouldn't you have told me about this?' he said, staring at the shed walls. There were puffy white clouds of spiders egg sacs dotted around. The corners of the room were scattered with dead insects. He hadn't ever noticed it before. Didn't it bother her?

'Because . . . ' she began, wrapping her arms around herself.

'Well?' he said.

She looked so small, so defeated, so colourless, he found himself wishing the whole thing away.

'Because I knew it would make you doubt us,' she said.

He stared at her a moment and then picked up his satchel.

'No,' he said. 'Those nut jobs could never make me doubt us. But you keeping this from me . . . ?' He shook his head. 'That's a good way to cause doubt.'

'Oh, don't say that, Dylan,' she said. 'Don't say that.'

But he was already on his way out, closing the shed door behind him.

9

Initially, Stephen rented an apartment in the French Quarter of New Orleans, next to a bar on Chartres Street, imagining that he would learn something from the eccentricity of the neighbourhood, but he merely hurried in and out of his apartment with his head down and began falling asleep at work. Street musicians, waitresses, strippers and sailors hung around outside his apartment at night, coming in and out of the bar noisily. He quickly saw the error in his snobbish naivety and moved to a suburb in Jefferson Parish along the Mississippi River, known at the time as Little Farms, where he rented a one-bedroom condo in a townhouse that had just been built. The tranquillity melted his ears. The year he moved in, the area was renamed River Ridge.

Robin also lived in River Ridge. So it wasn't just the strippers and sailors that drove him out of the French Quarter. He didn't tell Robin for a long while that he had moved though, for fear of seeming too enthusiastic. There were dozens of men pursuing her. Someone called Biff had put in a lot of groundwork and had even met the mother. When Stephen went to meet Robin from work, Biff would be already there waiting, arms folded, chewing a match. When Robin saw Biff, her face lit up and they linked arms and went up the street together. Stephen felt nauseous on these occasions and went home sadly to his condo, feeling as though he would never convince Robin of his worth.

After a year of hanging around her, getting no further than a shared milkshake or a peck on the cheek, he had a breakthrough. They were sat in a café drinking coffee. He had been working out too intensely and had pulled a muscle in his neck, so was sat rigidly and was wearing a clingy polyester shirt to show off his physique. He was beginning to tire not only of pursuing Robin but of living alone at River Ridge, of lifting weights to impress her. He wasn't fond of tight clothes and had decided that if this didn't work then that was it. She could have Biff and his chewed matches.

Although . . . he watched as she licked a dusting of chocolate from her top lip . . . She was achingly beautiful. She had started wearing black eye make-up. Maybe Biff liked it. Stephen did too. It made her look older, seductive . . . He tingled and looked away too quickly, aggravating his sore neck.

He couldn't take it any more. Maybe he would throw in New Orleans altogether and head back up to Boston where he fitted in and didn't have to resort to polyester.

'There she is,' Robin was saying. 'That's Mamma.' She was holding a small photograph out to him.

He reached out for the picture, trying to summon sufficient interest to respond. He sat up straight. 'That's your mom?' he said.

'Sure,' she said. 'You know her or something?'

He nodded. 'She's one of my patients.'

Robin's face expressed so many emotions, he scarcely knew which one to concentrate on. She looked pleased, impressed, grateful and shamed. She stared down at the table, her cheeks reddening.

'It doesn't matter,' he said. He didn't add 'that you're poor and your mother's a raving lunatic'. It was implied.

She was playing distractedly with the sugar shaker. 'Hey,' he said, lifting her chin with his hand. 'I love you, Robin.'

He didn't know why he said it. It just spilled out. Like the sugar that she poured everywhere in surprise, her eyes wider than her Alice band.

The year that followed was one of bliss. Was there a bad moment in it? He thought not. They went steady for all of 1975 and then married in 1976 on June the first.

It had to be that date. It was her mother's birthday. They had buried her by then, but she still had a say in things. Right from the start, she had a peculiar bearing on their relationship and he often reflected that had it not been for her mother's illness they never would have met.

He didn't particularly want to be married on Mamma's birthday — a woman who had battled mental illness all her life — but it was Robin's wish and there was little that he wouldn't do to please her. He even took his bride to see the Thibodeauxs in Manhattan since she was desperate to meet them. They, on the other hand, seemed indifferent to the experience and if they felt snubbed at not having been invited down to River Ridge for the intimate wedding, they didn't show it. They took their son and daughter-in-law to the Four Seasons for champagne, before sending them off with a case of crystal brandy glasses and a cheque as a down payment for their first home.

Robin chose the house. She fell in love with it as soon as they saw it: 403, Smoke Rock Drive, Jefferson.

He carried her across the threshold and they drank bourbon in his parents' crystal glasses on their first night there, lying out underneath the stars.

She talked that night about what she might do now that she was no longer caring for her mother. She spoke about this tactfully, so that no one could infer that she had resented her role as carer. Her love for her mother was deep, mystifyingly so, especially to Stephen who could not relate to parental adoration in the slightest.

He told her, with bourbon-fuelled intensity, that she could do anything — that she was bright enough, smart enough, beautiful enough to do whatever in God's name she wanted to do.

They made love, as though to bless his words and make them come true.

It couldn't have been more ironic, because she fell instantly pregnant.

And just like that — underneath the stars, dreaming of fulfilling her potential, drunk and euphoric — she became a carer again.

★   ★   ★

The christening was tomorrow. August was often rainy, but not this one. They had decorated the garden with bunting and had put a gazebo up just in case, but the weather looked set to hold.

Twyla was making the icing for the cake, when the phone rang. She picked the receiver up, propping it under her chin.

'Twyla?'

A waft of icing sugar rose, tickling her nose. 'Stephen,' she said.

'*Dad*,' he corrected. 'Everyone well?'

'Yes, thank you.'

'Huh.'

There was a pause. She took the opportunity to grind a cube of butter against the side of the bowl with the wooden spoon.

'Twyla, I've been thinking . . . ' he said. The butter gave way with a satisfying slump. She beat the icing quietly. 'I'd like to do something for you, something to help.'

She was about to tell him that there was nothing he could do, when she considered that there was something she could do for him.

'It's Charlie's christening tomorrow,' she said. 'Why don't you come? . . . Both of you.'

She flicked a drop of blue colouring into the icing and watched the liquid gather in a pool, tinting the edges of the butter mermaid-green.

'One moment,' he said.

There were voices in the background. A door was opening and closing. Footsteps were approaching.

'We'll be there,' he said.

As she hung up, she felt the rush of happiness

that often accompanied a good deed. She went out to the garden to find Dylan.

'Stephen's coming tomorrow,' she said. 'And Juliet. I just invited them.'

Dylan was fixing a string of bunting from the workshed to the back door. 'Well done, my love.'

'I need to pop out in a minute to pick up the wine glasses. Would you — ?'

'I'll stay,' he said.

'Oh,' she said. 'Are you sure?'

'Yes.' He smiled. 'I need to secure the gazebo. It's getting windy.'

'OK,' she said doubtfully, glancing about the garden as though trying to prove otherwise. It was a little breezy though.

★　★　★

It had been a mistake to not tell him about the letters. That was a fact. She always knew when she had reached the truth. It felt right and neat inside, like a spinning coin finally coming to a stop.

He was being off with her, distant, and she didn't know how to right the wrong.

She gripped the steering wheel tighter as she drove. Sometimes she held herself so stiff during the day that she ached by night.

'So we're going along the road to the supermarket, Charlie,' she said into the rear-view mirror. 'We're on a steep hill with trees either side. The trees are pretty.'

She glanced over her shoulder at him. He was moving his mouth with great effort.

'Tree,' he said.

'Hey?' she said, looking at him for too long this time.

The car swerved. She cursed to herself.

That was close. She nearly hit the kerb. She took a deep breath and focused on the road. But her attention went back to Charlie. She cocked her ear to listen to him. It sounded as if he had said —

'Tree,' he said.

This time it was clearer. She clapped her hand to her mouth, trying to contain her laughter, her exultation.

Don't make a big deal of it. Act naturally. Don't go crazy. Take it easy, for Charlie's sake.

This was supposed to be a natural step for him. If she hired a brass band to celebrate it, he would be overwhelmed, reluctant to do it again.

'Tree!' he said again, louder, more confidently.

And then he began to laugh, a high-pitched shrieky laugh, just as he had done at the beach when he first walked.

'Tree!' he shouted, slapping his bare legs, jerking about in his chair, pulling on the straps as though wanting to eject himself out through the top of the car into the sky.

It was the sound of his skin being slapped that did it — the happiness that sound evoked, like a baby splashing in the bath, like bare feet dancing on floorboards.

She looked for a place to stop the car. They were on a busy road. The traffic was thick and fast. She indicated and veered into the forecourt of a pub, her wheels spinning on the gravel.

She raced round to the passenger seat. He was waiting there in his turquoise shorts, his face turned towards her expectantly.

Look what I've done, Mummy! he seemed to be saying.

She unstrapped him and plucked him out of the seat and into her arms, feeling the blast of warmth that accompanied him. The back of his clothes were damp.

Call off the brass band if they must, but this was a big moment for him — and he knew it.

She rubbed her nose against his, kissed his forehead and cheeks.

'Yes!' she said, dancing around with him in the car park, as though there weren't traffic rushing by, as though there weren't people arriving for lunch at the pub, staring at her.

Was she out of her mind? Was she drunk?

'You did it!' she said. 'Yes, Charlie!'

He was laughing, his fluffy hair shining auburn in the sunlight, like a baby chimpanzee.

'Tree!' he said, squeezing his palms against her cheeks enthusiastically. He liked to squish her face. He was gentle, but she had learnt not to wear red lipstick.

'I love you so much, my little sweetheart.'

And she looked up to the sky and said a silent thank you thank you thank you to anyone there that happened to be watching.

★ ★ ★

He didn't mind half as much as she thought he did. He accepted why she had hidden it from him and realised that in the circumstances he might have done the same, that there wasn't a protocol for what to do when receiving abuse through the post.

Yet she was wary around him, no matter how much he tried to reassure her. She was making his favourite steak and red onion supper all the time, was smiling too often — even for her. Not that he minded — the smiles, the steaks. It was just that he couldn't get through to her that it was OK, that they were still in this together.

He shouldn't have said that about doubting her. He regretted it and had tried to take it back. It was one of the worst things to say to Twyla, and his trust and faith in her was such a hard thing to prove.

He would give it a while longer. Once the christening was over, things would settle down.

He had just taken a shower and was drying off in the bedroom when the front door opened and Twyla came bounding up the stairs. 'Dylan?' she was shouting.

He stood up, secured the towel round his waist.

'Dylan?' She ran into the room. 'You won't believe it!' she said, out of breath. 'Guess what just happened?' She looked pretty, rosy-cheeked. 'Charlie spoke!'

'No way!' he said, guilt rushing through him.

'I'll just get him,' she called over her shoulder as she raced from the room.

He should have gone with them, he thought, gazing after her. He should have been there when Charlie spoke. She was coming up the stairs again, carrying Charlie. 'Up we go,' she was saying. 'Up we go to Daddy.'

She set Charlie inside the doorway. Charlie approached slowly, his hands out to the side. He knew the wall was on the left, the bed on the right.

Dylan reached out to take his hand. 'Tell me what you said, Charlie boy,' he said.

Charlie liked being called that. He laughed, deep dimples appearing in his cheeks, like raindrops in sand. And then he remembered the task in hand and concentration clouded his face.

'Tree,' he said.

'Wow,' Dylan said, softly. 'Come here, Charlie,' he said, pulling his son towards him and kissing the top of his head.

And it was then, as he noted the vein at the top of Charlie's nose and the delicate folding of his ears and the freckle on his left cheek and the feathery eyebrows, that he realised that their little boy was an awesome configuration of cells and organs and liquids that were perfectly assembled and balanced, just the way they were.

★　★　★

The letter had been there since yesterday, unnoticed, containing the news that would change their lives.

She normally looked at the post as soon as it arrived, to check for hate mail. Yet in the bustle of organising the party, the post was pushed to the bottom shelf of the hallway dresser and forgotten about. It was Charlie who found it, the irony of which would have amused her under different circumstances.

The night before the christening she was getting Charlie ready for bed, when he wet himself and her dress. So she went downstairs to ask Dylan to watch Charlie whilst she got changed.

When she returned, Dylan was sat at the bottom of the stairs and Charlie was sitting on the hallway floor, chewing a letter.

'Hey, what you got there, Charlie?' she said, gently prising the envelope from his mouth. She glanced at the postmark. 'Oh!' she said.

Dylan had been gazing into space, his chin in his hands. They hadn't stopped all day — setting out chairs, decorating, cleaning, arranging glasses and plates. But now he stood quickly. 'What?' he said.

She could tell by his expression that he thought it was more abuse.

'It's from the Royal Square,' she said.

'Oh,' he said, looking relieved. 'Well, open it then.' He leant back, his leg propped against the wall.

She read the letter twice through before it fixed in her mind, before the words made sense.

Sometimes Charlie seemed to know when she was looking at him. Their eyes met now with uncanny precision.

'What's it say?' Dylan asked. 'Thank you for all the money but can we please have more?'

'Not quite.' She handed him the letter. 'They're ready,' she said. 'They'll operate.'

10

'So you need thirty thousand pounds,' said
Stephen, sipping his Pimm's cautiously as
though it had been spiked.

Twyla smiled, amusing herself with her
father's instructive manner of speech.

So you have a son.

So you live in Bath.

So . . .

'It seems unfair to ask you to pay even more,
Twyla,' Juliet said, craning her neck to join in the
conversation, since she was five foot tall. She had
twinkly eyes and a large yet modestly presented
chest. There was something of the cartoon
character about her, but Twyla hadn't worked
out which one yet. 'Aren't they going to take into
account all the fund-raising you've done?'

Betty Boop, Twyla thought.

'I don't think it works quite like that,' she said.

'And when's the operation?' asked Stephen.

'Two weeks.'

He raised his eyebrows. 'Why the rush?'

'The sooner the better,' said Twyla, staring
into the bottom of her empty Pimm's glass.
Would it be rude to suck the orange? Her
stomach was growling pitifully.

'And why's that, darling?' said Juliet.

Twyla, temporarily distracted by Juliet's term
of endearment, took a moment to reply.

'Because ideally he should have had the

141

operation long before now. His brain needs to learn how to see as early as possible.'

'And the risk?' asked Stephen.

Risk.

Twyla felt her cheeks burn at the mention of the word. She looked down at her feet which were squished into heels. Her feet had grown during pregnancy and her shoes no longer fitted as well.

'There's risk,' she said.

It was a real conversation stopper. The circle of guests next to them — several support group mums — happened to stop talking at the same time too. Silence hung limply in the air, until one of the mums laughed and the spell was broken.

'Well, I for one admire your spirit,' said Juliet. 'And to have put together this party too? It's inspiring.'

'Thank you,' said Twyla.

The party seemed to be going well. The Pimm's was strong, but no one had complained. It was a warm day and, whilst the marquee offered shade, most of the guests were glistening and red-faced. Charlie Ross, wearing a cream linen suit, was stood on the lawn holding Dylan's hand. Eileen was bent over talking to Charlie. And Bindy was playing with her necklace and yawning.

'Is that Dylan's sister?' said Juliet, following Twyla's gaze.

'Yes,' said Twyla, wishing that Bindy didn't look quite so bored. 'And that's his mother, Eileen, Charlie's grandma. She dotes on Charlie.'

Her father looked up at the mention of Eileen,

a pensive expression on his face that Twyla couldn't quite fathom.

'Could I use the bathroom?' said Juliet.

''Course,' said Twyla. 'First door on the left.'

She watched Juliet moving away, manoeuvring her petite form through the gatherings of guests. Then she glanced up at her father, wondering what they would talk about now that the affectionate part of the trio had gone.

'Twyla,' Stephen said, taking his sunglasses off. He bore the jaded look of someone who did too much reading. 'Let me pay for the operation.'

She looked about her as though her response lay in a scattering of letters in the gravel, if only she could assemble them quickly. 'I . . . '

Her uncertainty seemed to offend him.

'Why wouldn't you accept it, Twyla?' he said. 'You're my only daughter. Charlie's my only grandson. The money's there.' He shrugged. 'I can't think of one good reason to refuse it.'

Twyla looked over at Dylan for help, but he was deep in conversation with their neighbour.

She felt panicky — a disquieting fluttering below her heart. 'Excuse me,' she said, heading indoors.

Upstairs in the quiet of the bedroom, she kicked her heels off and sat down on the bed with her back against the headrest and her legs outstretched. Her heart was racing. She took a moment to let it find its natural pace before examining her thoughts.

It wasn't as simple as taking the money and being done with it. How to explain that to her father?

She hadn't taken anything from him in such a long time. Because by doing so she feared that he might think she was saying that everything had been all right — burying her mother in silence, uprooting to Boston and then England and boarding school.

Not taking anything from him was the only way that she could voice her disapproval. After all, you had to be really close to someone to shout at them.

And there was another reason why taking the money was difficult. It would mean that there was nothing stopping them from going ahead with the operation.

It had been easier whilst fund-raising. It had made their cause seem honourable, charitable. The more money that poured into the account, the more she felt as though it were a show of hands in support.

But in truth, the phenomenal total wasn't a show of hands, but mostly one huge hand belonging to a local multi-millionaire who was losing his sight and told Twyla that he thought what she was doing was remarkable.

She reached into the bedside drawer and took a pink envelope out.

It was the only letter of encouragement that she had ever received.

The note was written on rose-scented writing paper by a hand that was too old to attempt more than a few lines.

Dear Mrs Ridley,
I saw you on television this morning. I

watch too much telly but that's another story.

I lost my son, David, sixty-three years ago in a potholing accident. I used to tell him that if God wanted us to crawl around in the earth he'd have given us bristles like worms, and less fancy clothes.

There's nothing I wouldn't have done for my David. So if you want to fix your boy's eyes, then all power to you.

God bless.

From Mrs Jones, Portsmouth.

Twyla put the letter back in the drawer.

Through the ceiling came the sudden sound of samba music: Dylan's Brazilian album that he reserved for parties. She put her heels back on, smoothed her dress and returned downstairs.

Her father was still out in the garden where she had left him, with Juliet wrapped around his waist, swaying her hips to the music. Dylan was dancing on the lawn with Charlie, whose linen suit was more crinkled than a pug dog's face.

'Could I have a quick word, please?' she asked Stephen.

They went to the alley by the side of the house where it was quiet.

'We'll take the money for Charlie, thank you,' she said.

'You've discussed it with Dylan?' he asked.

'Not yet,' she said. 'I don't know what he's going to say. I'm just letting you know what my personal response would be.'

'Good.' He smiled. 'Thank you.'

He looked as though he were going to say something else. The unspoken hung between them and the narrow alley walls for a moment, and then was gone.

★   ★   ★

403 Smoke Rock Drive in Jefferson was where they had been happy. Sometimes when he couldn't sleep he imagined driving back along Mississippi River Road in his blue Ford Sedan, taking a left on to the tree-lined lot in the centre of Jefferson. He knew every bump in the road, every oak and cypress tree.

When he turned on to Smoke Rock Drive, he wouldn't be able to see Twyla right away. It was only when he pulled into their driveway that she came into view in her patchwork dress, with her palms pressed together expectantly.

She always waited on the front step for him, hidden by the gum trees and the Spanish moss. He thought the moss was ominous, the dangling silvery fingers shading their house — some called it tree hair — but Robin loved it. It wasn't moss, she said, but a flowering plant, a member of the pineapple family. It doesn't do the trees any harm, and it's protecting us.

At night, they could smell the fragrance of the Spanish moss and the summersweet shrubs. Robin was a keen gardener. She worked hard tending to the borders and then sat back to appreciate her efforts, watching the humming-birds dipping on to the summersweets.

If he was home early enough, he would sweep

Twyla off the front step and race her to the playground. On the way back they would stop at the bakery for a box of almond pastries filled with vanilla cream. They were Twyla's favourite and he could still taste the rich cream on his tongue.

When he was back too late, he crept through to Twyla's bedroom and kissed her forehead as she slept. On the morning after these nights, she always hurtled through to their room to check he had made it home safely, that he was still there. She would throw herself on him and nestle down under the covers between him and Robin.

All here, she would say. Good. Good.

How had he missed these signs? How had he missed the anxiety in his five-year-old daughter, the stillness in his once energetic wife, the sense of doom that was shrouding his home and had nothing to do with the Spanish moss?

He was still working at the mental health centre in New Orleans. His caseload was unrealistic and the pay dire, but he was learning a lot and was catching the eye of some important people. He commuted from Jefferson and was even finding time to take on a few private patients to boost his income, but it was a slog and he was ageing fast. He tried to be there for Robin and Twyla, but the days slipped by and sometimes he would put his head down on the dining table and fall asleep right there.

It's OK, Robin told him. Everything's OK.

He noticed that she had lost weight and felt bony, but she said it was because she had flu or a sickness bug. There was always some explanation. He accepted her reasons and fell asleep, vowing to speak to their neighbour, Jolie, in the morning. Jolie had a young daughter too and the women hung out together during the day.

But he never caught up with Jolie in the mornings — there wasn't time before work. And in the end it was Jolie who approached him.

I'm worried about Robin, she said.

Had he got to her first, it might have been different. But this way round, he was angry at the woman's interference, at her stupidity for not realising that a man in his position, of his profession, would have it covered.

Robin's fine, he snapped.

On his journey to work that day, however, he began to fret. He played through the moments of his time with them over the past months, flicking through them speedily as he did with the business cards Rolodex on his desk.

When had Robin last smiled?

Why didn't she want to try for another baby?

Was she eating?

Was Twyla eating?

What happened at home when he wasn't there?

He undid the top button of his shirt and wound down the window, feeling suddenly light-headed and hot. A police car and an ambulance were approaching him at speed down the highway. Everyone was slowing, allowing them to pass. He hit the brakes, feeling sweat trickle down his spine. And then it occurred to him.

He did a dangerous U-turn in the middle of the road and sped with screeching tyres back the way he had come, in the wake of the ambulance.

Please, God, he said aloud as he drove.

★　★　★

Stephen woke with a start. Juliet was asleep beside him, snoring softly. She shifted as he sat up, but then settled again. He consulted his watch. It was three o'clock in the morning.

He went through to the kitchen to make a tea and sat in the conservatory, beholding his reflection in the glass. It was a stormy, broody night.

What a sorry man he was. What a fool, full of grief and regret.

He studied his reflection — the stoop of his back, his heavy jowl.

He was old now. He had lived thirty-two years longer than Robin already.

'What are you doing up?' Juliet was standing in the doorway, wearing lime pyjamas that said *you snooze, you lose.* She could wear childish things like that — dice earrings, cardigans covered in moose heads — and still seem credible. Perhaps it was her diminutive form that lent itself easily to girlishness. Whatever it was, it gave her a versatility, a freedom that he found invigorating, even before dawn.

'Nothing,' he said.

'Come on,' she said, standing behind him and squeezing his shoulders to massage them. 'I know better than that.'

He sighed. 'It's Robin.'

'Robin?' Her hands retracted. 'What about her?'

'How she died.'

'Oh.' She sat down on the armchair opposite. 'Well, you saw Twyla at the christening yesterday. It's bound to stir up — '

'Regrets,' he said.

'Quite.' She rose to go through to the kitchen.

'I should tell her the truth,' he called after her.

She stopped and turned slowly. 'No,' she said. 'She's got enough on her plate. You've just done a wonderful thing, giving her the money for Charlie. Leave it at that.'

He listened to the sound of the tap running. Juliet wouldn't go back to sleep now, would start work on the conference she was speaking at. Sometimes he loathed her pragmatism, her ability to compartmentalise emotions, mostly because it was the thing that he most loathed about himself.

'Just before we change the subject . . . ' said Juliet, returning with a cafetière of coffee. 'What does Twyla think happened to her mother?'

The wind howled, rattling the conservatory windows, wobbling Stephen's reflection.

'Car accident,' he said, exhaling loudly.

'Well, there you go,' said Juliet, with a look of satisfaction. 'And that's exactly what did happen. So leave it now. Or you'll drive yourself mad.'

She was done. There was no more to discuss. She opened her laptop and began to type.

It wasn't exactly what had happened though. He shook his head unhappily and looked out of the window.

There through the glass, in the darkness of the garden outside, he could see Robin amongst the gum trees, underneath the Spanish moss.

She had died in a car, sure enough. But it hadn't been an accident.

★ ★ ★

The morning after the christening Dylan's phone rang at work and he answered whilst in the middle of writing an email. To his surprise, it was his mother, who launched straight into the reason for her call, without greeting or introduction.

'I've held my tongue long enough and I can do so no more!' she said.

'Hey?' he said.

'What you're doing is wrong. I know it's not you, son — that Twyla's got you wrapped around her little finger. But enough's enough. I can't stand by any more without speaking my mind. Stop this nonsense now before it's too late! Stop it, I say!'

He had never heard his mother so agitated and impassioned before. He was trying to think quickly — of something to cut her short, but words weren't forthcoming. It happened every time — as soon as someone got emotional he couldn't think straight.

'Mum . . . ' was all he could manage.

'Don't put Charlie through this operation. I beg of you. Make Twyla see reason!'

He hated himself for his lack of gumption, his inability to spar with his mother. He thought again of her coming through the doors of their childhood home — of her hair in rollers like a judge. She had always intimidated him, her and Bindy.

What kind of man was he? Not so long ago he had given himself the role of defending his family, and here he was unable to stand up to his little old mother from Cork.

There once was a woman from Cork
Whose son was a bit of a dork.

Bindy used to make up limericks and chant them incessantly.

'I'm going now, son, before I say something I regret!'

Dylan stared at the phone in his hand, before hanging up.

'Everything all right?' said a voice at his side. He looked up to see Molly standing there, hugging a file to her chest.

'Yes,' he said. Then he reconsidered. 'No.' He stood up. 'Don't s'pose you fancy an early lunch?'

She blushed deeply. The moment he said it, he regretted it. What if she took it the wrong way? Yet all he wanted was someone to talk to who wasn't his mother or his wife.

'I'll get my jacket,' said Molly.

On the way to the deli, Molly told him about her Sunday morning yoga class. She had just mastered the Firefly pose, she said.

They didn't sit down for lunch at the deli, but grabbed food to go. He found it easier to talk whilst walking.

'Charlie's having the operation,' he said, on the way back.

She stopped walking. 'On his eyes?' she said, screwing up her nose.

This was a silly thing to say. But he pressed on. 'Twyla's booking the operation today.' He glanced at his watch. 'Has probably already done so. In two weeks' time we'll be wheeling him into the operating theatre.'

Molly began to walk slowly. 'And you're having doubts,' she ventured.

He took a deep breath. 'Yes,' he said. 'I am.'

A truck was struggling up the hill out of the city, its engine grating with the effort.

'What do you think about it?' he asked.

She waited for the truck to pass before replying, its whoosh lifting the fringe of her hair. 'I couldn't possibly say,' she said.

They pressed the button at the pedestrian crossing and waited. The lights changed immediately, the traffic halting. They crossed the road and came to the narrow steps leading to the back of their office building. He motioned for Molly to go first, watching the back of her head bobbing as she went down the steps, his reflection appearing in the large gold clip in her hair.

'But you must have some opinion,' he said.

She laughed. 'Oh, I'm not falling for that trap!'

They continued side by side along the path. It was dark and smelt of damp earth and mould. 'It's not a trap,' he said. 'I just thought maybe you'd have a view.'

She stopped at the end of the corridor as they stepped into the bright light. 'No one can have a view on this other than you and your wife,' she said. 'It's what *you* think, Dylan.'

He looked at her. Her skin was completely unflawed — creamy, almost unreal.

What a lovely blank canvas. No conundrums, gut-wrenching dilemmas.

A teenager appeared suddenly on a skateboard around the corner of the road with a scrape and clatter, scuffing his foot rapidly towards them.

Dylan backed away from Molly, feeling as though he were implicated in some seedy liaison.

They began to walk again. 'That's the problem though,' he said miserably. 'I don't know what I think.'

'Then talk to Twyla,' she said.

'I have,' he said. 'We've talked till we're blue in the face. Now it's just a simple matter of yes or no.'

She shrugged. 'So which is it?'

★ ★ ★

That evening, Twyla greeted him with the news that the operation date was set for a week Thursday.

His stomach told him everything he needed to know. It didn't leap so much as lurch. Yet he couldn't bring himself to tell her that he still wasn't sure, that his doubt was growing rapidly now that the go-ahead had been given.

She told him about her conversation with the Royal Square, about what time they were needed and for how long and what they should bring. He knew that he should tell her about his mother's phone call. But to do so would send her into a spin.

He felt ill with indecision. He was sure that she would understand, was even possibly feeling the same way. No one would be absolutely certain of this, surely?

He went to sleep that night with his arm around Twyla, his mouth pressed into his favourite place at the back of her neck, but never having felt so far away from her; his mind filled with jellyfish eyes, judges in hair rollers and fireflies doing yoga.

11

There were some things in life that couldn't be fixed, Bindy thought. Some people were incapable of change, some conditions so terminal that their course was predestined at conception.

How their mother must have wept at the news that was delivered whilst her baby was still attached to her by its umbilical cord. Her newborn was severely disabled, so much so that it was a wonder she had the mobility to make it down the birthing canal.

Bindy was elsewhere at the time, not privy to the shock of the situation and not capable of comprehending it had she been included. Aged one, she would have been sat on a neighbour's floor, chewing wooden toys. Her mother was fresh from Cork and had no relatives to hand, so relied on the community and God.

Bindy used to go to church with her mother back then, twice on Sundays to the medieval tithe barn. They all had to go, Dylan too. Even Felicity, parked in the aisle beside them in her ugly wheelchair with its heavy wheels and grey padding. Fee had pasty skin and fair hair — startled tufts that looked as though they had been stuck on by a child with a penchant for cotton wool and glue projects.

Felicity had cerebral palsy. When Bindy heard this was what her little sister had, she knew it was important and that she should remember it so she wrote it down as *Sarah ball Paul, see?* to help her remember.

There was something else too that Fee had that Bindy remembered as *a pea leapt, see?* It made Fee shake and quiver, like the washing machine on spin.

In those days, Bindy used to pray like everyone else around her. She used to think that God would help them. But then Fee would start to moan and kick her legs like a baby calf, and their father would gesture for Bindy to wheel her outside.

On the front steps of the tithe barn, in the silence of the Sunday morning with the sound of muted prayer behind her, Bindy pulled strawberry laces from her pockets and sucked on them, watching the birds on the telegraph poles and the clouds pass by.

And she knew then, with her sister moaning beside her, hanging her limbs uselessly outside of the wheelchair to the point of nearly tipping the whole thing over, that what was happening here — right now on this step, with the birds and the clouds, the strawberry laces and the moans — was more real than anything going on back there.

Sometimes Felicity had a seizure and Bindy had to ram the heavy doors of the barn open and call for the priest to stop the service and for their dad to come help. Bindy hated those heavy doors — wished they had a flap for her to squeeze through, like the neighbour's cat.

The first time it happened Bindy was waiting

outside the post office with her sister. It was raining and Bindy was wearing a flared dress with a cherry motif on — one of those strange details from the past that life offered up like an obscure hors d'oeuvre — when Fee began to vibrate, white foam gathering at her mouth, her eyes rolling in her head, like drunken marbles.

Her parents had warned her about this. What was she supposed to do again? She tapped her head, trying to think.

Fee was rocking in her chair, the contraption rattling.

Don't let her swallow her tongue! This was what her mother had told her.

It felt like an incongruous piece of advice. What was Bindy supposed to do? Hold her sister's tongue, like a wriggling fish? Stop a stranger for help? Leave Fee and run inside the post office to get her mum?

Put her on her side. That's what she was supposed to do. But the chair was too heavy. How could she lay it over?

She began to kick the wheels — booting them, her teeth clenched.

Come on! Move it, you blasted demon! You evil sunnava —

'Belinda! What in God's good name do you think you're doing?' Her mother was stood there, scowling.

Bindy looked at her sister. The seizure had passed. Fee was peaceful, slouched placidly in her chair.

'Honestly, Bindy! I can't leave you alone for five minutes!'

The seizures got worse as Fee grew, exacerbated by her changing teenage body. Bindy was used to them by then, but their mother's depression had intensified, hanging like damp laundry around the ceilings of their home until Bindy felt so stifled she went outside to inhale.

And then the day came when the inevitable happened, changing the air in their home for ever.

For where there was once a burden, there was nothing now — a gaping hole that the wind rattled through at night.

There were no photographs of Fee that she knew of. How strange that was. A child who lived and breathed and then was banished to wispy memory.

No, there were some things that couldn't be fixed, no matter how much you longed or prayed otherwise.

Bindy had known this her entire life, from the moment she memorised *a pea leapt, see,* she could feel the sense of inescapability, of tragedy that they were being shuttled towards as surely as a river reaching the edge of a waterfall.

And when you got that far, when you reached the precipice, the only option that remained was to descend.

But Twyla was yet to learn that. She still thought you could defy nature and change fate.

She had to be stopped before she found out in the most tragic way possible — before the air changed, before the empty spaces grew so wide and sharp, they were enough to slice you in two.

159

* * *

He hadn't meant to follow them. He had followed them instinctively, like a thirsty rat to a watering hole, not pausing to consider the foolishness of his actions.

It was a cool day with drizzle in the air. They were at the bus station in town when he first spotted them. They were wearing red raincoats and were holding hands, absorbed in conversation. You could tell they were mother and son, so alike were they.

Then she turned round and looked in his direction, but she hadn't noticed him. She was glancing at her watch, anxious for them to get on their way.

The number fourteen arrived at last. She picked her child up and joined the queue.

He glanced at the route map. It was the wrong end of town for him. Wrong end? He lived right by here. He didn't even need to get the bus.

As the engine started, he grabbed a seat at the back and sank down, resting his hand on the camera which was hanging from his neck.

Why was he doing this?

He was curious about them. That was the only explanation he could give himself.

He watched as she talked to her son, pointed things out to him. The boy was gazing around impassively. Other passengers were watching them too. Granted, some might have been reflecting on her uncommon prettiness. But most were transfixed by the boy's inability to do what they could all do.

She stood to press the button sooner than he expected. They lived only halfway up the hill. He would have placed them higher, somewhere elevated.

Her step was light as they disembarked, not just because walking on a moving bus was like being on a treadmill, but because she had a weightless manner of walking that was almost like gliding. She held her son in her arms, her knuckles white with the effort of securing him.

As the bus departed, she crouched down to zip up the boy's coat.

He waited a few moments before getting off at the next stop, two hundred yards from theirs. Then he hurried back down the road, his camera banging against his chest.

Where were they? He spotted the flash of red as they disappeared down a gravel path.

He ran after them. When he reached the path, he looked around the corner.

The boy had fallen over and was howling with pain. He wanted to step forward then and offer to help, but how to explain his proximity to them? He couldn't just jump out.

What a stupid thing to do, following them like this.

She was brushing grit from the child's palms and examining his chin. She went through her pockets, then pulled out a first aid kit. All this she did routinely as though it were a regular occurrence. The boy recovered quickly and they set off.

He meant to part ways with them there, to turn round and wait for the number fourteen back to town. But he was so captured by them, he continued to follow.

He watched as they walked slowly along the road and up their driveway.

At the front door, she turned to look over her shoulder as though aware of someone there. But then she proceeded and he heard the door shut decisively.

★　★　★

When they got in, Charlie began to cry again. He had fallen so badly there was gravel embedded in his chin. She would have to soak it off with cotton wool.

From the moment he tumbled, things didn't feel right. Birds took off with a panicked flurry of wings. The rain fell more aggressively. The wind got up and tore at their jackets. And it seemed just for an instant as though something terrible was about to happen. She even glanced upwards for incoming catastrophe.

And now she knew what it was.

Dylan and his family were gathered unexpectedly in the lounge.

'Oh, hello,' she said in surprise, putting a hand to her hair to straighten it. She was wet through. 'I didn't know you were coming.'

'Twyla . . . ' said Dylan, immediately standing up.

They were drinking tea. Dylan had sliced up her fruitcake, yet no one looked to be eating it. There was something wrong with the set-up, but she couldn't think what.

'Twyla . . . ' Dylan said again. He looked strained, was shifting uneasily from foot to foot.

'Everything all right?' she said.

No one replied. Charlie appeared behind her, pushing his head between her legs.

'We need to get cleaned up,' she said. 'Charlie hurt himself.' She lifted him up so that Dylan could see his chin. 'Look.'

'Ouch,' said Dylan, ruffling Charlie's hair. 'Poor Charlie boy. That looks sore.' But there was something in his voice that disconcerted her — a stiltedness, an angst.

And that was what was wrong with the set-up: there was no conversation, no nothing. What were they sitting in silence for?

'Back in a minute,' she said.

As she carried Charlie upstairs, Dylan joined her.

In the bedroom, he shut the door behind them. 'I didn't know Mum and Bindy were coming over,' he said in a hushed voice.

'And?' She stepped past him to go through to the bathroom for the first aid kit.

He followed her. 'There's something I need to tell you,' he said.

As she patched up Charlie's chin, she noticed that her hands were shaking. She carried Charlie back through to the bedroom where she changed their clothes, towel-dried their hair.

'Mum doesn't want us to go ahead with the operation,' Dylan said. 'She rang me at work on Monday. I've been trying to find a way to tell you all week.'

She stopped with the comb dangling in her

hair and stared at him. 'What?' she said.

'She thinks I should try to talk you out of it.'

'I see,' Twyla said. 'And what do you think?'

'I . . . ' He hung his head.

'Oh, God,' she said.

'I'm sorry,' he called after her, as she picked Charlie up and left the room.

Downstairs, the lounge was still in silence. Dylan followed Twyla into the room where they sat next to each other on the sofa. Bindy and Eileen sat demurely on the opposite sofa. The only movement was Eileen's twiddling thumbs.

Twyla held Charlie on her lap. 'I don't wish to be rude,' Twyla said. 'But you don't normally come over on a Saturday. What exactly — ?'

'We want you to cancel the Royal Square,' said Eileen, looking Twyla straight in the eye.

Twyla composed herself before replying. 'We?' she said, her heart thumping.

Eileen nodded. 'Myself. Bindy here. And . . . Dylan.'

Twyla turned to look at the man next to her whom she suddenly didn't seem to know so well.

'Is this true?' she asked, feeling her temperature rise. They were going to do this here and now — discuss Charlie's operation in front of his family?

'I . . . ' Dylan began.

'Tell her the truth, son,' said Eileen.

'Quiet, Mum!' Dylan snapped.

His mother's back stiffened.

'I just don't know, Twyla,' he said.

'That's not what you said earlier,' muttered Eileen.

'I said, shut up, Mum!' Dylan shouted, jumping to his feet. 'I can't bloody well think straight!'

Eileen, shocked, fell silent.

He turned back to Twyla, his voice softening. 'I'm worried about the risks. He could lose his eyes.'

'But our surgeon's highly respected,' she said. 'We've gone through all this and it's fine, so long as — '

'He's too little,' he said. 'We can't put him through it.'

He placed his hand on Charlie's head then, as though blessing him. It was such a simple gesture that, for a moment, she could see how ludicrous her path was, how revolting the notion was of cutting open their child to give him implants.

And yet Charlie was sitting here on her lap now with a bloody chin — another injury from falling, like he did on a daily basis.

'You want this for him?' she said.

Dylan looked at her blankly, not understanding her meaning.

'Look at his chin,' she said. 'You want a life like that for him? A life of bruises and — '

'Nonsense,' said Eileen. 'All children fall and cut themselves, whether they can see or not. No one can give their child a life without adversity. It's impossible. And it's not what the Lord intended for — '

'For God's sake,' Dylan said, pulling his hair in frustration.

Twyla stood up, bristling with rage. 'I think

you should go,' she said.

'Yes,' Dylan said. 'We can't discuss this with you here.'

There was a terrible pause. And then Eileen and Bindy stood and gathered their coats and bags.

Bindy strode from the room without a word, but at the door Eileen turned, wavered.

She gazed at Dylan imploringly. And finally she looked at Twyla.

She looked small, standing there in her neat cardigan and slacks, clutching her handbag before her. 'Don't do this, Twyla. I beg of you. For Charlie.'

Twyla opened her mouth, stunned. 'You don't think this *is* for Charlie?' she asked.

Eileen sniffed and shook her head. 'No, dear,' she said. 'I don't.'

12

His Ford Sedan wouldn't move fast enough down the highway back to Jefferson. He clenched the wheel, the air buffeting through the windows, ballooning his shirtsleeves.

Come on, come on, he said, trying to follow the flashing lights of the ambulance. Where had it gone?

He passed a turn-off, a small road down to LaFleur Lake. By chance, he glanced down the road and there was the blue light.

He did another dangerous U-turn, cars swerving and beeping around him. Someone wound down their window and cursed him.

The turn-off was more of a track than a road. He put his window up. The dust was kicking up from his tyres.

He turned a sharp bend, and nearly went into the back of the ambulance.

He sat for a moment, surveying the scene, sweat sneaking from his hairline, his chest hammering. There was an ambulance, a fire engine, two police cars and a small gathering of people. The road was narrow at this end but about half a mile further on it led to a junction that fed into Jefferson. They used to come down here sometimes from the other end, down to LaFleur with Twyla on weekends to see if they could spot alligators. It was a pretty spot, a deep lake framed by tupelo and cypress trees.

There was a rapping on his window. He jumped.

'Sir?' A police officer was gesturing for him to wind down his window. 'You need to not be here,' the officer said, chewing slowly. 'You wanna turn round here and head back up the way you came?'

Stephen stared ahead of him as though he didn't understand a word the officer had said.

'You OK, sir?'

'I'm fine.' He undid his seat belt. 'I just need to get out the car. Has there been an accident?'

'Sir, you need to remain in your vehicle. We need to get a crane right where you are. So you go on and turn around and get yourself on your way.'

Stephen stepped out of his car, face to face with the officer. They were both sweating heavily. It was one of those tetchy days when the air curdled everything it touched. 'Just tell me if anyone's been injured.'

The officer set his jaw belligerently, but having looked Stephen up and down he evidently decided he looked important enough to warrant a concession. 'You could say that,' he said, folding his arms. 'Someone's done gone drove into the lake.'

Stephen felt relief flood through him. And then he considered: Jolie, their neighbour, had a car that Robin sometimes borrowed to run errands. It was a yellow Ford Pinto.

He strained to look past the officer, past the fire engine, standing on tiptoe for a glimpse. The policeman laid a hand on Stephen's shoulder.

'You need to return to your vehicle now,' he said, firmly.

Stephen saw that the officer's patience was waning. He got back into his car. 'The vehicle in the lake . . . ' he said, dabbing the back of his neck with a handkerchief.

'Yup?' the officer said.

'Is it . . . uh . . . a goddamn ugly yellow Pinto?'

The officer spat his gum into a bush and wiped his mouth with the back of his hand. 'Sure is, sir,' he said.

For the rest of his life, Stephen would remember that moment — why people described fear as their blood running cold in their veins.

To be sat by a lake in high summer in Louisiana shivering; that was something.

'My wife,' he said. 'It's my wife.'

*   *   *

He waited as the crane pulled the Pinto out of the water, its hood crumpled, dangling beneath it.

He didn't know why he watched. There was nothing inside the Pinto. A diver had already retrieved the body. It was somewhere beyond in a body bag. He didn't want to leave before Robin though. He wanted to leave with her. So there was nothing to do but watch the Pinto.

Someone put a blanket around him — a scratchy thing that hung heavily about him. He was frozen. He had to stamp his feet to make the blood reach them. This was what he remembered the most — his cold feet.

The officer stayed with him. Maybe it was a slow day. Or maybe he felt sorry for Stephen. Or maybe he thought Stephen was a big deal in his fancy suit and that there may be something in it for him. Either way, he stayed by his side and offered to drive him home. He even arranged for Stephen's Sedan to be towed.

They followed the ambulance nearly all the way home until it turned off to the hospital. The wrench that Stephen felt as the ambulance left them and drove away into the distance was more than he could endure. He gripped the sides of his seat and began to gasp for air as though oxygen were running low.

'Take it easy,' the officer said. 'Real easy. That's right. You're gonna get through this, sir.'

They turned on to Smoke Rock Drive. He knew when to look for Twyla, the exact moment that she would come into view.

As they pulled up outside number 403, Twyla was sat there on the front step, playing with her doll in the sunshine.

Jolie and her daughter were in their garden next door. Jolie was tending to her border of Indian Pink flowers. When she saw the police car, she stood up with her hand in the small of her back, her mouth flopping open.

'Where's Robin?' said Jolie, approaching. 'She borrowed my car hours ago, saying she was running an errand.' She wiped her muddy hands on her shirt. 'Has something happened?'

'Shush,' said Stephen, resting his hand on the side of the police car to steady himself. 'Not in front of Twyla.'

'Not in front of Twyla?' Jolie shrieked. 'She needs to know if something's done gone happened to her mammy! Oh no!' She began to wail. 'Oh sweet Jesus!'

Stephen pushed past his neighbour and headed to his house, leaving the officer to calm Jolie down. He sat down on the front step. His daughter looked at him without enquiry. She didn't need to know why he was home from work so early. She was just happy that he was here. 'Hi, Daddy,' she said. 'Shall we go get us some almond pastries?'

He never could bring himself to tell her the truth — that Robin accelerated and changed direction in order to smash through the fence at the lakeside. A family had witnessed it; a family just like his, sat enjoying a picnic, trying to spot alligators. Instead, they had spotted something altogether more horrific.

Never look for alligators. That seemed good advice.

She accepted his lie, that an accident had taken her mother from her. Her strength of spirit was remarkable, so much so that he asked a colleague to check her out. But the verdict was that her mental health was not feigned, but real enough. Optimism was her coping mechanism.

They left Jefferson almost immediately. Everything in Louisiana reminded him of Robin.

They packed up the house, giving Robin's clothes to Goodwill and their furniture to neighbours. Keeping it businesslike made it easier to forget the ghastly implications of the sold sign in the front yard. If optimism was

Twyla's way of coping, pragmatism was his.

He went back to congenial Boston with Twyla and for a short while he was composed there, if not happy.

Yet it felt wrong. Returning to Harvard felt as though he were regressing — trying to slot his motherless child into a world that no longer fitted them. So when the job came up in London, he seized it. An English education for his daughter and a fresh start for them in a land without summersweet, hummingbirds or alligators.

There was a price to pay though. Pragmatism worked well in business, but did little for hearts. He lost Twyla too the day that her mother failed to return from her errand. Because from then on she may have been smiling and bright, but she never sat there again on the front step, waiting for someone she loved to come home.

★   ★   ★

The phone rang Saturday night, cutting through the chilly air. He hadn't lit the log burner yet, had been intending to, but Juliet was out and somehow the shadows had grown around him without his noticing. His hands were cold when he picked up the phone. He reached for a blanket to drape over him.

It was Twyla. She was crying — so upset, she couldn't get the words out at first. 'Slow down, Twyla,' he said. 'Tell me again. Slowly.'

'They don't want me to do it,' she said, gulping for air.

'Do what?'

'The operation. Charlie's operation.'

He sat up, the blanket dropping from his lap. 'But it's all set.'

'I know. But they don't want to go through with it.'

There was a pause whilst she blew her nose.

'They?' he said.

'Dylan and Eileen and Bindy.'

'Huh,' he said.

How to advise her?

He gazed at the stack of wood in the basket by the fire. A woodlouse was making its way down between two logs, not realising the peril in doing so, the fate awaiting the wood. He always meant to check for insects in the logs before tossing them on to the fire, but he never remembered, was always too lost in thought.

And there, in that trifling louse, lay the truth: that he was too preoccupied with himself to save anyone.

He pushed aside the patient's notes he had been reading and reached for the tumbler of bourbon on the table. The case was particularly vexing — a woman whose agoraphobia was so chronic, he was at a loss as to how to help her.

'What does Dylan say?' he asked.

She sniffed. 'That we should cancel Thursday.'

'And what do you think?' he said. He took a sip of bourbon and waited for her response.

'That we should go ahead.'

'Then there's your answer,' he said.

The louse must take his chances on the logs.

The agoraphobe must take her chances out-doors.

'But if I do this, I could lose Dylan.'

'Not necessarily,' he said, rotating the glass on his knee, watching the golden liquor swirling. 'Not if Charlie can see.'

'But . . . what if . . . ?' She didn't complete the sentence.

'Twyla . . . ' he said. He pictured her standing before him as a child, her shoulders rosy from the sun, her hair crackling with static. 'What do you want to do?'

'To give Charlie this opportunity. Because, if I don't, I'll regret it for the rest of my life.'

'Then do it,' he said, putting his empty glass down heavily on the table.

★ ★ ★

Dylan turned the television off. He hadn't been able to focus on the programme. He was agitated, but chronically tired — a desperate combination.

There was a noise coming from above him. He opened the lounge door to listen. Twyla was on the phone in the spare room. Who would she be speaking to at this time of night?

He climbed the stairs and stopped halfway up, listening. He couldn't hear the words, but Twyla was crying.

The sound filled him with sadness. There was someone else out there whom she was turning to, and it wasn't him.

Who would it be? A girlfriend. Someone equipped

with the necessary emotional responses. Yet he had tried so hard to understand what she was going through, why all this mattered so greatly.

But when it came down to it, his preference was to leave Charlie as he was. And her preference was to change him.

How to resolve that?

He felt overcome with fatigue and was about to sit down on the stairs when the spare room door opened with a blast of yellow and he felt like a convict held captive under floodlights.

She stopped on seeing him, wondering perhaps how much he had heard. And then she made for the bathroom.

'Twyla.' He bounded up the remaining stairs. 'We need to talk.' He grabbed her sleeve as she went through the bathroom door, but she pulled herself away.

'There's nothing to discuss,' she said. 'You've made your feelings perfectly clear.'

'Clear?' he said, closing the bathroom door so as not to disturb Charlie. 'How can they be clear when I don't even know what they are?' He put his hands either side of her arms — clasped her there to summon her attention. 'Twyla . . . Can't you see what's happening?'

She felt small in his grip. Once more he was struck by how childlike she seemed — like that day in the snow, when she had stood in her red coat and wellington boots. She had brought Felicity to his mind. And she did so again now.

What was that similarity? Just physical — their mutual paleness, fairness? Or was it more than that?

'We need to stay strong,' he said. 'I love you.'

She released herself from him and went to the sink to splash cold water on her face.

'I haven't said no,' he said. 'I don't know what I think. But I need to be absolutely sure before Thursday. Do you understand?'

'Of course,' she said, her voice muffled by the towel she was wiping her face with.

They kissed good night — light numb kisses — and Dylan returned downstairs. He had to reach a decision by morning, even if he sat up all night to find it.

He went through to the kitchen to warm up a pan of milk and cinnamon. His mother used to make this for him. Not that he was a mummy's boy, yet still he reached for this when in need of solace.

If anything, he was a daddy's boy. His father had been a bolter. He had bolted at everything — when the toast burnt, when Felicity had a seizure, when Mum started to rant, and finally the big bolt: his departure.

Dylan took his drink through to the lounge and flicked the table lamp on before sitting down on the sofa, his hands around his mug. It was the end of the first week of September. There was a distinct chill in the air, a tension as summer held autumn off.

He thought again of his father, of the way he had walked out on them. Dylan was eleven years old. Felicity was barely cold in the earth. It must have been a horrible time, but he didn't remember it as such. His strongest memories were of playing seven-aside football in the frost, and a girl with braces who sat next to him in tutorial and kept Tic-Tacs hidden in the top of her knee-high socks.

An eleven-year-old boy's way of dealing with loss wasn't exactly the stuff that mental health manuals were made of. He had just pretended that none of it had happened, simple as.

It was what his father had done, after all. Twenty-five years ago his dad walked away, never to be seen again. Who knew where he was now, if he was even alive.

Dylan sipped his milk and watched the trees moving outside the window. He hadn't pulled the curtains yet, thought that he might feel less solitary if he could see signs of life beyond.

Why think of his father now, or Felicity, or the girl with braces?

What use was that?

Molly was right. This wasn't about anyone else. It was about himself and Twyla making a decision.

He thought of Molly and her creamy complexion, and all of a sudden he wanted to seek her out, to sit down with her and talk things through.

He put his mug down and rubbed his face.

It was Molly's apparent lack of complications that drew him, that was all.

She was a convenient escape route for his mind, and he wasn't about to take it, like jumping on a large inflatable chute from a burning tower block.

He was a better man than his father.

And so he continued to think, going over the facts about keratoprosthesis surgery, trying to concentrate on the most important thing: Charlie. For the answer lay within Charlie, within what was best for him.

When he stopped thinking, his eyes felt itchy, his limbs aching and cold. It was one o'clock in the morning. He went to the kitchen to rinse his mug out and as he switched off the lights he moaned, no closer to finding peace.

He climbed the stairs wearily, feeling utterly alone.

In the bedroom, he watched Charlie, who was asleep in his cot with his face pressed against the sheets, his blond hair angelic in the glow of the nightlight. Dylan crouched to adjust the blankets and found himself on his knees.

It was a long time since he had prayed. There was nothing else left for him to do.

'Please, Lord,' he whispered. 'Please tell me what to do.'

Twyla shifted behind him. He froze, worried that she had heard him. He didn't want to be seen in this position — desperate, out of ideas. He glanced over his shoulder and saw that she was still asleep.

There was something in her hand.

He prised it from her and took it to the nightlight. It was a handwritten letter, emitting a strange scent. He lifted the paper to his nose. Flowers of some kind.

Odd. Why would she have been holding this?

He leant closer towards the light and began to read.

In the end, despite Twyla's assurances that no stranger was going to make this decision for them, it was a stranger who determined their course, altered their lives.

People didn't often feel stirred to praise as often as they did to criticise. Few reached for their pens in admiration. Yet old Mrs Jones of Portsmouth had. And this made him realise that for every critic damning them, there was someone willing them on — someone who wasn't sufficiently moved to tell them so in writing but who regarded them with wonder and approval nonetheless. This realisation didn't make the outcome right or wrong, didn't answer any questions. It just made the arena more balanced.

He sat down on the bed and gazed at Twyla as she slept. Her face looked drawn, troubled.

And he saw then that Twyla's similarity to Felicity was their lack of control, their inability to do anything about their plights.

Both girls had been tossed about in early life by events beyond their control — by a hand that eventually defeated Felicity. Twyla had only managed to survive because she had worked out how to use hope and purpose to keep her going. To take that away from her now would destroy her.

He shook her arm. 'Twyla!' he said. 'Wake up!'

She sat up instantly. 'What?' she said. 'Charlie?'

'He's fine,' he said, pointing to their son in his cot.

'Oh,' she said, looking about her sleepily. 'Then what?'

He took her hand. 'Let's go for it.'

'Hey?' she said, drawing the covers up to her chin.

'The operation.'

She stared at him.

'You're right,' he said. 'We have to do this, or we'll never know what could have been.'

She was motionless for a moment longer. And then she leapt up, abandoning the bedcovers, clasping her hands around his neck. She was kissing his face and saying thank you. And he laughed with relief that a decision had been reached, that he hadn't taken the inflatable chute route but had stood firm. He held her tightly and nestled his mouth to her neck, kissing her, daring himself to believe that this time next week, Charlie would be able to see for himself just how pretty his mum was.

13

The moments in Bindy's childhood when she was free were so rare, so exquisite, they stood out like illuminated exhibits in a display case. She could remember the afternoon she drove her bike up and down the driveway, the tassels on her handlebars twirling in the sunshine; the time she played Indians, crawling through the grass with a wooden dagger in her mouth; dancing with her dad at a wedding.

The rest of the time, she was Felicity's carer. It was never officially so — no one declared her a carer, gave her praise or credit, or told her teachers that she wasn't really poorly again but had to stay home to help Fee because their mother couldn't get up. Their mum was the official help. She told the healthcare specialists that she had everything under control. And she did, when they visited. She made the tea, laid out the Nice biscuits, fixed her make-up and wheeled Fee into the room with a look that said *Aren't I a charm?*

But when the visitors left, she slumped into her chair and fixed her eyes on Bindy, who stopped picking the scab on her knee or colouring in, and instead wheeled her sister out into the hallway, anywhere away from their mother who needed some quiet.

Bindy didn't miss that much school. It was just that when she went she found she couldn't stop yawning, couldn't follow what they were talking about. She was too tired to keep up, and bored senseless. It seemed so pointless.

She shared a room with Fee who moaned all night because her joints were aching. At first Bindy found the noise maddening, sharing a room with someone who made yelping noises like a seal. But then her father told her that Felicity wasn't a seal but a human with deep emotions, like everyone else. Fee just couldn't express herself with words.

On learning this, Bindy spent a few weeks prodding her sister curiously, wondering whether she could provoke a reaction, whether there was a secret code to her language. One yelp for no, two for yes. But it was useless. Fee might have been feeling a multitude of emotions, but there was no code, no way to unlock her thoughts.

From then on, Bindy stayed by her sister's side whenever possible, trying to speak for her. For the idea that Fee was trapped inside a useless bag of skin saddened Bindy so much, she wanted to do something about it. So when Fee moaned, Bindy took to telling visitors things like, *Fee says could you shut the window 'cos she's getting a crick in her neck.* Or on bolder days, *Fee says that hat with all the plastic grapes and cherries on is ridiculous and does nothing to flatter you.*

There was only a year between the sisters, but Dylan was four years younger than Fee. Bindy suspected that his arrival wasn't planned, such was their mother's shock at Felicity's condition. Either way, Dylan was left to get on with things by himself, which he did rather well. Right from the start, he separated himself out from them, just like their father. Both men were there, part of the household, active contributors in conversations, yet they left the room when things got ropy.

And they often did. By the time Fee was in her teens, their mother took to her bed more regularly. Bindy brought food to her on a tray, squinting in the gloomy light, trying not to absorb the stale air, the toxic depression. Her mother refused to open the curtains or a window, and refused to eat.

Fee's seizures were intensifying, and Bindy was supposed to be choosing GCSE options at school. Dylan had joined a football team, and came and went as he liked. But at least Bindy was sleeping well now. She was so used to Fee's noises, they lulled her to sleep, like birds calling to roost. Thoroughly exhausted, she would have slept on a train track.

She knew exactly who to take it out on: their father. He wasn't home enough. He was a floor manager at a biscuit factory, and brought home boxes of broken biscuits once a week — custard creams, Jammie Dodgers. Small consolation. The boxes appeared more often the less their dad was home. He started taking extra shifts on weekends. When he wasn't at work, he slept on a fold-out bed in Dylan's room, since Eileen didn't want him near her.

Somehow their mum blamed their dad for Fee. She never said as much because it would sound insane, but still the blame was there and slowly she pushed him away and turned more to her Lord. In the midst of one of her depressions, she would stumble around the house grasping her rosary beads. When she made it downstairs, she relentlessly cross-stitched wall hangings as though there were gaps in the plaster that needed covering. *With the help of God small things grow.* Yeah right. The only thing growing in this house was mildew.

There was an atmosphere of doom around Felicity that intensified during those teenage years. Other people could feel it, even strangers. They gave Fee and her wheelchair a wide berth. Dogs circled her cautiously. The whole house seemed to hold its breath in anticipation of tragedy.

Bindy was sure that Fee could feel it too. When she lifted her sister into bed at night, Fee seemed to cling more tightly, to moan more plaintively, as though she were saying, *I'm scared, Bindy. What's going to happen to me?*

★ ★ ★

Bindy unscrewed the lid of her hipflask and sat down on the bed. She thought about Fee more than was recommended. There wasn't a day that passed when she didn't think of her. And now a memory had stepped forward that tightened her ribs — a memory that she had considered lost.

It was the only time she ever saw her sister cry. She hadn't known that Fee could cry, that she even knew what tears were. The tears looked planted on her face, oddly detached, as though someone had put them there as a prank. There could be no other explanation to Bindy's young mind.

They were at the fair, all five of them together in a rare occurrence — one that she would have added to her display of illuminated memories had it been happier. Their mum bought Felicity a red balloon and tied it to the arm of her wheelchair. Fee rocked herself in delight, kicking her feet, moaning. She loved that balloon. They were all pleased.

But on the way home, the string untied itself slowly, with no one noticing. When they turned around, Fee was crying silent tears, her mouth open, gaping. No one could do anything about it. They just stood and watched the balloon drifting away from them into the breezeless evening sky.

★   ★   ★

Paul arrived at his brother's house early evening and was just taking his coat off, when his phone rang. He shot his brother an apologetic look before leaving the room to take the call.

In the hallway, amongst the cardboard boxes of baby gear — a cot by the looks of it, a pram, a colourful mobile of safari animals — he spoke to his boss. She had just received a tip-off that the Ridley boy was being operated on on Thursday, and wanted him to go round there first thing in the morning to get a photograph.

'The Ridley boy?' he asked warily. There was only one Ridley on the *Herald's* radar that he knew of.

'The blind boy,' his boss said. 'You know the one.'

He did indeed.

There was a clatter of saucepans in the kitchen beyond. The aromas — coconut, onions, chicken — were teasing his stomach. His sister-in-law was a chef — a pregnant chef. Was there a more ardent type of cook on the planet?

'They won't agree to a photograph,' he said.

'And how would you know?' his boss said. 'Go ask! I'm running the piece either way. Apparently the op's risky for kids. Locals will be interested to hear that. They've a right to know how things have progressed.'

He hung up and stood staring at the boxes, at the gear that had begun to accumulate over the past few weeks.

The Ridleys had been like that once, he thought. They would have ordered loads of stuff — maybe mobiles and visual toys. And then half of it would have been useless for their son.

Maybe that's what it was all about for them: making everything less ineffectual, more mean-ingful.

He went back into the kitchen, where his sister-in-law was dipping her finger into a sauce to taste it, her oversized hair tamed in a bandana. It was only when she turned that you saw the huge bump. 'Was that your boss?' she asked, serving up supper. It was stir-fry — a Caribbean concoction.

'Yep,' he said, taking a seat.

His brother handed him a large glass of wine.

186

Paul drank it as though it were water, before checking himself.

His boss always rattled him. Less than two years into this job, and he was already looking for work elsewhere. Perhaps he was better suited to wedding photography or school portraits. Something less morally dubious. Or maybe he could go back to being a lawyer . . .

'What was so urgent it couldn't wait?' his brother said.

'The Ridleys,' Paul replied. 'They're having the op this week.'

'The Ridleys?' his brother said, blankly. He was a carpenter who had chosen that occupation because he could work alone, with wood. His hands were calloused, his hair speckled with wood shavings and his connection with the world tenuous.

'The blind boy,' Paul said.

'Never heard of him,' his brother said, tucking into his food.

Halfway through the meal, when their hunger had been sated, Paul set down his fork. 'Would you do what they're doing?' he asked his sister-in-law.

He didn't have to clarify what he meant. They had discussed it several times of late, along with anyone else who read the papers. The argument had a *would you, wouldn't you* quality that most people enjoyed, even if they weren't parents, weren't in the same position, weren't remotely qualified to judge.

'It's impossible to say for sure,' she replied. She touched her hand to her belly as she spoke. 'But I don't think so.'

'We won't need to anyhow,' his brother said, putting his hand on top of hers in mutual appreciation of the bump. 'Nothing wrong with this one.'

'But what if there was?' Paul said. 'Heaven forbid.' He held up both his hands to fortify his words. 'No one ever thinks this will happen to them. That's what makes it so difficult when it does.' He took a gulp of wine. 'But what if you did have to make that choice? I mean, who are we to judge anyway?'

'Hun,' said his sister-in-law, wiping her mouth with a napkin, 'you're getting yourself way too caught up in this. You need to get yourself a good night's sleep.'

'I'll try,' Paul said, smiling wryly.

★ ★ ★

On his walk home, Paul kept playing his boss's words over in his head. He vehemently disagreed with her. The public didn't have a right to know about the Ridleys. No one had the right to opine about such a personal matter. Yet it didn't stop them.

At first the *Herald* coverage was sympathetic in order to lure Twyla Ridley to them. She would have welcomed the exposure that increased her fund-raising total. Yet the balance was tipping and it wouldn't be long before his boss would subtly imply criticism, with the focus shifting from the miraculous to the foolhardy: *mother presses ahead with controversial quest for son to see . . .*

His boss wasn't so much reporting the news as stirring debate. And nothing sold papers like passing judgement on parents.

A child had died locally last month after choking on a take-out chicken nugget. The *Herald* had reported the tragic incident and soon their website was heaving with debate. Someone wrote that if the child hadn't have been eating junk food, he would still be alive — if only parents fed their children properly. This wasn't a lone psychopathic voice. The comment had received over fifty likes.

No one had 'liked' the comment at the bottom that Paul added however:

A little girl choked on an apple when I was a child. Do you think her parents were happy that it was a healthy snack?

He wished he hadn't written it. He was so incensed, he had wanted to take action. But posting a silly comment online wasn't action.

Perhaps his past in law really was calling him back. It wasn't just Twyla Ridley and her plight that had captured him, but his desire to make the world a better place in some small way.

Working at the *Herald* certainly wasn't doing that.

He wouldn't descend on the Ridleys in the morning, but would email them first to ask if they would consent to a photograph. His boss would never know, and it would save him disturbing the Ridleys. He didn't want Twyla Ridley to think that little of him.

As he walked home, he gazed up at the sky. Unusually for the city centre, he could see the North Star and the Plough. It was a crisp autumn evening, the sort that made you pull your coat closer around you but not want to button it yet.

The ancient sky was unchanged from old, just like humans. The public were poised like a Roman crowd, eagerly awaiting the fate of the gladiator, Twyla Ridley. They would feast their eyes and then go home satisfied that their lives were so much better, that they were so much more fortunate and clever.

★　★　★

The day before the operation, Twyla arranged for no one to call, for none of the health specialists or any family to visit. She had refused a photograph in the press and had asked that no article be printed about them. Whether her request would be met was neither here nor there. By tomorrow, it would all be over.

All the commentary had been heard, the hate mail read, the family arguments settled, the financial transactions made, the train tickets bought, the hospital bed booked.

It was all set.

The weather had turned. Autumn was trying to creep in whilst none of them were looking. The leaves were curling on the trees, like licked stamps. There was a chill in the air and most days were filled with blue sky and grey clouds in equal measures — with warm and cold air. Soon the balance would tip and summer would be overthrown.

Dylan was due home any moment. Things were good between them again, although there was an understandable tension in the air.

His mother was noticeably elusive and probably wasn't going to ring to wish them well. Perhaps it was too much to ask, but now that a decision had been reached Twyla wished that Eileen could at least have bade them good luck.

At least her father had backed them, albeit financially, as was his way. But it was something. And in this case everything, for without the money there would be no tomorrow.

She kissed the back of Charlie's head and smoothed his hair. He was sat on her lap playing with his alphabet zoo. They were taking him to feed the ducks after lunch, to distract themselves and keep things as normal as possible.

They hadn't told Charlie about tomorrow, felt that doing so might frighten him. As far as he was aware, he was going on a train ride to the capital city of England. The surgery itself was fairly short — a few hours at most — and Charlie would be under general anaesthetic. By the time he woke up, he would be in recovery with minimal discomfort.

He twisted in his seat, his nappy crackling. 'Tree?' he asked.

This was his way of asking to go in the garden. She kissed his cheek. 'Good idea,' she said. 'Come on.'

They left the lounge hand in hand and went through to the utility room. Twyla opened the back door, the sunshine streaming on to the mat.

She had only just sat Charlie down with his back against the rosemary tub when the front door bell rang. She frowned. The social worker normally came at this time, but Twyla had made herself clear about today.

She looked doubtfully at Charlie. 'I'm going to leave you for a second,' she said. 'Don't move. OK?'

It wasn't the social worker at the door. It was a man in a tweed jacket bearing a badge with indecipherable writing on it. 'Good morning,' he said. 'I'm from All Saints Church of Redemption and Salvation.' He reeled the words off mechanically. 'I understand that you wanted — '

'I'm sorry,' she said, 'But I don't have time for this today.' And with a smile, so as not to offend, she began to close the door.

But then she heard him say something and she swung open the door again. 'What did you say?' she asked.

A butterfly fluttered near and then away again, disorientated.

'That you should pray for Charlie Ross before it's too late,' he said.

She stared in amazement at him. She couldn't think of a response — a polite one — so she closed the door without further to-do.

She made her way back down the hallway, bewildered. She had no idea how people imagined that they had the right to —

She came to a halt in the garden and stood blinking about her.

'Charlie? Where are you?'

★ ★ ★

There was no way out of their back garden. Charlie was here somewhere.

He must have followed her indoors when the doorbell rang. She went back into the utility room. 'Charlie?'

She traced her steps through the kitchen, down the hallway. All the doors were closed and he wasn't able to reach the handles to open them. The stair gate was closed so he wasn't upstairs. All the cupboards had child locks on. Everything was sealed, secure.

She went back outside. 'Charlie?' The sky had darkened. It looked like it was about to rain. What did he have on? The green top with the monster logo, and blue shorts. 'Charlie!'

Where would he go if inclined to leave? Was there a small place that he would be tempted to poke about in?

She got down on her knees where she had left him. If he had tried to follow her, he would have toppled over the fence on to the gravel. He knew about that edge, wouldn't have tried it.

Where else?

Little places.

There weren't any little places. No gaps — nowhere he could squeeze.

Behind her workshop? The shed was only inches from the stone wall behind it. She dropped to her knees and lowered herself to peer underneath the workshop, which was propped up on bricks. 'Charlie?' she called.

There was barely enough room for a rat to

crawl underneath. She hurried indoors, grabbed a torch and returned outside. Lying out flat, she held the light underneath the shed. The torch was dead — the batteries had gone. She flung the torch aside. He couldn't be under the shed. There wasn't room.

She stood on the rosemary pot to climb the wall. Scraping her knees, she clambered to the top where she stared at next door's neat mosaic paving. 'Charlie?' He couldn't have climbed there.

She turned and ran to the opposite wall. This wall was higher. There was no way he could have scaled it.

She looked all around again. How else could he leave?

Her eye settled on the disused gate at the back of the garden. It led to a path that was once used by residents, but was now overgrown with weeds. The gate was too high for Charlie, but an adult could reach over and unbolt it from the other side. Charlie couldn't have climbed it. There were no footholds in the wood.

She approached the gate. There was just enough room for her to slide between the shed and the neighbour's wall to reach it.

It was dark. She didn't have to venture forward more than a step to see it there at the bottom of the gate, spilling into the gloom — a shard of light.

'Oh no,' she said. 'Oh God no.'

The gate was open.

'Twyla? Charlie boy? Ready for the ducks?'

Dylan was home.

She wavered. If she stopped to tell him, they would lose precious time.

She pushed the gate open, ramming it against the buddleia. The path was barely visible through the undergrowth. She moved forward, lowering her face from thorny vines.

Someone else had trodden here, had pushed the undergrowth aside as she was doing now. There were crushed nettles, snapped branches.

She followed the down-trodden path, going the length of the eight semi-detached properties that stood between their house on Orchard Drive and the main road.

She had stopped calling for Charlie. It didn't feel safe to do so now. Instead, she talked to herself in a shallow whisper. 'Help me, Charlie, love. Tell me where you are.'

She reached the main road as though emerging from a rabbit hole and stood staring at the traffic thundering past.

What if Charlie had somehow made his way here alone? Would he know not to step off this pavement? Had she even told him about road safety yet, about how dangerous cars were?

Horror muddled her thoughts, like a crazy spinning top.

He couldn't have been knocked down. There would have been a dreadful commotion. She would have known about it.

Then what?

She hastened down the main road, passing the

car lot where men with scrawny arms hand-washed cars when they weren't sitting on sofas, playing cards. She didn't think to ask them if they had seen anything.

Charlie hadn't made that journey alone. The undergrowth was crushed at her eye level in some parts. If he had made the journey at all, he had been carried.

As she turned the corner and ran along Orchard Drive, she began to shiver involuntarily. She was wearing a thin T-shirt. A splash of rain landed on her bare arm. Charlie would be so cold without a coat. When had she last changed his nappy? And what about food? They were about to have lunch.

It began to rain heavily. She ran up their driveway and tried the handle of the front door. It was locked. She hammered on the door with the flats of her hands. 'Dylan?' she shouted. 'Dylan!'

Someone a few doors up was getting into their car. They paused to look at Twyla and she turned away, her wet hair flapping about her, clinging to her neck.

Dylan opened the door and looked stunned. 'What on earth . . . ?' he said, helping her into the house. Her teeth were chattering loudly. He grabbed a coat from the rack and bundled it around her. 'What's going on?'

She wiped her eyes, leaving black mascara trails on her fingers. 'I . . . ' she said.

'What?' he said.

'I can't find Charlie.'

He stared at her. 'Hey?'

'He's gone,' she said.

'Gone?'

'I don't know where he is,' she said.

'When did you last see him?' he said, raising his voice.

'About ten minutes ago. And then he was gone.'

'Jesus Christ.' He rubbed his face in agitation and then grabbed the phone.

Twyla sat down at the foot of the stairs, feeling weightless, as though floating.

'I need to report a missing child,' Dylan said into the phone. 'He's twenty months old . . . Yes it's very urgent! . . . He's blind.'

A trickle of rain ran from Twyla's hair down her spine. She was feeling nauseous. She cupped her hand to her mouth and kept it there.

'Thank you,' Dylan said. 'And hurry!'

He hung up. He was wearing an old pinstriped suit that he didn't often wear. The colour had drained from his face, leaving him with a strange grey pallor.

'Tell me what happened,' he said.

'He was in the garden . . . And then he was gone.'

'How?' he said. 'How did he go? When? Where?'

'About ten minutes ago,' she said. 'Wait.' She pressed her temples. 'It was eleven-thirty, eleven-forty.'

'And?'

'Someone rang the doorbell and I left Charlie to answer it . . . only for a moment. And it was a man.'

'A man?'

She nodded. 'A religious door-to-door caller. He said something about me praying for Charlie before it was too late.'

'Too late for what?' he said.

She pushed her wet hair away from her face and gazed at him, unwilling and unable to answer.

'Do you think he was distracting me whilst someone took him?' she said.

'From where?'

'From the garden,' she said.

'You were in the garden?'

'Yes.'

'You didn't tell me that,' he said.

'I did.'

They stared at each other before Dylan went through to the lounge. She followed him. He tossed his suit jacket on to the sofa and stood looking out of the window. 'I can't believe this is happening,' he said. 'How did he get out of the garden?'

'The back gate was unlocked,' she said.

'The back gate was unlocked,' he repeated slowly, as though trying to learn a foreign phrase. 'We never use the back gate. Why was it unlocked?'

'I don't know,' she said. 'I went along the path just now. It was all trodden down. I think someone carried Charlie along there.'

'Oh, Christ,' said Dylan. He began to pace the floor. 'What was the man like?'

'I don't know . . . Short. Weird-looking.'

He stopped. 'This is about the operation, isn't it?' he said.

She didn't know what to say.

She looked out the window. A white feather was slowly falling from the sky to earth. She watched it as it drifted down, curled like a miniature boat. It looked enigmatic, removed from its previous owner, nothing to do with the bird that was soaring above, oblivious to its loss.

14

The police arrived promptly. Two officers worked diligently through the process, gathering a description of Charlie Ross and recent photographs; details of where he was last seen; a list of his acquaintances; a list of the specialists who worked with him, and an outline of his typical day.

It was too pedestrian for Twyla. She kept consulting her watch. Charlie could be anywhere by now. Dylan's winter coat was still bundled around her shoulders. Her hair was damp and her skin smelt of rain and terror. The clock was ticking loudly. Otherwise the room was quiet as the policemen worked, their radios crackling unfathomably.

One of the officers told her that they had to assess the level of risk before they could do anything else.

'Level of risk?' said Twyla. 'He's blind!'

'And you have grounds to believe that he's been abducted?' he replied cordially.

She threw off her coat feeling suddenly claustrophobic. 'Yes,' she said. 'I told you about the hate mail. And the religious man. I told you what he said about praying before it was too late.'

'There are plenty of people who'd like to stop tomorrow from happening,' said Dylan. He was stood by the window, watching out for Charlie.

He had rolled up his shirtsleeves. There was a line of sweat on his back.

'And we intend to look into that as soon as we've finished here,' said the officer.

'But shouldn't we be out there now searching for him?' said Twyla.

'Of course,' said the other officer. 'Once we've identified the risk.'

'Oh for goodness sake!' said Twyla, her hands coiling into fists of frustration.

'Look,' the first officer said, shutting his notebook with a decisive snap. 'I know this is highly distressing, but the best thing to do is not panic. Ninety-nine per cent of the time, these things have a simple explanation.'

Once satisfied of the facts, the officers looked around the house and the garden. They went along Orchard Drive knocking on doors. They poked about the bushes to the front and back of the house, looking for hiding places for a toddler, and examined the trodden-down path behind the workshop.

And then they uttered the words she had dreaded hearing: that they would be back shortly and in the meantime she should try to remain calm, that they were sure Charlie would show up.

★　★　★

Dylan watched the police car pulling away. If they weren't back in half an hour he was phoning his old school friend who was a policeman. His friend worked in traffic, but might be able to make a few calls for them. In the meantime, they had to wait.

His stomach was bubbling, his mouth trembling, as though he were being broken down cell by cell. It reminded him of a science museum trip he had taken as a boy where he discovered that television was thousands of dots of light. He was able to believe now for the first time that he really was mostly water and molecules, not a solid person at all.

He turned to look at Twyla. Her head was droopy, her limbs lifeless, as though she had abandoned herself. All that remained was a startled expression around the mouth.

He knelt down before her. 'Twyla,' he said. Her took her hand. It was morbidly cold. 'Why don't we get you out of these wet clothes?'

He tried to pull her to her feet, but she wouldn't yield, was back-breakingly heavy.

'You'll catch cold and that won't do anyone any good,' he said. 'Charlie will need you when he comes back.'

This seemed to work. She eased herself up as though she were much older than she was, and walked noiselessly from the room.

'What are we going to do about the operation?' he called after her.

There was no reply.

He went to follow her upstairs and saw that she was standing in the utility room at the window. The back door was open, the wind fluttering the fly curtain she had installed to keep germs out of the house, away from Charlie.

How painstaking she had been: the door

wedges, the foam on sharp corners, the Braille labels.

The fly curtain rattled now, a gentle sound, like Charlie shaking it to be let back in.

'Do you want me to cancel the Royal Square?' he said.

Once more, she didn't reply.

He eyed the garden uneasily. Charlie's spade was propped against the pot of rosemary. It sickened him to see it there. Charlie loved to dig; Twyla had given him a mud pot of his own to poke about in.

Dylan would have to ring the Royal Square and explain. Someone had to.

What would he tell them? He would have to tell the truth and beg some understanding — an open invitation to take up Charlie's operation slot as soon as he returned and was fit to travel.

Why wouldn't he be fit to travel?

He clenched his jaw and took a moment to calm himself.

'Come on, love,' he said, pulling her away from the window. 'The police will be back any minute.'

He escorted her upstairs, unable to decide whether she was inhumanly heavy or inhumanly weightless or both. Whatever it was, she didn't feel like Twyla any more.

★　★　★

Twyla listened to the water running in the bathroom. She was sitting on the edge of the bed, following a crack in the wall with her eyes.

The police would be back any moment, Dylan said — she just had time for a quick bath to warm her up. If she didn't she would get hypothermia and would be no use to Charlie when he returned.

He was saying one thing and doing the other.

He didn't really think Charlie would be back shortly. If he thought that, he wouldn't have phoned the Royal Square. He thought she didn't know that he had cancelled them, but she had heard him murmuring into the phone and guessed what he was doing.

She put her hand to her forehead. It felt damp. All of her felt damp, a fine mist of perspiration coating her body.

Charlie would be cold without his coat.

She listened, checking that Dylan was still running the bath, before slipping downstairs.

A police car was outside, several cars. Doors were slamming. A mobile phone was ringing. She could hear voices — lots of them. Blue lights were flashing noiselessly through the frosted pane of their front door. It didn't feel like an allied force arriving, but as though invaders were creeping forward to storm their home.

She had already gone through the details with them. She couldn't sit there again, filling out forms, making cups of tea. Dylan could do it. Besides, she would only be gone a moment.

She wouldn't wear a jumper or coat, for her son had neither. She stepped into a pair of old shoes and pulled the back door shut behind her.

She retraced her steps — through the gate, along the path. This time she stopped to ask the men at the car wash if they had seen a little boy with blond hair, and she called into the Chinese takeaway to ask the same. She stopped an elderly man at the bus stop and a mother with a pram, and began to knock on every door in the neighbourhood until her hand was sore from knocking and her throat was sore from talking and the sun was tired from shining and had sunk.

★   ★   ★

Twyla could remember staying up all night once when she was a student. It was a dare amongst a group of them — an experiment to see how long they could sit up for and what would happen to them when they did. Nothing did happen except that they stumbled about goofily at breakfast the next morning, sniggering, and fell asleep in lectures. It had seemed daring, experimental and deviant. But Twyla saw now that it was none of those things — that it was sad that some people sat up like that every night without choice, fixed rigid through illness, fear or both.

The outside world looked no different through the night. Once darkness had fallen, it looked exactly the same at ten o'clock, two o'clock or four. And when it was over, there was no bell that rang, no signal to mark the end of one day and the dawning of the next. The two days merged smoothly like the tide rolling on to the beach, dragging the sand with it, leaving no trace of boundaries, no definitions, no edges.

By five, there was a patch of light above the

trees, but it was impossible to say whether it was the lights of the city, or dawn approaching, like a tribe of natives carrying fire torches. Even the road had finally stopped. There were a few cars throughout the night but five o'clock was a strange neverland — a moment when the cogs stopped and all was still and the world was handed back to nature.

Would she ever sleep again?

By six, the glow above the trees was unmistakable, but it had changed shade to an indigo that was tingeing the whole sky a watery litmus paper colour.

By six-twenty, the birds were singing and the sky was an eerie grey.

By six-thirty, the sky had won and was blushing pink.

And it was then that Twyla rang her father.

It took him a while to answer. He would be asleep, slow to stir, fumbling for his dressing gown.

Eighteen rings. She let the phone ring, picturing him making his way through his plush house, his hair on end, his spectacles on the tip of his nose. He would take the call in his study, as he always used to do when she had lived with him. She hadn't visited his home in Highgate, but knew he was bound to have a study there — that people didn't really change, even when their environment did.

She remembered him saying years ago that he had a friend high up at Scotland Yard. She had no idea how he knew such a person. Perhaps they had studied together — psychology majors at Harvard.

He listened to her account, pausing to make notes as though she were one of his patients, his fountain pen scratching. Sometimes as a child, she had stolen through to his study to try out his selection of pens, betraying her presence there with splodges of ink on her fingers and on his expensive writing paper. He didn't seem to mind. That was one thing about him.

Another thing about him was that he was born in Louisiana, and so was she. They were family. And when it was a matter of blood — unlike money — she had no hesitation in begging.

'Please help,' she told him, her face tight with dried tears.

'I'll do my utmost, Twyla,' he said. 'But my contact is long gone at the Yard. He retired years ago.'

'But surely there's someone you know? Something you can do?'

She held her head in her hands. She could hear Dylan shifting about. He had gone to bed, but she had heard the door handles going and the floorboards creaking all night and knew he had barely rested.

'Leave it with me,' he said.

'Thank you,' she said. And then, 'I love you.' But she was saying it to an empty line because he had hung up some minutes ago.

★   ★   ★

The new day brought a detective sergeant, a dozen constables and as many Alsatians. The sergeant made it clear that the case was deemed high risk due to Charlie's impairments and the suspicious circumstances surrounding his disappearance.

The police, joined by a specialist team, set about searching the house even more thoroughly. They went into the attic and out to the workshop. They opened every door, every drawer, ransacked every item, turned everything out until Twyla felt as though her own body was being turned over, her insides hanging out.

It was disorientating, sitting there in the lounge with everyone moving around her, sitting still like she was instructed to do in case there were any changes.

Dylan was out with a search team, trawling the fields with the Alsatians and a growing body of volunteers. She could have done with him here, would have welcomed his arm around her, his hand in hers. But to keep him here was selfish when he was needed elsewhere. And so she sat alone.

Charlie would have been there now, she thought, glancing at the clock. Right now, they would have been preparing him for surgery.

Each passing second boomed in her ears, every tick of the clock provoked her, until she wanted to smash up all the clocks and run out into the street screaming.

But she didn't. She sat there sedately, waiting.

Early morning, a team of forensics in puffy suits arrived. They didn't introduce themselves, but began poking about as though they were familiar with the house and came here all the time. When they went upstairs, she took umbrage and followed them. Yet when she reached the top stair, she didn't have the gumption to antagonise them so went to the bedroom on the pretext of finding something.

In truth, there was nothing in the bedroom or in any room that she needed. She looked at the house perplexedly, wondering why there were things like coffee and cake tins, lampshades and books. Who had any need for them?

When she came out of the bedroom, she was alarmed to glimpse a man in the bathroom taking samples from Charlie's toothbrush — scraping fragments of her son into a plastic container.

Her legs grew heavy, rooting her to the spot. 'What's that for?' she asked.

'Just a precaution,' the man said, snapping a jar lid shut and turning his back on her.

The detective sergeant was calling for her downstairs.

He wanted to go over the facts again. This time he probed further: Charlie's medical history and the impending operation; his language and physical limitations; a list of friends and family. Who came to Charlie's christening? What was Charlie's mental health like? What was the state of her marriage? Were they happy?

Twyla put her head in her hands, trying to pick over his words.

'Hell of a coincidence, don't you think?' the sergeant said, pursing his lips. He had full lips that somehow didn't fit his bony face. 'Charlie going missing the day before his operation?'

'Yes,' she agreed.

'It stands to reason that Charlie's disappeared because someone didn't want him to go through with it.' He chewed the end of his pen.

'Yes,' she said again.

'Can you give me the names of those who were opposed to the operation?' he said, flicking to a fresh page in his notepad.

'Everyone,' she said.

'Everyone?'

'Pretty much,' she said. 'It was only really me that wanted it. Even Dylan was unsure.' She composed herself, smoothed the surface of her jeans, wiped her damp hands.

'And what about his family?' he said, consulting his notebook. 'Eileen and Bindy Ridley? How did they feel?'

'They wanted to stop it.'

'They told you that?'

'Yes. On Saturday. They begged me to stop the operation.'

'And were you tempted to?'

'Yes,' she said.

'But he was still having the op?'

'In the end, I wasn't going to let criticism stop me. I wanted this for Charlie.'

'Fair enough,' he said. 'Well, I'll need you to make a list of everyone who opposed you, even if it does amount to everyone you know. Do you think you can do that?'

'I'll try,' she said.

He stood up, his knees clicking. 'If it's any consolation, I think what you were doing for your boy was very brave.'

It was the sort of approval that she would have

been thrilled to hear yesterday. Yet now she made no response, barely acknowledged it.

They left the lounge. Forensics had gone, leaving the door open and a trail of muddy footsteps on the hallway tiles. A cold breeze entered the house, stirring their trouser legs. She drew her cardigan closer around her. How cold Charlie would be without his coat.

'Sergeant,' she said. 'You're going to find him, aren't you?'

'We're going to give this all we've got,' he replied.

She tried to smile, but it went wrong and her lips trembled with the effort. 'Thank you,' she said.

'You get some rest.' He turned to go and then stopped. 'I need you to remember the name of that church. Think back to what that man told you.' He tapped his head. 'It's in there somewhere.'

'I know,' she said. 'I've been going back over it. But I just can't remember.'

'You will,' he said. 'Trust me. Keep the faith.'

★   ★   ★

Faith.

What did faith feel like to a mother missing her child? If lampshades and books were irrelevant clutter, then abstract notions didn't stand a chance. What use was faith to the bereft?

She couldn't remember when she had last drunk a cup of tea, eaten anything solid. As time ticked on, the sense of disorder only grew.

211

She was watching the shapes moving on the television that evening, when the doorbell rang. Dylan went to answer it and returned with someone behind him. He stepped aside. It was his mother.

'Twyla ... I'm so dreadfully sorry,' Eileen said, holding out her hand and swaying in her little lace-up boots, but making no move forward.

Twyla nodded to her in greeting.

Eileen pulled a scrunched-up tissue from her pocket. Other tissue balls toppled to the floor in its wake. Dylan bent to retrieve them for her.

This small act of kindness made Twyla want to cry. She reached for the throw beside her, pulled it over her. If she could have vanished, she would have.

'Thank you, son.' Eileen's wicker basket was at her feet, crammed with Tupperware and tea towels. 'I've brought you some stew,' she said.

'Let's go warm it up,' said Dylan, taking his mother's arm.

Twyla tucked herself into the lambswool throw, feeling its fine hairs tickle her skin. Night had fallen, was groping behind the curtains, reminding her that another endless stretch of darkness was beginning.

To think of Charlie somewhere out there and not here was unbearable. What she would do to have him here with her now. Just to touch him, to have him here.

'Please, Twyla.' Eileen was bending down to offer Twyla a tray of steaming food. 'Eat something, my dear. Get your strength up . . . for Charlie.'

Twyla gazed up at Eileen. 'Could you give me a hug?' she said.

Eileen gave a gasp of surprise. 'To be sure!' she said.

Twyla cried, her tears wetting the collar of her mother-in-law's blouse. Eileen didn't smell like Twyla's mother but there was, ever so dimly in her bones, an ethereal, maternal aura that Twyla craved.

Eileen, tapping Twyla's back woodenly as though beating time, was more comfort than she could have imagined.

★ ★ ★

The house was clean and tidy. Eileen had cleared up supper and had done the laundry, laying out Charlie's dinosaur pyjamas in his cot. She said that if they were ready for him, if they made his home journey smooth, he would return.

Tomorrow morning, Eileen would appear on the doorstep with her basket of things that a woman of a certain age and mindset regarded as essentials in a crisis: skimmed milk, fruitcake in foil, lentil and bacon soup.

None of these things mattered to Twyla, but if they were of reassurance to Eileen then fine. Let Eileen do what she needed to do. Let the house fall down. Let the fridge go bare. Just bring Charlie back.

Dylan was sat on the sofa opposite, his chin thick with stubble, his expression vacant.

It was midnight. She was still sitting underneath the throw, with the lounge curtains open so that she could keep an eye on nightfall. Her stew had grown cold, had been heated again and eventually abandoned on the floor.

'Dylan,' she said, dropping the cover from her shoulders and standing. She moved towards him cautiously. 'I'm sorry.'

'Don't be,' he said — magnanimously, she felt.

He had every right to be furious with her; she wanted him to be furious. Being nice was making it worse.

'If I hadn't pursued this,' she said, 'if I hadn't pushed for it, Charlie would be here now.'

'No.' He shook his head. 'It's not your fault.'

He sat forward and held his head in his hands. He sat like that without speaking for a few minutes. And then suddenly stood. 'I'm going to try to get a couple hours' kip,' he said. 'I think you should too.'

'I'll be up shortly,' she said.

He nodded and left the room.

★　★　★

At two o'clock, she woke on the sofa with a sore neck.

Her forehead was damp with perspiration. She had dreamt of Charlie Ross.

They were at the park and it was dark. There were lumps of ice in the river and there was snow underfoot, the wet creeping up their trouser legs. You should have brought your coat, she kept saying, tutting. Charlie was trying to say something to her. He looked so cold. She bent closer to listen. But then there was a noise behind them and she turned, and when she looked back Charlie was gone.

She turned to the side table to pick up the list she had started compiling for the sergeant. It wasn't very comprehensive. There must be other names she could think of. Why was it so difficult? If only she hadn't destroyed all the hate mail.

And yet, not everything was gone. There was one line that had been repeated so often it had lodged in her mind.

She opened up the laptop and typed the Proverbs quote into Google.

Nothing. Just pages of religious text and biblical references. She added 'Bath, UK' to the search. The computer was clicking, whirring as though thinking.

And then the results appeared.

Welcome to All Saints Church of Redemption and Salvation, Bath.

She recalled the name of the church as soon as she saw it. It was exactly what the man had said two days ago on her doorstep.

Her eye ran down the page. There, at the bottom, amongst the photographs of smiling parishioners and their mission statements and core values, was Proverbs 3:7.

15

There was only one church in the area called All Saints. It was an attractive church in Bath stone with an old-fashioned iron gate, above which a beautiful gas lamp was suspended. Schoolchildren walked past the church every day, running sticks along the rails; ravens perched on the roof tiles; leaves gathered in the forecourt.

Yet despite its welcoming exterior, there was something peculiar about the place. No one was ever seen passing through the tall gates, or witnessed leaving. The sound of a congregation singing hymns didn't float out through open windows on Sundays, nor was there the subdued murmur of communal prayer. The property was locked up and silent.

All Saints' administration was handled at home by members of the congregation. The church building was a façade of sorts. It was rarely used for services, given that All Saints believed in preaching on the streets and not behind walls.

The church had over two hundred listed members, all of whom had to be willing to knock on doors or preach the word of God with a microphone in the shopping precinct.

Once Twyla saw the name, she knew where she had seen it before. She had darted past that board in town many times using Charlie's pram as a buffer — the board that said, 'Save Your

Soul Before It's Too Late!'

She understood now why the man had told her to pray for Charlie before it was too late. This was the church of warnings. It should have been called the Hourglass Church, as though there were a huge timer set on its roof, where the sand was trickling down with ghastly consequences.

How could All Saints' members bear it? How could they think of things in such drastic terms — that there was a day of judgement, a way of saving one's soul? What did that even mean?

These were the questions that Twyla would have asked, but the police had some simpler questions that they wanted answered that Friday morning. Twyla had given them the name of the church first thing and an official inquiry into All Saints had been launched.

The family liaison officer said that the lady in charge of administration was claiming that it was impossible to say who had knocked on the Ridleys' door. It could have been anyone.

'Someone there knows Charlie by name,' the officer told Twyla. 'Someone knew where he lived and that he was having the operation the next day. It won't take us long to dig him out of whatever hole he's hiding in.'

It didn't conjure up the most pleasant of images, but it was fitting. The man had seemed worm-like, translucent. Or maybe she was just projecting that on to him. As the days wore on, it was hard to trust her own judgement or anyone else.

She was glad of the officer's company. Eileen

was currently out in the kitchen, but since Twyla's display of affection towards her the night before, was keeping her distance. Eileen, who believed in boundaries — nay, she invented them — probably felt that Twyla had taken things a step too far. Bindy was phoning frequently for updates and to offer help, and Stephen was on his way now. But the one person who could ease her mind was not here.

Dylan was out walking, looking for Charlie. He was keeping himself moving and being useful, he said. And whilst it was vital to keep looking — the police had stressed this very point — she couldn't help but feel that he was also removing himself from her.

But, as she said, she wasn't to be trusted. He might simply be out looking for his son.

★ ★ ★

Paul went to the public gardens most days between jobs. It was his favourite spot in the city. He had grown up in Bath and had fond memories of coming here with his parents as a child.

He tended to sit underneath the elm with his book propped on his knee, his eyes drowsy with insomnia. Invariably, he dozed off after reading several pages and was woken by the alarm on his watch summoning him to work.

Today, however, he was too preoccupied to attempt reading. His boss had just told him about the missing Ridley boy and he had come straight to the park to clear his head. She wasn't going to run a piece on it yet, however tempted, because there was another missing person occupying the headlines. Two stories would topple the balance, she said.

Balance? Paul thought.

There was nothing balanced about this.

The other missing person was a local MP's son called Jones who was seventeen and suspected to have drowned in the river. Once found — and his boss said she hoped they'd bloody well get on with it — they would run the Ridley piece which she had all prepared.

He glanced behind him at the entrance to the garden just in case. Twyla Ridley wouldn't come though, not now, not without her son.

He felt deeply sorry for her. And sad that he might not see her again. His only hope had been bumping into her here — for her to have finally realised that of all the trees in the city, they had both chosen the same one.

⋆   ⋆   ⋆

Dylan spent all of Friday walking, looking for Charlie across the fields, through a wood, around the lonely outbuildings of an abandoned farm. He told Twyla he would be on his mobile, that he would get a taxi home if needed urgently. He couldn't bear sitting around the house. Besides, Stephen was on his way to offer Twyla moral support today. She wouldn't be alone.

He glanced at his watch to confirm the date, although he was well aware of every day, every hour, every minute that had passed since

Charlie's disappearance.

The police were doing their best, but had nothing. The forensic reports were inconclusive. The press had been informed, but wouldn't get involved because of a missing MP's son that was all over the local news. Charlie wasn't the only missing child in the world. There was a queue, as with most things in life. Even in this small city, there was another lost soul out there — already lost in the worst possible way by the sounds of things.

He kicked a stone angrily along the lane, a cloud of dust rising. He imagined at that moment that he was gigantic, omnipotent — that he could cause dust storms and thunder and hail, that he could hold the earth in his fist and crack it like a Kinder egg and pick over its contents to find his son.

But then the opposite happened and the focus panned out with alarming speed, reminding him of his insignificance, like an ant standing at the edge of the Grand Canyon, and he suddenly felt utterly vanquished.

He sat down on a tree stump in the middle of a field and looked about him. He had no idea where he was. So much for getting a taxi home urgently. He peeled off his jumper and flapped his shirt. It was a warm day.

He picked a blade of grass and chewed on it. It felt good sitting there in the field: simple, sweet, part of an innocent system of growth that wasn't interfered with by anyone, aside from the occasional tractor.

This is what he had wanted for Charlie. A

simple life — a family just enjoying spending time together, hearing each other's stories, caring for each other. It was what he had been deprived of as a boy. His childhood had been a conflicted, messy time.

Was that why he was drawn to Molly?

Was he even drawn to her?

He shrugged. What the hell did it matter now. What did any of it matter now?

There was no one around — not a bird or a beast that he could see, aside from a ladybird on a large flat leaf beside him. He blew a gust of air at the ladybird and it took off with a blur of wings.

Then he cradled his head in his hands and cried.

★   ★   ★

Stephen looked up at the house. As usual, he was tired from the car journey. Really it would have been so much easier to get the train, but he hadn't thought of that until he was halfway down the M4. Besides, he liked being in control and one didn't get that with public transport.

He was here today to offer Twyla his services, not that he could be much help. She had told him he didn't need to come and yet he felt he had to. So here he was.

The grandmother answered the door. He hadn't expected to see her. He tried to remember her name as they stood there smiling awkwardly at one another.

She had been attractive once. Her eyes were

the colour and softness of a grey cashmere sweater. She had an upturned mouth with no sign of sullenness. And yet Stephen had consulted with enough patients over the years to spot depression when he saw it. Some people wore it outside their skin, like a fancy overcoat to show off, whilst others, like this lady — Elinor? Elsie? — wore it deeper, as though they had swallowed the misery to hide it. That trick had only ever fooled him once, with tragic consequences. Now he was alert to its existence, keen to spot it.

'It's Stephen, isn't it?' the grandma said. She was wearing a lacy apron. 'I would shake your hand, but I'm in the middle of making scones.' She held up her hands, which were coated in flour. She had a lovely Irish accent, one that suggested grace and goodwill. 'Do come in.'

As he stepped into the house, Twyla appeared in the hallway. The grandmother hurried back to the kitchen.

Twyla stopped in front of him, holding her shoulders high as though the coat hanger were left in her shirt. She looked much thinner than when he had last seen her.

'Thank you for coming,' she said. She turned and walked back down the hallway. Was he supposed to follow?

Through the kitchen they went, past the grandmother kneading scone mix — Twyla pausing to pluck two mugs from their hanging hooks — through the utility room and out into the garden, where there was a wrought iron table and chairs — the spindly sage green type that

222

were fashionable in Paris. On the table was a stack of magazines and a teapot.

Twyla took a seat, poured two mugs of tea and sat staring up into the sky.

'Is that my tea?' he asked.

She shrugged, not rudely but vaguely. He took this as a yes and sat down to join her. In truth, he was parched. The traffic had been awful coming into Bath from London.

'You look thin,' he said. 'Are you eating?'

She shrugged again.

'It must be a help having . . . ' What was her name? ' . . . Dylan's mother here.'

'Eileen,' she said.

'Yes, Eileen.' He nodded. 'And where's Dylan?'

'Out walking.' She took a sip of tea.

'Walking?'

'Looking for Charlie,' she said.

She was petite and frail sitting there in the morning sunshine. He was struck by how greatly she resembled her mother, perhaps more so today than he had ever seen before.

He shifted uncomfortably in his seat. Even after all these years, it pained him to recall Robin's fine qualities. It was easier to credit her with none, to not mourn or long for what had been lost.

He followed Twyla's line of vision to see what it was that she was gazing at. It seemed to be the pots of herbs.

So the religious door-to-door caller had distracted Twyla long enough for Charlie to be taken. He wondered how long it would take the police to track the man down.

'It won't be long before they find him,' she said.

'Who?'

'The religious man.'

He gazed at her. He wouldn't use the word 'psychic', since he detested it. He would say 'intuitive' instead. She was intuitive, like Robin. 'There's been a development?' he asked.

'I remembered the name of the church. The police are working on it now.'

'Well, why didn't you say?' he said.

'Because nothing may come of it.'

'Huh,' he said. 'And the police are doing a good job?'

'So far as I can tell,' she said. 'How can you tell?'

'Have they contacted the press?'

She looked at him blankly. 'We have to wait our turn,' she said. 'There's another boy missing. An MP's son.' She set her mug down, as though struggling with its weight. He would have to encourage her to eat something before he left. 'They think he might be in the river.'

'Poor chap,' said Stephen.

He looked at his daughter, at the frown lines etched into her pallid skin, at the freckles smattering her cheeks. He could still see her as she was at four years old, sat screwing up her nose to examine a flower or pulling his beard to see if it would break. But the beard was gone and the four-year-old with it.

At that moment, the phone rang. She sloped off, giving the impression that there was nothing of interest to discuss with anyone.

He took the opportunity to speak with the grandmother indoors. 'I'm worried about her,' he said in a low voice.

Eileen wasn't going to stop what she was doing. She had finished the scones and now she was washing up, her hands moving rapidly. A classic example of using distraction to cope.

'Oh, she isn't always like this,' she replied. 'She was bright earlier. And then she crashed about an hour before you came. By teatime she'll be up and running again, making lists and what not.'

'Lists?'

'Yes. She loves a good list.' She turned and wiped her hands on her apron.

He felt a tingle of annoyance, of jealousy, at the knowledge that this woman displayed about his daughter. He opened his mouth to come back with some prior knowledge about Twyla, something from her childhood perhaps, but Eileen was ploughing on.

'She's a wonderful optimist, your daughter,' she said. 'She's determined to get through.' She untied her apron and hung it on the oven rail, before going through to the utility room to pull laundry from the washing machine. 'You've got to admire her for that.'

As she drew level with him, she stopped and gazed at him. 'I looked her name up when she joined our family. It means 'twilight', doesn't it?' she said. 'It's very pretty and unusual. Did you choose it?'

He stared at this woman — at this amicable Irish woman who was stood where he should have been stood, knowing what he should have known — and he wanted to sob. A psychotherapist, at the top of his profession, wanting to bawl.

'No,' he said. 'It was Robin, her mother.'

'How nice,' said Eileen, as though discussing how to get sponges to rise. 'Well, I'd best get upstairs and start the ironing. Will you be staying for supper?'

'Huh?' said Stephen, gazing after her for she was already halfway down the hallway. 'Um, yes. Please. Sure. Supper.'

The lounge door opened then and Twyla appeared. On seeing him, she smiled widely and ran towards him — a flash of blonde hair, freckles and light.

'They found him, Dad!' she was shouting, as she flung her arms around his neck. 'The religious man! They've got him!'

* * *

The police emailed Twyla a photograph of the suspect. She was able to identify him right away. He was called Collins and lived in Midsomer Norton, a town ten miles south of Bath. He had been brought in for questioning and the family liaison officer would visit them as soon as they had any news.

She rang Dylan immediately to get him back from his walk. He ran home, arriving out of breath, his forehead glistening. On seeing her, he did something that pleased her greatly — he grabbed her hand and squeezed it.

They had supper with Eileen and Stephen — a

226

shepherd's pie that Twyla could barely taste in her agitation. And then they waited in the lounge with Stephen, flicking listlessly through television channels and magazines. Every now and then Eileen came in with trays of tea and biscuits. She was keeping herself occupied with chores, slipping about the house, trying not to disturb them. The only signs of her presence were the neat piles of folded clothes that she left behind her, like worm casts at the beach.

Finally, when it was black outside, Stephen said he ought to be heading home. He said he would be back again Sunday to take Twyla out for some fresh air and keep her mentally occupied, so long as Dylan didn't mind.

'You can always stay here if you need to, Stephen,' Dylan said, shaking his hand. 'Save you keep driving up and down?'

'No need,' said Stephen. 'It's really no bother.'

Then her father turned to her. 'Y'all need to try to get some rest,' he said.

She gazed up at him, startled by his tender tone, by that little escaped 'y'all'. 'Thank you for coming,' she said.

In the end, the family liaison officer didn't arrive until after ten o'clock at night. He was apologetic, but there was something else clouding his face — a knockback that he was preparing them for.

'I'm sorry to say that Collins has been released,' he said.

'What?' said Dylan, jumping up.

'Why?' Twyla said, standing also.

'He's legit,' the officer said with a downward

shrug of his mouth. 'He said he was told to call round.'

'Hey?' Twyla said, her cheeks burning. 'That's impossible!'

'Apparently not.' The officer balanced on the backs of his heels before swaying forward again. 'He claims he was told you wanted to see him, that you needed guidance.'

'Guidance?' said Dylan.

'Yep. All Saints got a call last week from an acquaintance of yours. They didn't get a name, but were given an exact time to call and were told you'd be expecting them.'

'But who would have done that?' asked Twyla.

'Lord knows,' the officer said. 'We were hoping you could tell us that.'

The room fell quiet.

'None of this makes sense,' Twyla said, sinking back down on to the sofa.

'So what now?' Dylan asked, joining her. She didn't need to ask him how he was feeling to see that he was disheartened, the way he flopped down resignedly.

The officer sighed, tugged on the short bristles of his beard. 'I'm not entirely sure. But I'll be able to update you first thing.'

They saw the officer out, thanked him for his trouble.

Eileen had left an hour ago. It was just the two of them standing in the gloom. It had been a long while since it was just them at home alone. The last time would have been — she thought about it — the night Charlie was born.

She reached for Dylan's hand, but there had

been another shift. The Collins lead had energised him, had temporarily abated his fear, given him hope.

Now they were back to nothing. And she sensed that he had drifted from her again.

16

Bindy drove too fast for her mother's liking. Eileen was sitting there, handbag on lap, gripping the handle on the ceiling as though she were going up in a ski lift.

Bindy couldn't help it. Her mother's primness made her want to act more irresponsibly. She knew she took the corners too fast and that her mother crossed herself before getting into the car next to her.

Maybe this was how it was with parents when you got to a certain age. If they wanted it one way you did it the other, no matter what you believed to be best. It was nature's way of trying to prove that you were old enough to make your own decisions, without parental interference.

They were off to a church event, which Bindy had offered to take her mother to by way of distracting her. Eileen wasn't needed at Dylan's today. Apparently he had said something about it being Saturday and that they would muddle through without her. But their mother would go mad without something to occupy her. She looked ashen, like a prime minister going through a war, ageing rapidly overnight. Maybe tomorrow she would wake and all her hair would have fallen out. That happened sometimes.

Bald or not, Charlie being missing was hitting her hard. Only one thing had hit her so hard before and it was the thing that none of them could talk about.

They hadn't agreed on it as such. No one had decided that Felicity would never be spoken of again. It had just unfolded that way. Bindy had read about grief in the magazines in the dentist's surgery at work — about the different ways that people responded to it. Some built shrines, dedicated rooms and mantelpieces to lost ones; others shut it all down. Somehow her family had felt the same way about how to grieve. And this unspoken consensus was the thing that united them, despite their differences.

Then along came Charlie Ross. Their mother doted on him, not only because he was her only grandchild but because his disability linked him to Felicity. The fact that Charlie was born on Christmas Day augmented their mother's belief that the boy was her saviour, her second chance.

And now the sweet boy had been missing for three days. It was horrendous. Eileen was twitching constantly, wringing her hands. Yet she had wanted this, had prayed for her Lord to intervene and stop the operation from taking place. It sounded sick to say so out loud, so Bindy restricted it to her private thoughts, but really, her mother should have been careful what she wished for.

'Dylan's out a lot,' Eileen said.

Bindy glanced sideways at her mother, trying to decipher her tone. It was impossible to tell. Her mouth was firmly set, her eyes cast upwards.

'Keeping himself busy?' Bindy suggested.

Eileen said nothing.

Dylan would remove himself from trouble. They both knew it. The longer Charlie was missing, the greater would be his desire to run away.

He had done exactly the same thing before when tragedy struck. Weeks, months had passed before he had joined them at the dinner table. He couldn't stand what they represented when they were in the same room together — the enormity of the combined loss. She knew as much, without his saying. It was all over his eleven-year-old face. And it was there again now.

Twyla had been an obvious bride for him, a way for him to make the break from the past that he needed, to prove that adversity could be removed with the right amount of energy and positivity.

See? he seemed to be declaring on his wedding day, holding his luminous bride's hand high. *Life doesn't have to be all crap and gloomy. I'm making a break for it. Watch and learn!*

Except that it had backfired. Because little had Dylan realised that his wife's positivity and desire for perfection would be the very thing to undo him.

What he hadn't — couldn't have — foreseen was that he would have a disabled child too. Fee's presence, his gloomy past, was there beside him every step of the way, like a ghost sewn loosely to his skin.

'Do you think we should speak to Twyla?' Bindy asked, pulling into the church car park.

'What about?' said Eileen.

'About Dylan. About how he reacted before when . . . ?'

'When what, Bindy?'

Bindy undid her seat belt glumly. It was useless.

As she entered the church and smelt the faint scent of frankincense, she watched as her mother was embraced by friends. She was glad that her mother had found a place where she felt a sense of belonging and comfort. Because Bindy had found no such place of her own.

She sat at the back, hidden in a dark corner, gazing at the stained-glass window on the left side of the church. It depicted a mother in blue with her back bent, urging her children forward to Christ.

Bindy drew her coat closer around her. The church was cold. She could see her mother looking about for her. The tea was being poured, the cake was being sliced, but Bindy wasn't going to join them.

She gazed at one of the children in the window — at the blonde curve of her hair, at the way the light hit her, illuminated her in particular, choosing her above the others. It was just where the sun happened to be at that moment.

So it was with Twyla. It was not of her own making — that optimism, that lightness of touch. She hadn't had a say in it, hadn't devised it that way. She was just one lucky woman. Somehow she had got through the past unscathed. Her mother may have died when she was little but she had been too young for it to dig deep, for her to truly feel the wrench of separation. She couldn't even remember most of it, she said.

Yet all that was set to change.

Bindy folded her arms defensively, her heart beating faster as her shameful thoughts crept forward.

It was terrible and she wouldn't have wished it this way for Charlie's sake, but she would be interested to see how well Twyla fared when things went wrong. The hardest thing to do in life was to stay afloat when calamity hit.

Bindy had been held up by Dylan for too long against his wife and found lacking.

Don't turn into bitter old Bindy!

Look away, children!

Children . . . Ah. She closed her eyes. She hadn't wanted them. Maybe she would have had she not known Fee, had she not already been a carer for so long that the idea of doing so again was deeply unappealing. Maybe if she hadn't been convinced that when you loved someone that much, when you yearned to make their life more comfortable, it always ended badly. Maybe then she might have had children.

But she had known Fee. And she had known the pain of loss. And nothing could change that now.

She knew the course that Twyla was headed for so well, she could have drawn her a map.

She had been like Twyla, a long time ago. Dylan had forgotten. She too had wanted to change someone's life for the better, and she had been making progress too. Felicity's speech therapist was trying to teach her to communicate with sign language, and Bindy had been looking into getting a voice synthesiser. She was working on finding solutions, alongside trying to revise for her GCSEs and keeping an eye on Dylan and getting their mother up and dressed of a morning, and watching for their dad's key turning in the lock at night in case one day it didn't.

Bindy bent her head and clasped her hands together. Anyone taking the time to look up from their teacups and fruit loaf would have thought she was deep in prayer.

But pray was the last thing she would do. She found no comfort in it now.

Her heart quickened even more until it was racing so fast she could feel it in her throat.

It took courage to go back there, to think back to that day. Yet she wanted to now, at last.

It was the morning of her GCSE biology exam. She hadn't revised for biology. The brain was a meaningless mass, the reproductive organs a waste of molecules.

She woke with a gasp and sat up, clutching the sheets in a sweat. She had dreamt that she had missed the exam — had got the time wrong and everyone was pouring out of the school hall, jeering *Missed it, Ridley, you loser!*

She yanked the curtain aside to allow enough light to see her alarm clock. Eight in the morning. Thank God.

She slumped back down under the covers.

'Fee,' she whispered.

Felicity was sound asleep.

She considered this. It was unusual, but not unheard of. Fee normally began to moan just after dawn. But today she was in a deep sleep. Good for her.

She threw the covers off her bed and stepped into her slippers. The bedroom was in darkness but she could have made her way around it blindfold. Felicity was a tidy roommate, so few were her belongings and needs. No make-up, no Morrissey posters. Just the wheelchair and some eczema cream.

'Fee?' She put her hand on her sister's head, brushed her hair from her face.

To her surprise, her face wasn't there. She wasn't lying on her side as usual. She was face down.

She felt Fee's forehead. It was cold. The covers had come off her in the night.

A shiver of fear ran through Bindy.

She pulled Fee on to her back, lifting her at the shoulder and hip bone, her contours sharp even in a velour nightie. Then she sat down on the edge of the bed and picked up her sister's frozen hand and gripped it tightly.

Finally, she brought herself to look at her face.

Sweet Fee with her ashen skin, her eyelids translucent, her lips tinged blue.

'Oh, no, Fee,' she said, beginning to cry. 'No, Fee!'

When they finally discovered them, Bindy was in bed with Fee, holding her sister in her arms, trying to warm her up.

★　★　★

For weeks, all Bindy could think of was *Sarah ball Paul, see?* and *a pea leapt, see?* The words went round her head in a moronic, senseless loop.

236

Felicity had died from SUDEP — sudden unexpected death in *a pea leapt, see?*

No one knew the cause of death with SUDEP. Some thought it was because the *a pea leapt, see?* wasn't being controlled well enough. Some thought it meant that a seizure had caused breathing problems, or problems in the brain or heart. No one knew for sure.

Sudep, sudep, sudep.

It was like a skipping rhyme that Bindy skipped up and down the stairs to, down to breakfast, on the way to school, in and out of the funeral.

⋆   ⋆   ⋆

'Bindy!' She felt a hand on her back — a stern hand, followed by her mother's voice. 'What in heaven's name do you think you're doing?'

Bindy put a hand to her face. She was crying.

She wiped the tears away. 'Sorry, Mum. It's because of Charlie. I'm sure everyone will under — '

'Don't make a fuss in public!' her mother said, clicking her tongue. 'You're embarrassing me!'

Bindy watched her mother return to her friends and settle again, picking up her cake plate.

She gazed up at the stained glass. The girl in the image was still lit up.

Hang on to the light, Twyla, she thought. Hang on whilst you can.

Because any minute now, the wind would blow and the sky would shift and the sun would move, and she would be in darkness. Just like the rest of them.

★ ★ ★

The journey to Midsomer Norton took forty minutes. The bus was hurtling along at speed now that it had got out of Bath and was heading down the hill on the main road towards Wells. The countryside was luscious even though autumn was beginning to strip the trees, like a giant thief with a swag bag full of leaves.

Dylan would be out of the shower by now, reading her note. She hadn't told him where she was going. What she was doing could get her into trouble, but what the heck. The case was going nowhere. It was Saturday and the leads had run dry. The liaison officer had assured her that they weren't going to give up. Hang tight, he said.

Hang tight? Was that supposed to reassure her? It sounded awful.

The bus arrived in Midsomer Norton high street, the engine convulsing to a halt. She pulled her coat about her as she headed up the hill. She hadn't been to Midsomer Norton before and was still no closer to being able to describe the town because she walked without seeing, her mind on her mission.

She stopped outside the house. Her mobile was vibrating in her pocket. It niggled her, like a child tugging on her arm. *Don't, Twyla. Don't!*

She walked up the pathway, rang the doorbell then waited. He took a while to answer, the bristle draught-excluder making a hissing sound as he pulled the door open.

'What are you doing here?' he said. He was wearing a mustard-coloured jumper and corduroy trousers.

The familiarity of his face, the association with the most awful day of her life filled her with dread. 'I need to talk to you,' she said.

'How did you get my address?'

Her phone was vibrating again. 'From the website. I saw the details of the prayer group that you hold here. I hope you don't — '

'I want you to leave,' he said, closing the door.

She stuck her foot forward to stop the door. 'Please,' she said.

To her astonishment, he forced the door shut.

She crouched down. 'That's not very religious,' she said, through the letterbox.

'Go away,' he said.

'I thought you wanted to help me,' she said. 'Isn't that why you called round on Wednesday? To offer me religious instruction?'

About five minutes passed. She stood looking up at the sky, stamping her feet. She had all day to kill. She had nowhere else to be. Her once finely tuned life of appointments and nap times was now clockless.

The door opened with a hesitant creak. 'Do the police know you're here?' he said.

'No,' she replied. 'It's a personal visit.'

He tilted his head as though trying to weigh her up. 'Ten minutes,' he said, holding his fingers up to indicate ten. 'And that's it.'

She followed him into the house. For a religious man, he lived in the dark. The lounge was barely lit and smelt mouldy. He motioned for her to sit on a wooden chair, whilst he sat on a battered armchair.

It could have been a nice home, but had been left to ruin and there was a strong sense that time had little meaning here too. She wondered how he afforded a place on his own with apparently little in the way of work, aside from spreading the Good Word. But it struck her that maybe he couldn't work, that he was ill in some way. He had a nasty outbreak of psoriasis on his neck. Perhaps it had flared up in the stress of the police interviews.

'Why are you here?' he said, rubbing his hands together as though trying to keep warm.

She looked at the crucifix above the fireplace, at the Bible on the table, at the lack of ornaments. Wasn't he lonely? Perhaps he had a wife or children, but she doubted it.

'You're my only hope,' she said.

He shifted in his chair, a look of something passing over his face. What was it — pride, satisfaction?

'Oh?' he said.

'There must be something you didn't tell them. Something you can give me.'

He dropped his hands limply either side of the chair. 'I went through this with the police,' he said.

She looked again at the mahogany crucifix. It was an intricate carving of roses and thorns. She had never seen one like it before.

'What did you mean,' she asked, 'when you said that I had to pray for Charlie before it was too late?'

He blew out his cheeks in a dismissive manner. 'I regret saying it,' he said. 'It's a phrase that we use at All Saints. We were merely interested in your son as a case study.'

'A case study?'

'We clip things in the press that interest us so we can investigate them and respond officially, if needs be.'

'I see,' said Twyla. 'But why the interest in Charlie?'

'I think you know the answer,' he said, with a smile.

She had a feeling he was going to tell her.

'You were violating God's wishes,' he said.

If he wanted her to react, to defend herself, she wasn't going to oblige. She nodded, keeping her expression neutral.

He pressed on. 'We became interested in Charlie some months ago. So when the request came for us to visit you, we saw the chance to spread our doctrine.'

Something about him was mismatched. It was the way that he spoke. He appeared lowly and yet eloquent. She glanced around the room and saw a bookshelf of gold-embossed hardbacks. It didn't prove or mean anything, but still she found him perplexing as an overall package.

He was looking at her and smiled weakly, holding up his ten fingers again. There was something deeply childish about him.

'It's all right. I'm going,' she said, taking his cue and standing up. 'But please let me or the police know if you think of anything else.'

He extended his hand to her. 'I don't suppose

I can interest you in a prayer meeting today? Free coffee and biscuits.'

'No, thank you,' she said. 'I don't pray.'

'Then we will pray for you.'

She wanted to tell him not to, but didn't want to argue with her only source of hope.

As she turned to go, she thought of something. 'Mr Collins?' she said. 'What did you use to be? I mean, in the way of work?'

He paused before replying, once more a strange look passing over his face. 'I was a doctor,' he said.

'Ah. That explains the books.'

'The books?'

'Nothing,' she said, wishing she hadn't mentioned it.

'Good day,' he said. 'And may God bless you and have mercy upon you.'

* * *

When she got home, Dylan was waiting on the front doorstep.

'How long have you been sitting here?' she said.

He glanced at his watch. 'Two hours,' he said. If he was angry, bored or otherwise, nothing in his expression hinted at it.

The wind was getting up. Leaves were falling from the trees, landing by her feet with a scuttle.

'I went to see Collins,' she said.

'Collins?' he said. 'Whatever for?'

'I thought he might be able to tell me something.'

242

'And?'

'He had nothing to tell me. It was useless.' She kicked at a leaf, scrunching it with her foot.

'Well, that's that then,' he said.

She looked up at the sky. It was completely white. An aeroplane was making its way noiselessly across the sky.

'Where is he, Dylan?' she said.

'I don't know.'

'He's coming back to us, isn't he?'

'I hope so,' he said.

She went into the house and smelt the air. It was dry and smoky. She opened the kitchen door and saw that the coffee pot had come on as programmed for their eight o'clock brew, but no one had tended to it and it had burnt itself dry.

★   ★   ★

Robin had suffered from post-partum psychosis, as her mother had done before her: severe mental illness after childbirth.

There was less awareness of the condition back then. It was now known to be able to cause paranoia, delusions, the inability to separate dreams from reality. In Robin's case, her fantasy was that there was nothing wrong with her — a fantasy that she played out so well she had everyone fooled, including her husband.

Stephen had always dreaded the day when Twyla became a mother, knowing that he would have to arm her and her healthcare providers with this information. So it had come as a shock to him to hear that she had already given birth.

Yet perhaps it had worked for the best. Had he told Twyla about her mother's condition whilst she was expecting the baby, the knowledge might have done her more harm than good.

He had intended telling her at their first meeting last year — the day he visited with the kaleidoscope gift — but Charlie's disability rendered such a thing impossible. Twyla had enough to contend with without living in fear of a mental illness that she may or may not have inherited. These things weren't always handed down. The gene could have died with Robin, drifting to the bottom of LaFleur Lake, where it remained amongst the swaying weeds and the largemouth bass and bream.

He observed her closely at their every meeting, but she was adept at masking her thoughts. She gave him no cause for concern, yet even the soundest mind would be tested given recent events and now with Charlie missing. He was almost tempted to tell Dylan about Robin, but the extra burden at such a time would be counter-productive. Besides, he couldn't bring himself to go behind his daughter's back for a second time.

The door of his study opened. Juliet came in, flicking the light on and halting before him with a look of suspicion. 'What were you doing sitting in the dark?' she said, her black earrings dangling, like hungry spiders.

'Thinking,' he said.

'About what?' She perched on the edge of his desk, playing with the smooth pebble that he had used for years as a paperweight. It had come all the way from Louisiana. They had picked it up on a trip up to Fontainebleau State Park a few months before Twyla was born.

He reached forward to take the pebble from Juliet and held it in his hand, remembering the deer that had walked around the campsite at the state park; the children raking for clams at the beach; how Robin had been in awe of the twilight lighting the old sugar mill ruins and the oak grove, inspiring her to choose Twyla's name.

He sighed. 'I should have told Twyla the truth about her mother a long time ago,' he said.

'Oh, darling,' she said. 'Why think of that now?'

'I should have told her at the time,' he said.

She moved behind him, draped her arms over his chest. 'But you didn't,' she said. 'She was just a child. She couldn't have coped with the truth.' She pulled him round in his swivel chair so that he was facing her. 'You did what you thought was best.' She tapped his nose lightly. 'Don't forget — it was your loss too.'

No one could speak as nimbly about loss as Juliet could.

'I've just lit the log burner,' she said. 'Come . . . ' She tugged on his arm to get him to stand. 'Don't sit in here in the gloom. Leave the past in the past.'

They left the room, Juliet telling him that everything was going to be fine. Before he closed the door behind him, he turned to look back at his desk.

He could see Robin standing there, tossing the pebble into the air, laughing.

She used to do that — lean against his desk, plucking up things like his pen or the pebble or his elastic band ball and playing catch with it in the air. It always felt to him as though she were literally making light of his work. She didn't have a lot of time for his profession, didn't believe in it. Perhaps, in hindsight, she had been right not to. It hadn't done much for her, or for her mother.

'One moment,' he said to Juliet. He returned to his desk and laid the pebble carefully in his drawer, turning the key in the lock.

17

She hadn't been inside her workshop since Charlie had gone. The last people to enter it were the police. She hadn't been in to check what sort of state they had left it in.

She stood outside for a moment, her hand on the door, wondering what it would feel like inside. Some people said they could pick up vibes from walls, could read the rhythms and history of a building, like taking its pulse. What would they say with their hand resting on the wooden door here, as she was doing now? This had been her special place — a place where Charlie sat at her feet whilst she worked. Could anyone feel that, feel the warmth that had once lain inside, or had it seeped out through the cracks in the floorboards, soaked into the earth?

With a deep breath, she opened the door. It was unexpectedly warm inside and stuffy. The days were balmy, with autumn creeping forward each day ever so slowly and imperceptibly, like a child growing.

The police hadn't turned the room upside down. It appeared exactly as she had left it — the wicker chair, the workbench, the tools and materials waiting for her return.

She flicked the radio on, turned it to a murmur and sat down at the workbench. She didn't want to listen to what they were talking about, or hear the music or opinions. She just wanted meaningless noise.

She steadied her hand and picked up the pencil torch, but did nothing with it. Without Charlie she couldn't function. The bola necklaces were meaningless. She had no desire to make them, could see no worth in doing so. For if her mother was in the chime, then so too was Charlie — a magical possibility that she had carried with her her whole life, just waiting to meet him in the flesh.

Years ago, she had read that baby girls were born with their eggs already stored in their ovaries. The idea had horrified her at the time. But then when she fell pregnant she had thought of it again, how her baby had been a part of her from the moment she arrived on earth.

It was little wonder that mothers loved their children so.

It began to rain outside, large drops hitting the shed walls and windows. Her father was coming soon to take her out. Anywhere she fancied, he said. She thought maybe the public gardens. It was the only place she could think of.

She used to love it when it rained as she worked, the cosiness that it lent her workshop. Now it reminded her of Charlie, of how cold he would be outside in his shorts, without a coat.

★   ★   ★

He couldn't believe it when he saw her. He didn't recognise her at first. She was stood halfway down the steps in a turquoise coat that was billowing in the wind.

It was the colour that caught his eye. It reminded him of the sea in Turquoise Bay, Australia. He hadn't thought of there in a long time. He had been travelling with a girl who had ginger spiralled hair and knew the shores of Western Australia better than anyone else he met. She was gone now, like all the rest of it, packed away with the sand and soggy towels.

He wouldn't have recognised Twyla because she was so thin. She was with someone whom he hadn't seen before. The man was standing sideways on to her, as though uncomfortable talking to her. She was pulling away from him, already with one foot in the park, ready to break free. Something about the stilted manner in which they parted said father and daughter to him, so he settled for that.

He looked down at his book, but could still see the turquoise coat that was heading his way.

She stopped in front of him abruptly. 'Oh!' she said.

He kept his book upright before him, as though engrossed in its contents.

'*The Art of Acceptance*?' she said. '*How to be happy with your lot, without settling*?'

He was so startled that he put his book down, immediately regretting doing so. Without his prop, he felt unguarded. His forehead was sweating, and it was a cold day. 'Eh?' he said, for want of something more profound to say.

'The title of your book,' she said, pointing.

'Oh . . . Right.'

He was mortified. Caught reading sappy self-help stuff in public by the woman whom he inappropriately fixated on.

'So what's the secret?' she said.

'What?' He couldn't think straight. His mind was rambling.

Turquoise.

Self-help.

Ginger spirals.

Soggy towels.

All the times he had daydreamed about this moment. And now it was here, he realised that he hadn't prepared a speech, had no idea what to say or do.

'The secret?' she said.

'What secret?'

'Of how to accept your lot without settling?' she said, with a trace of impatience.

'Oh,' he said, trying to shrug. The action came off too tight and awkward, like a shoulder spasm. 'I don't know. I'm only on page five.'

This was clearly a lie. He was holding the book halfway through. He dropped it carelessly on to the grass, crossed his arms and gazed up at the sky as though fascinated by cloud formations.

'We normally sit here,' she said. 'Underneath the tree.'

'So do I,' he said. 'Whenever I can.'

'Funny that we've never seen you,' she said. 'This is our spot.'

'Perhaps we come here at different times. What time do — ?'

'We put a blanket down right here. And I sit here with him.' She was pointing to the area about her, underneath the elm, behind his deckchair. She sounded much aggrieved, as though he were trespassing.

'With Charlie Ross?'

The moment he said it, he wished he hadn't. Her face clouded. She pushed her hands into her pockets and turned away.

He had blown it. And yet she didn't walk off.

He stood up. It was sunny now but blustery. It had rained earlier and the grass was still shimmering with moisture.

He daren't stand too close to her. He looked at the back of her turquoise coat — at her hair which was quivering in the breeze, at the label which was sticking out of her jumper. He wanted to tuck it back in. He wanted to tuck all of her neatly into his life.

'You don't recognise me, do you?' he said.

'Should I?'

'I was there when your baby was born,' he said. 'I took your photograph. I'm Paul Walden.'

She turned back around to face him. She was smiling. 'You saw Charlie when he was born.' She said this with awe, as though telling him he was the first man to walk on the moon, or to have scaled the Himalayas.

Had he been less decent, he would have recognised this for the plus that it was. But he could see that this woman was not only never his in the first place, but wasn't anyone's now. She was beyond reach, no longer in possession of a body. All that remained was that light that he wanted to trap underneath a cheese dome and keep by his bed to see him through winter, like the jars of sunshine you could buy in novelty stores.

251

'I read about you in the paper,' he said. Then he considered that this sounded creepy. 'I think most people did,' he added.

'Quite a story.'

She was pretty, this close up. Even with her having lost so much. She still had so much there.

He wanted to tell her that he cared for her, that he wanted to take care of her, even though he didn't know her; that he felt her pain keenly, almost as though it were his own.

There was so much to say. But he merely said, 'Are you OK?'

She laughed bitterly. 'I've had better days.'

Her eyes were green. What an idiot he was. He didn't even know the colour of her eyes. If that wasn't a reality check, nothing else was.

'I wouldn't wish it on anyone,' she said. 'I hang on to my sanity on a daily basis.'

'I'm sorry,' he said, inadequately. 'Is there any news? Any breakthroughs?'

'No,' she said. 'There's nothing.' She bit her lip and looked away.

'That's a shame.' Again, woefully inadequate. He wanted to compensate for it. 'Can I . . . If it's not too odd a question . . . Can I help you in any way?'

She didn't look startled or put out by his forwardness. She appeared to be considering the offer. 'No,' came the inevitable reply.

She was wearing faded yellow gloves. She tapped her hands together in an odd mannerism, as though heralding the end of her conversation on the matter. She struck him suddenly as

Edwardian — frail, genteel, the sort of character in an opera who keeled over from tuberculosis.

All this he was thinking, so he didn't notice the old man returning until he was stood right next to them.

'Twyla?' the man said, surveying them both with interest.

'Hello, Dad,' she said.

Aha!

'And this is?' the old man said.

He braced himself. How would she describe him?

A park weirdo?

My stalker?

'Paul Walden,' she said.

She had been listening! He wanted to scoop her up and kiss her. Instead, he picked up his book from the grass and slipped it into his coat before the father clocked the title.

The father extended his hand. 'Stephen Thibodeaux,' he said. He was wearing leather gloves and was formidable, tall, professional-looking. A legal eagle, Paul thought, a political powerhouse, a . . . 'And how do you two know each other?' The father spoke without apparent judgement, yet raised his eyebrows and pursed his lips, waiting for the response.

Paul waited also, wondering how she would reply.

'We're old friends,' she said.

There was a pause and then her father touched her elbow. 'Shall we?' he said. And they moved away without further word.

He was folding up his deckchair when he

heard a voice behind him. She was stood there, slightly out of breath. 'Can I borrow it?' she said.

'Borrow what?' he asked.

'*The Art of Acceptance*,' she said, looking about for it.

He reached into his pocket for the book and handed it to her. 'Here you go.'

She nodded a thank you.

'Don't tell your father it's mine,' he called after her.

He watched her leaving until her turquoise coat had vanished from sight. She didn't look back.

He carried his deckchair over to the area where the chairs were gathered by the wall, restrained by a rusty chain, like football fans leaning forward to jeer.

She had finally noticed him, with her son gone. But the circumstances were too sad and it didn't feel like much to celebrate.

At least, he thought, as he left the park, she now had a small part of him with her, tucked inside the pocket of her coat. And there had to be some comfort in that.

★   ★   ★

They found the body of the MP's missing son at three-thirty in the afternoon. The abbey bell was ringing with poignant timing, summoning its congregation to evensong. As the last bell struck and reverberated around the city, a hush of ghastly anticipation fell.

Dylan was at work at the time, checking

correspondence, making arrangements for colleagues to handle his work in his absence. He had come in on Sunday afternoon when no one would be there. He couldn't face anyone — found his emails, even his own handwriting, disconcertingly removed from him. But to his dismay there were three designers in the office, handling an urgent project. They were polite, subdued around him. Evidently they knew about Charlie and were unsure how to broach the matter.

And then one of them noticed the gathering of people outside on the riverbank below. So they all went to look out the window. They were four storeys high and, as Dylan looked down, he felt as though his blood were draining from his body and pooling in his feet.

He pushed the window open for air. It was very quiet. Several men in black were working down by the river. A diver was in the water. People were gathering — tourists with neon backpacks and locals with shopping bags who were hanging back nervously but unable to tear themselves away. Some were taking photographs on their phones. One of the men was shooing them off, flapping his hands.

In those minutes, watching the diver circling the water, Dylan became weightless with terror. His vision was wobbling, searing. He couldn't see or think clearly.

What if something like this had happened to Charlie?

What if it *was* Charlie?

Oh, God. No. Not Charlie. He clutched the

windowsill in panic.

The body was being lifted, water draining from it.

And then he realised something. The body was far too big for Charlie.

'Oh, thank Christ!' he said, laughing and then looking over his shoulder by way of checking himself, of checking who was watching him. Because relief was not something that many people were experiencing at that moment.

He felt a hand on his arm. It was Molly.

The body was being laid out on a stretcher in a body bag. 'Poor lad,' Molly said. 'Must be the Jones boy — the MP's son.'

The MP's son; someone else's tragedy, someone else's life destroyed.

Guilt propelled Dylan away from the window and he sat down with a sinking feeling, as his adrenalin, his trepidation shrank. All he was left with was grief, and the nausea of knowing he had been pleased that someone else's child was dead and not his.

'God,' he said, putting his head in his hands and moaning.

Molly was whispering something to the other junior. There was the sound of the water cooler glugging. A plastic cup appeared before him. He took it gratefully, sipped the icy water.

'I think we'll call it a day,' the senior said. 'We can crack on again first thing in the morning.' He put his hand on Dylan's shoulder. 'You OK?'

'Fine,' said Dylan.

What else could you say? Certainly not the truth.

'Well, just leave everything to me. Don't worry

about this place. Just concentrate on — '

'Thanks,' Dylan said, cutting him off. He didn't want to hear it said out loud.

The senior and the junior left at the same time. The body would have prompted them to recall that work was fundamentally irrelevant. On the streets below the onlookers would be dispersing, clutching their jackets closer around them, holding their bags a little tighter. The air was charged, vital with death — with the stern reminder that it had served the city.

It was just the two of them left in the dusky light of the office.

'I'm so sorry,' said Molly, after some time.

She knew not to say anything more. He was thankful for that.

'I thought you went to yoga on Sundays,' he said. He had drunk the water and was clutching the empty cup in his hand. He crushed it and it sprang back into shape.

'Sunday mornings,' she said.

'Oh, yes,' he said. 'Of course.'

He stood up. He felt better now. He threw the cup in the bin and looked out the window again. Molly stood by his side.

There were a few lingerers on the riverbank. The ambulance had gone. The diver was still there and a few of the men in black. Otherwise it was over.

He could have done something about it, could have flicked her away, rebuffed her. But he didn't. When she reached for his hand, he took it and they stood like that, quietly watching the men working.

Twyla stood for a moment taking in the scene before her. Dylan was wearing jeans and an old sweater. Beside him was a woman in a shirt dress and ballerina flats. Nothing much appeared to be going on. They weren't even talking. But then the woman reached for his hand and, to Twyla's horror, he accepted it.

'Dylan?' she called out.

He looked at her in shock. 'What are you doing here?'

Twyla stared past him at the woman who was assembling her belongings and couldn't have left the office quicker had the carpets been pulled up underneath her.

Twyla waited for the doors to close before turning to face Dylan. 'Who is she?' she asked.

'Molly Carpenter,' he said. 'A junior.'

'And you've taken to holding hands with her?'

He put his hands in his pockets and looked anywhere but at her. 'No,' he said. 'She was helping me.'

'Helping you?' she said. Her heart was bouncing as though trampolining. She had never liked trampolining — the fact that the harder you bounced, the higher up it threw you.

She put her hand on the nearest desk to support herself and saw that she was leaning on a design mock-up for moisturiser. Maybe it was Molly Carpenter's work. Molly Carpenter, who looked entirely ordinary, plain, who had been holding Dylan's hand.

Dylan was rifling through some paperwork on

his desk. 'They just found the Jones boy,' he said. 'I was in shock.'

'And that's why we came to find you,' she said. 'So you weren't on your own.' She glanced about the room accusingly. 'But I can see that I needn't have worried about that.'

'We?' he said.

It took her a moment to realise what he was referring to. 'Me and my father,' she said. 'He's downstairs in the car park.'

'Oh,' Dylan said, reddening.

'We were on our way home, but then we saw the police and someone told us they had found the Jones boy.'

The poor Jones boy. Suddenly, she wanted to go home. 'I'll see you later,' she said.

'Twyla!' He hurried after her. 'You have to understand. This isn't . . . '

'Isn't what?' she asked.

When he didn't reply, when he floundered helplessly, too tired or beaten or guilty to give a solid response, she left.

On the car journey home, the family liaison officer rang her mobile. She didn't want to speak to him, was too distracted by what had just happened.

'Guess who preaches at All Saints?' the officer was asking her.

'I don't know,' she said.

'The woman who accosted you in the supermarket,' he said.

'The old woman?'

'Yep. She knows Collins. We missed it cos we thought she was batty. Turns out that she has

259

moments of lucidity and still occasionally preaches.'

'OK . . . ' said Twyla, trying to process the information.

'She's the missing link,' the officer said.

'She is?'

'Someone didn't want Charlie to have the operation. Let's call them 'A'. The old woman didn't want that either. She had a go at you and you told A about it. A then realised that the old woman was an ally. They approached her and she led them to All Saints and to Collins.'

Twyla fell silent. Her father was driving beside her — his hair combed back, his suit spotless. The interior of his Mercedes was pristine and archaic. The car glided along the road, so soundproofed and padded, as though the rules of gravity or time didn't apply to them, as though there were no world beyond.

'So I need to think about who I told?' she said.

'Just park it for now,' he said. 'Until we say otherwise.'

She hung up.

'Everything all right?' Stephen said.

She didn't answer. She was thinking about who she had told about the old woman: Dylan, Ofelia, her father, her next-door neighbour, the support group, about a dozen friends, Eileen, Bindy, most of Eileen's friends at a church fund-raiser.

It was possible that about fifty people knew. And then there was the media coverage. If it weren't for the fund-raising, the old woman would never have known about Charlie.

'What's wrong?' Stephen asked.

'Nothing,' she said.

Stephen pulled up outside the house. 'Are you sure you don't want me to come in?' he said. 'You must be feeling shaky after — '

'No,' she said. 'I'm fine. Dylan will be home in a minute.'

'Very well.' Stephen let the engine run. It droned smoothly. 'I've every faith that this is going to turn out all right,' he said.

She nodded. There was that useless word 'faith' again.

'I'll give you a ring when I'm back home,' he said, pulling away.

Inside the house, she went through to the kitchen to put the kettle on and stood drumming a spoon on the counter.

What would she say to Dylan when he got back? Should she let the whole thing go — put it down to trauma, to exceptional circumstances? Or was there more to it?

There was a noise — a strange moaning sound. She stopped drumming and listened.

There it went again. It sounded like . . .

She dropped the spoon with a clatter and hurried through to the utility room to look out of the window.

'Charlie!' she shouted.

She lurched towards the back door, rattling the handle feverishly. It was locked.

She hurried back to the kitchen and yanked open the cupboard to retrieve the keys. Then ran to the door and swung it open, skittling the row of wellington boots.

There was Charlie, amongst the herbs, digging in his pot of mud.

She stumbled towards him across the gravel, scaling the steps to the elevated lawn in one leap. 'Charlie!' she said. 'Charlie!'

She grabbed him from the lawn and into her arms. She kissed his cheeks, his chin, the crook of his neck, tasting his enchanting skin, smelling autumn in his hair.

'I don't believe it!' she said. 'You're home, Charlie! You're home!'

She held him with crushing intensity, held him above her with her arms outstretched to make him laugh, spun him round in a twirl, and kissed him until there were blotches on his skin — emblems of her exuberance. She said his name over and over, relishing the pleasure of saying her son's name as she held him in her arms.

She suddenly stopped and looked at her watch.

The police would want to know what time Charlie had returned. Time was important again now that he was back. She felt it — the lurch as the carousel began, as everything became purposeful and scheduled once more.

She set Charlie back down and crouched before him. 'Are you all right?' she asked.

She didn't know what she expected from him; some sort of sign perhaps. But he was simply looking at her with a queer half-smile.

'You're here,' she said, squeezing his arms to emphasise the words. 'You're back!' She wanted to say more — to tell him she had feared that he had been harmed or worse. Yet couldn't alarm him. There was no telling what was going through his mind. And yet he seemed happy enough — was back to digging in his pot.

A raven took off from the aerial on the roof with a loud twang. The noise made her jump. She turned to look at the gate. It was the same as before — slightly ajar. Charlie had been returned the way he was taken. She wouldn't touch any of it this time, would go nowhere near the gate or the path.

The sky clouded over. It was getting cold. 'Let's go inside,' she said.

She took his hand, expecting his teetering toddle but he was more stable. They walked across the lawn together, Charlie barely needing her support.

Once inside, she turned the key in the back door and took Charlie's hand to go through to the kitchen. His skin felt cold and clammy. There was a different smell about his person, telling her that he had been elsewhere.

Her mouth felt dry. She swallowed uneasily.

She set Charlie on the kitchen top, his head barely skimming the row of mugs hanging from hooks.

Then she placed her hands on his knees to hold him steady. 'Sweetheart,' she said, 'let me look at you.'

Her heart began to pound. 'Now you look at me,' she said.

Charlie Ross set his eyes on her for the very first time and smiled. She gasped so loudly that he jumped, setting the mugs wobbling on their hooks.

He frowned at her, a furrow appearing above his eyes that were no longer milky, but ocean blue, and so clear that when she bent closer she could see beyond the surface to the strange mechanisms below that looked like lobster pots wobbling on the seabed.

★　★　★

'Twyla?' Dylan entered the kitchen and stopped abruptly, stunned.

Charlie was sitting on the kitchen top. Twyla was holding on to his knees. She looked pale and radiant at the same time.

He looked at Charlie and then at Twyla and then back at Charlie again. 'Charlie?' he said, incredulously, as though it couldn't be him.

But it was him all right. Charlie was right there in front of him, in his shorts and top, waving as though saying, *Hello, Daddee!* like any other day.

Dylan couldn't process it quickly enough, or at all.

'What?' he said.

And then it hit him. Charlie was back. Charlie was home.

He gave a yelp of joy and grabbed Twyla and Charlie and pressed them all together. 'Oh thank God! You're back, Charlie boy!' he shouted. 'You're safe! You're home!'

When he broke away from them, when he set Charlie delicately back on the counter, like returning a china figurine to a cabinet, he noticed that Twyla wasn't looking happy.

He didn't want to ask what it was. Surely it wasn't that silly incident earlier? He intended to clear that up as soon as he —

'Dylan,' she said.

'What?'

'Look at Charlie.'

Something in her voice made his stomach dip. He hadn't considered this — hadn't had time to think yet, that Charlie could be harmed in some way.

He turned to look at his son. 'Charlie boy,' he said, quietly.

Charlie gazed at him directly.

'Bloody hell,' Dylan said, backing away into the oven. 'What's happened to him?'

18

'How can this be?' Dylan said. 'I don't understand.' He flicked the kitchen light on and tilted Charlie's face upwards, peering at him. 'He's had the keratoprosthesis surgery, hasn't he?' His heart begin to race uncomfortably. 'What on earth . . . ?'

Charlie kept his eyes on him, watching him intently.

The poor boy.

Dylan's stomach turned over at the thought of it — of Charlie being taken off and worked on by someone. But who would have done that to them, to him?

'We must call the police,' Twyla said.

'Yes,' said Dylan. But he didn't move. He was thinking of that day at work when he had looked up the procedure online, of how anxious it had made him. His son now had that telescope inside his eyes and looked to be wearing blue contact lenses on top. Yet Dylan could still see the weird jellyfish-like object below.

He thought of how upset Twyla was when the boy at the supermarket called Charlie an alien. What would kids say when they saw Charlie now?

For a moment he forgot himself and stared at Twyla accusingly. It was her who had wanted this, not him. But she looked so aggrieved, so gaunt, he knew that to turn on her now would be inexcusable.

Instead he went to phone the police.

As he dialled, he thought again of what he had read about the risks.

Glaucoma. Bleeding. Infection. Scar tissue. Detached retina. Inflammation. Drooping eyelids. Did any of this apply to Charlie? Was he in any danger?

What the hell was going on?

The detective answered. 'Charlie's back!' Dylan blurted, taking the phone through to the lounge. Twyla followed, leading Charlie by the hand. 'He's here! And we think he can see . . . That's right. We think he's had the op. Yes — he can *see!*'

Twyla was setting out Charlie's play rug and his basket of toys, but Charlie was reluctant to move — was standing at the edge of the rug.

The detective was reminding Dylan of procedure. Dylan was agreeing, muttering arbitrary responses — yes, no, fine. But he was starting to feel sick to his stomach.

He hung up the phone. They were to remain exactly as they were and to touch nothing.

That wouldn't be a problem for Charlie. He was still standing motionless, even though his mother was offering him a toy car.

'How long will they be?' she asked.

'Fifteen minutes max,' Dylan said.

'Wait,' she said, reaching forward to Charlie. 'What's that?' She pulled a piece of paper from Charlie's shorts and unfolded it. 'Oh my goodness,' she said, standing up. 'Dylan . . . Look.'

He read the note. It was very concise: the date, the type of prosthesis used, the medications prescribed and aftercare required. The information was abbreviated and technical — mostly incomprehensible. *PKP, IOL, IE, RPM, fluoroquinolone, trimethoprim, 0.005% benazlkonium chloride.*

They would have to get someone to translate it for them. Armed with this information, perhaps he could plan a way forward. He could consult with the Royal Square. And there were specialists locally who could help — experts who were already familiar with Charlie. They wouldn't be on their own.

It was a start. He felt marginally better.

He carefully folded the note back up and lay it on the coffee table. 'We shouldn't have touched that. Or Charlie,' he said.

His tone was angrier than he had intended to be. Twyla looked up quickly at him.

Since Charlie's return, she had been watching him quietly. She was waiting for an accusation, a word of resentment thrown her way. But he wouldn't allow himself to do that. Because once he did, there would be no way back.

They stayed like that — frightened to move or to touch any evidence — until the police arrived noisily outside.

There were more police cars now than when Charlie disappeared. They were parked in their driveway, in the neighbours' driveways, on the verge opposite, blocking the turning circle at the end.

Police flooded the house, like black ants on a picnic. The adrenalin in the air was palpable.

'Come on, people!' the sergeant shouted,

bounding up the doorsteps, the wheels having barely stopped spinning on his car. 'Smithy — go round the back of the house and along the street. Amos, take a look at the boy. I want samples. Wicksy, work with the Ridleys. Get the names of those specialists. I want them here and I want them here five minutes ago. Nobody touch anything unless it's your job to do so. Nobody do anything unless I say so.' He clapped his hands. 'Now let's get to work!'

Charlie was being led by the hand into the dining room by one of the forensic team. Dylan and Twyla were steered into the lounge by a female officer. 'I need you to find me the contact details of Charlie's medical consultants,' she said. 'We need them here urgently.'

Dylan warmed to the practicality of this bit, the sense that they were doing something about the situation. They were able to reach all their usual consultants, plus the leading eye surgeon in the region, and a London-based specialist who would be joining the consultation meeting later by webcam.

Dylan was impressed by the police's efficiency, by the speed at which things were moving. He found himself beginning to feel more energised, more hopeful — even slightly hysterical at times. There was a strange ecstasy at the heart of crisis that kept popping up inappropriately, like a clown at a funeral.

When their work was done, when they could be of no further help for the time being, he asked the police officer if he could phone his mother. When the officer consented, Twyla stood too. 'I'll call my father,' she said.

They reached the door at the same time. 'Dylan — ' Twyla said.

'Charlie's back,' he said, cutting her words short. 'He's home.'

There was no more to say than that. It was all he knew.

'Yes,' she agreed, frowning slightly.

★   ★   ★

The specialists eventually began to pull up in muddy Volvo estates, in the sort of cars that suggested a life in the country with children and golden retrievers. They set up a debate area in the lounge abound with webcams, laptops and paperwork — the air thick with argument, statistics, medical vocabulary and accents, as specialists dialled in from around the world.

In the meantime, the social workers, psychologists and forensics were examining Charlie Ross and had determined three things: that he was returned via the back gate; that no one witnessed his return; and that he was bearing no signs of abuse or neglect.

The eye specialists quickly determined that Charlie could see. Yet it took them well beyond nightfall to reach this conclusion on a theoretical level. The disharmony wasn't about whether or not he could see, but the means by which it was possible. They would need to examine him further in the morning, but for now they concluded that Charlie had undergone kerato-prosthesis surgery in both eyes.

Who would take the risk with such a young child? they argued.

Well, the Royal Square, for one.

Yes, but the Royal Square didn't do it. So who?

What about the risks? one of the specialists kept saying. Infectious endophthalmitis, sterile vitritis, retinal detachment, vitreous haemorrhage . . .

His ominous words grew with the shadows that were leering around the lounge walls.

Who indeed, Twyla asked herself, would have operated on a toddler with such a low likelihood of success, with such a daunting list of risks attached?

She sank lower into her seat and bit her nails, as she waited for the experts to turn and point at her.

You would have!

You would have taken that risk!

What sort of a mother are you?

But no one said that. This wasn't about her. They were coming up with an healthcare plan for Charlie — were discussing the level of medication and type of lenses required.

Charlie was still next door in the dining room. His examinations were over and the social worker was playing with him, keeping him entertained with a box of plastic stickle bricks. Twyla hadn't seen stickle bricks for years, not since she was a child — blocks that were covered in bristles, like upside-down woodlice.

She looked at Dylan. He was engrossed in the discussions, writing in a notepad. She wondered what he was thinking, how much he was holding her accountable.

But now the specialists were rising and buttoning coats. Laptops were closing, webcams blackening, foreign connections cut.

Dylan was talking to one of the doctors about the appointment in the morning at the eye centre in Bristol. Yes, the doctor was assuring him, they would be preparing a comprehensive aftercare plan. None of this was going to be guesswork. They wouldn't be left to struggle alone. Business cards were procured. Hearty handshakes.

The police and other staff were withdrawing too. Voices were hushed, briefcases and specimen jars were snapping shut. Outside, car doors were closing quietly, wheels crackling on tarmac.

The sergeant, who had been sat in the lounge all along, listening to the specialists' debate, was showing signs of leaving when he sat back down.

'At the beginning, we thought this was about who didn't want the operation,' he said, looking at Twyla and Dylan in turn. 'But now it's turned into something else all together.'

Twyla opened her mouth to reply, but was struggling to think of anything that made sense.

Charlie was drowsy in her arms, reaching up to tug listlessly on a tangle in her hair. She pulled his hand away, thinking how good it was to feel his skin, however sticky it was. She wanted to bath him — to make him hers again, to go to bed and discard this scrappy day. For what had at first glance appeared benign and heartening was becoming more uncomfortable by the hour. Charlie's homecoming was like being offered a yellow fluffy blanket to wrap yourself in, only to discover it was fibre-glass — thousands of tiny shards of glass that itched and lodged in your lungs, like lethal candyfloss.

'What is it that you're thinking, Sergeant?' Dylan asked. Dylan was standing with his back to the fireplace, his hands clasped behind him, his mouth taut with apprehension.

'Well . . . ' The sergeant began. He looked very tired, but was evidently determined to press on. 'Perhaps you could tell me what involvement you've had with medical research groups,' he said.

The question startled Twyla slightly. 'Medical research?' Dylan said. And then left the room. 'Wait one moment,' he said, over his shoulder.

He returned promptly, carrying a file. 'Bear with me,' he said, going through the file. 'Here you go,' he said, handing the sergeant several sheets of paper.

'And these are . . . ?' said the sergeant, putting his glasses on.

'Letters from medical research programmes. We only received four, I believe. Is that right, Twyla?'

She nodded. She had forgotten about the letters. They had arrived shortly after her award, during the height of the hate mail. She had handed them to Dylan who filed them along with all the other medical paperwork.

'Stockholm . . . Dundee . . . Brussels . . . Belfast,' said the sergeant, reading the letterheads in turn. 'Why didn't you tell me about these?'

'We forgot about them, I guess,' Dylan said.

'There's been so much going on.'

The sergeant folded the letters slowly and put them into the inside pocket of his suit jacket. Then he stood up.

'Those letters are very useful,' he said. 'Thank you both. I'll trouble you no further tonight. You get some rest.'

'Can I just have a quick word?' Dylan said, following the sergeant from the room.

The two men stood in the hallway. 'It's abuse,' Dylan was saying. 'A violation of human rights.'

'Absolutely,' the sergeant said. 'I've no intention of letting things slide.'

Dylan was lowering his voice now. Twyla couldn't quite hear.

Then she heard the front door close and Dylan's steps down the hallway. He didn't return to the lounge.

She picked Charlie up and walked through to the kitchen where Dylan was washing up the huge pile of coffee cups. She was surprised they had that much china.

'Do you think it's too late to bath him?' she asked.

Dylan glanced at the clock above him. 'Should be fine for a quick splash,' he said. 'Might do you both good.'

She nodded and took Charlie upstairs. They were both yawning, their foreheads pressed together dozily, Charlie's hands clasped around her neck. Once more, she was struck by how good it was to feel him, to hold him again, and she afforded herself a short-lived flutter of joy, like an autumn leaf on its final descent to the ground.

As she ran the bath, she unwrapped the eye shields from the cellophane. The specialists had left them with an emergency healthcare plan to tide them over until morning. They were to administer Charlie with antibiotics, and steroids to prevent inflammation. The two biggest enemies at this stage were glaucoma and infection. Most of the other uglies had already been eliminated.

Yawning again, she ran the bath, lit candles and turned out the light before climbing into the tub with Charlie. He would be sensitive to glare for some time, the doctors said, so it was best to keep the lights down for now.

She sat at one end of the tub with her knees drawn up to her, and Charlie at the other end, the goggles incongruously large on his face.

Even by candlelight and with the eye shields in place, she could see the mechanism in his eyes — the ring with circles punched around its circumference, like the dialling face of an old-fashioned phone.

As she watched Charlie, who was happily splashing about, slapping the water with the palms of his hands, something came to her — a recollection.

She thought of the moment when the midwives asked whether she wanted Charlie delivered on to her chest or cleaned first. She had imagined that what they were really asking was whether she was a natural earth mother who would love her baby any which way he came to her.

She hadn't ever really answered the question.

But she could see quite plainly now that the answer was no.

★   ★   ★

Dylan had been sitting for a while on the sofa opposite Twyla in silence. He hadn't felt like speaking, hadn't trusted himself yet. But now he knew what he had to tell her, what she needed to hear.

He sat down beside her, his hand on her knee. It was just after midnight. There was a strong wind outside, moaning down the chimney.

'I've been thinking . . . ' he said.

'Dylan . . . '

They had both spoken at the same time. They smiled.

'You go first,' she said.

'No, you,' he said.

'OK. Well, I was just going to say that I'm sorry.'

'You've said that many times,' he said. 'And it's OK.'

'But if I hadn't — '

'We both agreed to the operation,' he said. 'It wasn't just you. We thought we were doing the right thing.'

'Yes, but not like this.' She bowed her head. 'I wanted to be there when he opened his eyes. I wanted to be there for him.'

'I know,' he said, squeezing her hand. 'Which is why I told the sergeant that I'm expecting him to step things up. He mentioned that we could do a press conference. Would you be up for that?'

'A press conference?' she said, looking at him in alarm. 'After all we've been through?'

'But it could help us find Charlie's abductor,' he said.

She was holding herself taut. It was all too much for her. And yet he couldn't let it go.

'Twyla,' he said. 'I know it's a lot to take in, a lot to think about, on top of everything else, but . . . '

Now was the time to tell her the last bit, the summary of his thoughts.

'I've been . . . ' he said. He searched for the right word, for a better word, but couldn't find one in time. ' . . . Angry with you.'

'Oh,' she said, smiling sadly. 'I guessed so. And I don't blame — '

'When Charlie went missing . . . ' He shook his head. 'I thought the whole thing could have been prevented.'

He paused, gazed at her.

Was she ready to hear this?

'If I don't find who did this to us, if I don't have someone else to blame, then I'm worried I'll blame you,' he said.

There. He had said it. He blew his cheeks out in relief.

He expected her to retaliate, to defend herself. But she said nothing.

He took her hand once more, stroked it gently. 'I supported you all along the way,' he said. 'So support me with this. Please. Let me try to find who did this.'

She nodded. 'I'll help with the press conference, if that's what you want.'

He sat back, happier for saying his piece.

Yet later, as he cleaned his teeth, he beheld the goggles that were drying off on the airer above the bath, and he cringed.

The implants were in Charlie's eyes.

Would Dylan ever get used to that?

As he got into bed and stared at Charlie who was snoring in his cot, he felt deeply troubled.

It wasn't just the thought of someone having done this to their child without their consent. It was the knowledge — the full confession at last — that he hadn't ever wanted it done in the first place.

19

The appointment the following morning was agonisingly long. Two consultants examined Charlie. Afterwards, Twyla, Dylan and Charlie waited in a cafeteria. Several plain-clothed police were on-site but hanging back diplomatically. Everyone wanted to know which exact procedure had been done, using which type of implant and by whom.

Charlie, seated in a highchair, was eating a flapjack without enthusiasm. He looked thin-cheeked, sallow. The social worker was meeting them later with a child psychologist to verify that Charlie was emotionally well after his ordeal. He could be suffering from a delayed reaction, they had said yesterday.

Twyla stirred her coffee as though it were an effort. She hadn't managed to get much sleep, no more than a fitful hour or so. She had sat up by Charlie's cot, going back through everything from his birth to now, examining her motives. She couldn't shift the sense that she had brought this on them, had inflicted this on her son.

Charlie pushed his plate away. 'Don't you want any more, sweetheart?' she said. He shook his head and began to steer a toy car along the table, amongst the sauces and shakers, almost upsetting a vase. Normally, she would have reprimanded him, yet was reluctant to do so now. She was tiptoeing around, afraid to upset him, as though there were a big deficit to pay off before she could go back to bossing him about.

Dylan was on the phone to his boss, asking for a week's holiday. 'That's very kind,' he was saying. 'Thank you very much.' He hung up the phone. 'He's not putting the week through as holiday. And he said to let him know if we need anything else.'

'Mr and Mrs Ridley?' The consultant's secretary appeared behind them. 'Please come through when you're ready.'

Twyla's stomach churned.

The consultant met them in an air-conditioned room containing potted plants and bookcases of medical manuals. He had been there with them last night — was the consultant who had said the least.

They all sat down and, as the consultant began to speak, the door opened and a plain-clothed policeman slipped in with a nod and hovered in the corner behind them.

'The surgeon who operated on Charlie used the Boston K-Pro keratoprosthesis,' the doctor said.

'One moment, please,' said Dylan, pulling a notepad from his jacket. 'The Boston K-Pro?'

'It's a superior product and the prognosis is extremely good.' The consultant leant back in his chair, which gave a little jerk before lowering itself. 'There are risks, as I'm sure you're aware. However, in Charlie's case things are looking pretty positive.'

Twyla glanced at Dylan's notepad.

He had written: 'POSITIVE'.

She looked at Charlie, who was going through a basket of toys on the floor. He had discovered a ragged board book and was settling down to look at it. As he opened the first page and bent closer to see the illustration of a bear in a forest, he gave a coo of pleasure. He brought the book to Twyla and placed it on her lap.

'Tree,' he said, pointing to the illustration, looking up at her. 'Tree.'

'Yes, Charlie,' she whispered, nodding, blinking back tears.

The consultant sat upright again, leaning his elbows on the desk. 'It's important to realise that the risks tend to be small and rare. With the appropriate level of care and vigilance, you should be fine. However, you'll need to look out for signs of swelling, redness, puffiness, discharge.'

Charlie sat back down and continued to thumb through the book at Twyla's feet.

'I'll provide you with syringes,' the consultant said. 'You'll need to sterilise them. I'll be prescribing antibiotics in the form of prophylactic eye drops, which you'll administer three times a day.'

'Prophylactic . . . ' said Dylan, writing with increased speed.

'There was talk of steroids,' the consultant said, forming his hands into an arch, 'but I don't think they're necessary in Charlie's case.'

'So should we dispose of the steroids we were given last night?' Dylan asked.

'Yes, do,' the consultant said. He held up his hands. 'No steroids.' He smiled lightly. 'All this

281

will be written up for you before you go home, Mr Ridley.'

'Ah. Thank you,' said Dylan, nodding, but still writing.

'We'll make you up a fresh kit of equipment and medication. Keeps things nice and simple.'

Twyla smiled at him, but he looked away, picked up the medical notes. This wasn't an intimate place, despite the personal matter being discussed. When you entered these rooms it was impossible to tell the thoughts that went through the doctors' minds, whether judgements and aspersions were cast.

'A bandage soft contact lens must be worn twenty-four seven,' the consultant said.

'Disposable lenses?' Twyla asked.

'No,' he replied. 'We'll be fitting the lens at each appointment.' He paused, pursed his lips. 'This is very much a suck it and see situation. None of us have been through this procedure with a child of Charlie's age, or of any age for that matter.' He cleared his throat as though signalling the end to his digression. 'I'm also going to give you a couple pairs of eye shields to be worn around water and on extended trips outdoors.'

'And how long will he need those for?' Dylan asked.

'Two months,' the consultant replied. 'We'll review at the next consultation. We'll need to see Charlie every month for six months. His eye pressure's good currently, but you'll need to see the doctor fortnightly to check for glaucoma. And then he'll see us every three months for the rest of his life. He'll also need to continue with the prophylactic eye drops for the rest of his life.'

There was a pause as everyone absorbed the information, the enormity of the undertaking — the life sentence.

Charlie looked up enquiringly, unsettled by the sudden quiet, the book still open on his lap.

'So,' the consultant said, pushing back his chair and standing up. 'Everything's clear?'

'I think so,' Dylan said. 'Presumably if we have any questions . . . '

'You can call me any time,' the consultant said, moving towards the door to see them out. The policeman made no sign of moving, was presumably going to talk with him after they had left.

The consultant shook Dylan's hand. Then he turned to Twyla, who was holding Charlie in her arms. Charlie was still clutching the book. She tried to prise it from him, to put it back in the toy basket.

The consultant put his hand on Charlie's head. 'That was my book as a child, can you believe,' he said. 'But you can keep it.'

'Really?' said Twyla. 'That's — '

'I've been intrigued by this case,' he said. 'In many ways, it's revolutionary, remarkable.' He smiled, but this time it wasn't as clipped as before. 'Enjoy your son, Mrs Ridley. And your new life together.'

Dylan asked if he could remain a moment with the consultant and the policeman to go through the case details.

As the men consented and the door closed

behind them, Twyla did her best not to cry as she sat down in the waiting room with Charlie in her arms, who was still gripping the doctor's book as though it were the deeds to Legoland.

★ ★ ★

Paul saw on the news that the boy was back. She wasn't interviewed. Only the detective sergeant spoke. But they showed a photograph of Twyla Ridley and the boy.

It was funny to see the picture of her there on the screen, to view her as everyone else did. They would all process her the same way: young woman, happy-looking.

He was in the pub on a *Herald* social evening when the newsreel played. He asked his colleagues to hush up so he could listen. He still couldn't hear. He went right over to the television, asking the barman to turn the volume up.

The reporter was outside the Ridleys' home. It was raining. 'Toddler Charlie Ross Ridley was returned unharmed to his family earlier today. Police are continuing to work on the case. But for now, where Charlie Ridley has been and why remains a mystery.'

That was it. He returned to his seat, unsatisfied.

He opened a packet of peanuts, tugging at them absently, gazing at the screen. 'You seem very interested in that story,' one of his colleagues said. She was from Leeds and he could never remember her name.

'Hmm?' he replied.

What did she want him to say? That he was in love with the Ridley woman, the married woman who had just been reunited with her abducted child who used to be blind and now wasn't?

'It's scientific experimentation,' said his boss.

'What is?' Paul said.

'The Ridley case that you're so obsessed with,' his boss said, laughing her croaky twenty Camel Lights a day laugh.

'And why would it be that?' he asked.

She shrugged. 'I've been in this job long enough to recognise the patterns.'

'What patterns?'

She pulled a cigarette from the packet and tapped it end down on the table. 'First there was that teenager who was kidnapped by the hospital in Chicago last spring. And then there was that young girl in Mexico. There's been dozens of others too. Not many make the headlines though. They're all in collusion: medical researchers, hospitals.' She stood up and grabbed her jacket.

'But why?'

'Why?' She laughed scornfully. 'For profit! And to use the kids for research . . . Don't look so shocked!' She put her cigarette to her lips. It bounced up and down as she spoke. 'Stay long enough in this job, you realise there's nothing that people aren't capable of.'

He really didn't want to stay long enough in this job to earn that kind of world view.

'Just going for a smoke,' his boss said, and left.

'Do you know the Ridleys?' the woman from Leeds asked him.

He pretended not to hear and took a long

drink of beer, gazing at the television screen. The news had moved on to a feature about sheep farming.

When he got home later, he felt dejected and alone. But he didn't have time to entertain self-pity for long. Because his phone rang and his boss's abrasive chatter cut through the stillness of the room, reminding him of a laughing kookaburra.

* * *

He grabbed the opportunity to do the job before anyone else. He had already told his boss that he would like all the Ridley jobs, since he had a personal interest in the case. 'I bet you do,' his boss had said, thumbing through the photographs of Mrs Ridley.

He assured his boss that his interest in the case was purely professional.

He didn't feel very professional today. His hands were clammy. He hoped no one would talk to him so that he could observe things without distraction.

Interest in the case was huge. The boardroom at the police station was crammed with journalists, their voices booming around the walls. The man next to him was talking about the case in the Chicago hospital that his boss had mentioned. It was suffocatingly warm. There were no windows open or air-conditioning. Many of the reporters were sporting underarm wet patches and were fanning themselves with gadgets and notepads.

Twyla entered the room and a hush fell. Behind her was her father, the man whom he had met at the park. He felt a swell of pleasure, since he alone was acquainted with the main cast. But the pleasure was soon quelled because in the father's wake came the husband.

He wasn't sure where he had placed the husband in his mind. He had fantasised that there was no husband any more, that he had been neatly disposed of somehow. Yet there he was, firm-jawed, handsome, by her side.

He felt ghastly about it.

The Ridleys were consulting with police staff at the front of the room. Then they took their places at the head table, with the husband sat right next to his wife, his hand on top of hers.

Paul wanted to rush at them, to tear them apart. But he sat still and waited for silence as the leading detective sergeant of the case addressed the room.

'Thank you all for coming,' the sergeant said.

Paul eased himself along the wall, sliding between bodies to get a good picture. The only way to do it was to suck in his chest. When he reached the front, he crouched down, balancing his camera on his knee.

'Charlie Ross Ridley was returned to his parents late yesterday afternoon. When they last saw him, he was blind. And now he can see.'

There were excited murmurs around the room. The sergeant began to go through the details — of when the boy had gone missing, what he had been wearing. Reporters were scribbling down the facts, their pencils making snake-like hisses on paper.

'We're following several lines of inquiry, but would ask the public to please come forward with any information that might be of use.'

'Do you have any hunches, Sergeant?' a journalist called out.

'I'm not able to disclose specific details,' the sergeant said. Someone groaned. The sergeant gathered his paperwork and stood up to signal the end of the announcement. Behind him, a photograph of Charlie Ridley was displayed on a large screen, with the information number to call.

Paul watched Twyla. He wasn't sure that she had been listening. She appeared to be elsewhere, focusing on the ceiling. She was wearing a pale pink jumper with pearls dotted about it. As the cameras flashed, so the pearls caught the light.

'Is this medical kidnapping?' shouted a reporter from the middle of the crowd.

'No further questions, please,' said the sergeant, holding up his hand. 'Thank you.'

'Twyla,' someone called out hurriedly from the back. 'How do you feel?'

'No comment,' she said. Her reply was barely audible. Only those at the front could hear her.

'Sorry, Twyla?' the journalist was shouting. 'What did you say?' But she had risen and was moving away, her husband steering her by the elbow.

The press were all talking at once. Some were discreet, others less so. 'Lab rat,' Paul heard someone say.

When he got out to the foyer, he was surprised to see her standing there on her own. She appeared to be waiting for someone.

Even more to his surprise: she was waiting for him.

'I thought you might be here today,' she said. 'I wanted to give you this.' She opened the flap on her bag and pulled out his book.

The Art of Acceptance. Had he really been reading that?

'Here.' She handed it to him. 'I shouldn't have taken it from you. I was going a bit crazy with Charlie missing.' She frowned. 'I was clutching at straws. I'm sorry.'

So he was a straw.

He couldn't bring himself to meet her gaze, thought that if he did, he wouldn't be able to look away again.

'You didn't have to return it,' he said, not moving to take the book. 'You should keep it.'

People were milling around them, talking loudly until they noticed her and lowered their voices. She glanced sideways at her husband and father who were waiting outside on the pavement. The afternoon sun was ebbing away, lending a sad pink tinge to the sky — the same colour as her jumper.

He admitted to himself then that he had been completely stupid and wrong. He had no claim on her. He had been carried away on a whim, misled by loneliness.

The man with the claim was stood some yards beyond, wearing a wedding ring, waiting for her to go home with him.

'Please,' she said, handing him the book. 'Take it. It's yours.'

'OK,' he said, feeling disproportionately sad.

She turned and left, hurrying off.

He remained in the lobby for a short while afterwards, wondering what to do with himself for the rest of the day, shamelessly holding *The Art of Acceptance* in full view for anyone to see.

★　★　★

Her father came down from London again to lend a hand with the press conference. She had told him not to, that it was silly him keeping coming up and down, that there wasn't anything he could do. But then the police told her that it would be helpful to make a show of unity, of having family around them. And so Stephen had driven down once more.

Eileen looked after Charlie whilst they were gone, and also oversaw to the social worker and child psychologist visit in their absence. It had gone well, she told them later. No problems with his mentals, as she called it, and there was a chicken pie and apple cake in the fridge for their supper.

It had been such a long day. They saw Stephen off, then Eileen. And then they bathed Charlie, administered his eye drops and put him to bed. They disposed of the steroids as instructed, cleared a space on the kitchen counter for the syringes and goggles, and refrigerated the antibiotics.

By the time they sat down for supper, they

were on the ten o'clock news — a glimpse of themselves at the press conference and Charlie's photograph for all to see. They watched it dispassionately, before turning the television off and beginning to eat.

They had decided to open a bottle of claret. They ate quietly, slowly, enjoying the nourishment of food and wine.

When they had finished, Dylan set his plate aside and looked at her. 'So,' he said. 'We survived the first day.'

'Yes.' She glanced at the ceiling. All was quiet. Charlie had gone to sleep immediately, exhausted from the day's events.

'More wine?' Dylan asked.

'Please.'

She listened to the satisfying glug glug glug of the bottle as her glass was filled.

'What did the police say at the hospital earlier?' she asked.

'Not much,' he said, setting the bottle on the coffee table. 'They're currently contacting all the leading eye surgeons in Europe. It could take some time, especially to do it thoroughly.'

They sat side by side, holding hands on the sofa, like a teenage couple.

She sipped her wine. It felt intoxicating — the tranquillising sensation of alcohol on a fractured nervous system.

They finished the bottle in silence, neither feeling the need to talk.

Until Twyla realised that there was something large that had been left unsaid, unresolved, amid all the chaos.

'Can we talk about Molly?' she said.

It was half past eleven. They should have been in bed, but their once carefully timed life of routine and appointments had been dismantled and this new one was horribly ill-formed, shapeless.

'What about her?' he said.

She hesitated. How to ask him, but not to make it into something it wasn't? 'Do you work closely with her?' she said.

He put his empty glass down. 'Not really, no. Why?'

'Because you were holding her hand?'

'Look,' he said, laughing. 'I told you — it was because of the shock, of finding the body.'

But there was something in his laugh that she didn't like: something defensive.

'Do you like her?' she asked.

He folded his arms. 'As a colleague,' he replied, 'yes.'

'And there's nothing more?' she said.

'No.' He shook his head. 'Nothing.'

'So tell me about her.'

'What about her?'

'I dunno,' she said. 'What's she like? What are her hobbies?'

His cheeks were flushed. They were both too tired for this — irrational, vulnerable.

'Actually,' she said, 'don't.' She was going to tell him not to answer her questions, not to say anything but to come up to bed with her and get some sleep.

But he had begun to reply. 'Hobbies?' He paused, smiled. 'Yoga. She's just mastered the Firefly pose — ' He broke off. 'What?'

'Oh, God!' she said. 'You *do* like her!'

He laughed again. 'Don't be so stupid!'

'Well, how do you expect me to feel?' she said, standing up. 'Charlie's missing and I walk in on you holding hands with someone at work? How would you feel if it was you, Dylan, hey?'

Dylan stood up, looking suddenly sober. 'I'm sorry,' he said.

It had been a mistake to drink wine. And a mistake to mention that woman's name.

'I just needed someone to talk to.' He stared at the carpet. 'I had Mum on my back. And I didn't want to upset you. And Molly was there. She's a good listener. And — '

'And I'm not?' said Twyla.

'I didn't say that,' he said, moving towards her. 'I just found her easy to talk to. And then when she took my hand, I let her. It didn't mean anything. It was just that she was a friend and I needed one.'

She gazed at him. 'But you had me,' she said.

He had no reply.

They said no more.

They checked on Charlie, pulled the bed sheets up around them and turned their backs on each other. And for the first time in their married life, there was no good-night kiss.

'Good night, my love,' she whispered, realising that it would be dangerous to leave things like this, without a word of reconciliation.

But Dylan made no response. He was asleep.

She knew better than to trust herself late at night, when her viewpoint was distorted. Yet she felt it anyway: the disquieting premonition that they were about to be undone.

20

Stephen was filling in an insurance form, the sunshine streaming in on his desk, when he realised with a start that he knew nothing about his family's medical history. He had always written 'N/A', without knowing whether it was true. But now he stopped with his fountain pen poised over the tick box, wondering whether his father was diabetic or prone to indigestion or high blood pressure.

He was ashamed to admit that he didn't know. In fact, he couldn't say very much about Stephen Thibodeaux Senior at all.

He eyed the phone, deep in contemplation, fiddling with his tie. It was many years since he had spoken to his parents, having become increasingly reliant on their efficient letter system.

It took a long time for them to pick up. He glanced at his watch. It was breakfast time in New York. They would be sitting at their elongated table, sliding the silver toast rack to one another, whilst perusing the *Times*.

At eighty-seven years old, with the help of domestic staff, they were managing to hang on to their apartment. As they weren't short of money, he had never had to worry about them. Money had been in the Thibodeaux family for so long it was more than a problem solver. It was a means of communication, of easing awkward social situations. 'Looking down on us because we're from the Deep South? Well, here's my Platinum card.'

'Hello?'

He barely recognised his mother's voice.

'Mother?' he said. 'Is that you?'

'Who is this, please?' she asked.

For God's sake. Who else would be calling her 'Mother'?

'It's Stephen,' he said. 'How are you?'

'Stephen,' she said unemotionally. 'You got my letter then?'

'Letter?'

'I asked Greta to post it a fortnight ago. When did it arrive?'

He looked at the tray on the side table where the post amassed. It was some time since he had gone through the tray, what with everything that had happened of late. Juliet normally filtered arrivals into three piles: personal, financial, professional.

At the top of the personal pile — the sole arrival in that category — was his mother's letter. He recognised the American handwriting, the familiar scroll of his birthplace.

He opened the envelope quietly, slipping his letter opener along the seal. The note was written on personalised Thibodeaux stationery.

'Hello? Stephen, are you there?'

His eye fell on the crux of the matter, layered within the standard pleasantries.

I am writing to inform you that your father passed away yesterday morning. It was sudden and attributed to old age.

'Father died?' he said.

'Why, yes,' she replied. 'I thought that was why you were ringing. Don't tell me the letter didn't get there yet? I hope that Greta — '

'And you chose to tell me by letter? What about the funeral?'

'Last Tuesday.'

He pinched the top of his nose. 'Mother, don't you see?' he said. 'This is . . . '

'Yes, Stephen?'

He was about to say that it was all wrong, that it had been a waste of associated genes, that they may as well have been strangers. His father had lived and died and was no more associated with Stephen than his postman or dustbin man. In fact, the latter was better acquainted with Stephen because he knew from his rubbish what he liked to eat and drink.

What was the point in telling her this now — an eighty-seven-year-old widow whose biggest preoccupation was whether her maid could be trusted to post a letter on time?

'Are you all right?' he asked.

Recently he had been harbouring the notion of flying out to see them some time with Twyla and Charlie. Twyla could have met her grandparents before undertaking that trip to Cape Cod they had talked about. He could see now, however, that this was sentiment talking, that such a thing was unfeasible.

'Of course,' she said. 'Your father went peacefully, and I myself am in good health.'

So pragmatic. Was this how he was? Was this how his daughter saw him?

'Let me know if you need anything,' he said. He didn't expect her to take him up on the offer.

As they were ending the call, he thought of something. 'Mother?'

She heard him just in time. She was still there. 'Yes?'

'Maybe we could speak on the phone occasionally?'

'Phone?' she said. 'What's wrong with letters? It's what we've always done, Stephen.'

He hung up, overcome with disappointment and sorrow.

So the old man had passed.

Their long-distance transatlantic relationship that had been spun out for over sixty years had finally drawn to a close; a relationship remarkable only for its ability to leave everyone completely unmoved.

There was a noise downstairs. Juliet was home.

'What are you doing?' she said, entering his study, resting her bag on the floor. She was wearing a long jumper with a poppy across her chest. All of a sudden, her childish fashion annoyed him.

'Are you OK?' she said. Her nose was as red as the poppy. It was cold out.

'My father died.'

'Your father?' she said, looking about the room as though for a corpse.

'Yup.' He held up the letter for her to see.

'You were told by post?'

'Yup,' he said again.

'Oh, I'm sorry, darling.' She dropped her

shoulders in sympathy. 'Is there anything I can do? Shall I book the flights?'

'Good idea,' he said. 'Get them for last Tuesday.'

'Last Tuesday? Oh.' Her mouth formed a circle as realisation dawned. She moved behind him and placed her hand on his back, stroking it soothingly. She smelt of cold air — the sort of faint scent that lingered about a person after coming indoors on a chilly day. 'Let me pour you a drink and a bath.'

'No, thank you,' he said, pulling away from her to stand up. 'I'm off to Bath.'

'Again? It must be costing you a fortune in petrol, Stephen.'

'Which is why I'm going to stay for a few days.'

'Stay?' she said. 'Where?'

'At the Royal Crescent Hotel, if they'll have me.'

Juliet stared at him for a moment before moving to retrieve her handbag, to continue on with her day. He had annoyed her.

'What's so urgent this time?' she asked, her hand on the doorknob.

'Nothing,' he said. 'I just feel that I should be doing more to help her with Charlie. It's a lot to take on.'

'But she's got her husband.'

'Yes, and he went back to work today. She needs my help.'

'She said that?'

'Not in so many words.' He put his suit jacket on and ran his fingers through his hair.

'Oh, just go,' Juliet said, flapping her hand.

Stephen sighed and went upstairs to pack. As he filled his overnight bag, there was a tap on the bedroom door. Juliet stood there looking up at him. 'Would you like me to come with you?' she asked.

He couldn't say the words, couldn't tell her that she had no place in Twyla's life, that he wasn't sure if he had a place there either.

'How long will you be gone for?' she asked plaintively. 'I'm sorry. I don't mean to be pathetic.'

'It's not pathetic,' he said.

It occurred to him that this was a painful situation for her. She hadn't wanted children. It was a calculated decision, yet Twyla was a delicate subject between them. Perhaps not because Twyla was his offspring, but because she was Robin's.

'So how long?' she asked again.

'I'm not sure,' he said. He stooped to kiss her on the forehead. 'As long as it takes.'

Juliet left the room and Stephen closed his case, picked it up and made his way downstairs.

He had to do this. His father had died a complete stranger to him. That couldn't be what happened to him and Twyla.

Any day now, a cheque would arrive accompanied by a personalised complimentary slip. It would be the sum that had been settled on him in the event of Stephen Thibodeaux Senior's death.

It would be the penultimate cheque. The final one would arrive when his mother passed away.

He realised that he had forgotten the point of his phone call, that he had meant to enquire about their medical history. There was no point writing to ask. By the time a letter flew all the way to Manhattan and back, no one would care about the answer.

★　★　★

Dylan stood watching the rain hitting the window. There were leaves strewn all over Bindy's garden, like debris after a party. Summer had gone on for so long that many of the leaves hadn't had time to turn golden before falling. It made the view seem messier, more wasteful somehow.

It was Saturday morning. He had been back at the office for one hard-wearing week. There was a backlog of work, but he had wanted to be at home sorting things out there. Charlie had back-to-back appointments and consultations. He was adapting to his new ability and was giving the doctors no signs for concern as of yet. Twyla was handling it well, taking it one conscientious step at a time. Yet things were very strained between them. They needed a conversation to clear the air, but there had been little opportunity to do so. She was rightly preoccupied with Charlie. On the occasions he had found her resting, alone, she seemed beyond discussion, weary in the extreme. And he had been meeting with the police after work nightly for progress updates, sometimes coming home well after supper.

He couldn't help but feel that being in the office with Molly was the worst place he could be. Yet how to get around that? He had to go to work, and Molly was there. And besides, there was nothing going on between them. Office friendships, when one or both of the individuals were married, were tricky. There were all sorts of boundaries in place that both parties went to pains to adhere to. Even the most innocent person would writhe guiltily when nearing the boundary: lingering eye contact, a shared smile. Let alone holding hands . . .

He felt awkward with Molly now. And she in turn was less prone to blushing and had moved four desks away in a sudden desire to be near natural light.

He would miss the nasally laughter, for he knew that their friendship was over. Passionate affairs ended with smashed crockery, the occasional stabbing or gunfire; so office friendships ceased with the subtle reorganisation of seating arrangements.

To give Twyla a break, he had offered to bring Charlie to Bindy's for the morning. Really, he wanted to talk things through with his sister. Not that she was a relationship guru. But she was better than no one.

Yet, on arrival at Bindy's, he was dismayed to find his mother's car in the driveway. Talking to Bindy would be impossible now.

'Well, it's a miracle that he can see,' his mother was saying. 'But it wasn't of the Lord's doing, to be sure.'

Dylan turned to look at his mother, who was

kneeling on the floorboards to build a tower block with Charlie. Bindy's house could have done with a few carpets and rugs to soften the feel. He glanced up at the ceiling, which was high and bare, aside from a small chandelier that looked alone and rather shocked, as though singled out for ridicule.

'It's a miracle, Mum,' Dylan said. 'Let's just settle for that.'

Each passing day, they were realising the magnitude of the situation, of Charlie's vision. Charlie could play with any toy, not just carefully selected ones. It was difficult to resist the temptation to go out and buy the whole toy shop at once. Charlie could have anything! He could kick the softball back to Dylan now — had even caught it last weekend — and they had walked up to the recreation field to find conkers; simple things that only days before had been impossible for them to do.

'How are the investigations going?' his mother asked. She had risen from the floor and sat drinking a mug of tea. Bindy, sitting in the corner of the room, was reading a magazine by the light of an austere-looking lamp — the sort of thing a surgeon might use. She was in every way a comfortless being, Dylan thought.

'Not very well,' he said.

'Oh?' his mother said. 'Don't they have any leads?'

'Not at the moment,' he said.

'But what about the medical research thing?'

He shrugged. 'They've interviewed every eye surgeon in the country and beyond.'

'And?' she asked.

'Nothing. The operation appears to be traceless.'

'Nonsense! Nothing is traceless. What about the Collins man?'

'What about him?' said Dylan. 'They've got nothing on him either.'

Eileen frowned. 'But surely you're not going to let this rest, son?'

Dylan gazed at her. She was wearing a cream argyle sweater and cream corduroys — an odd outfit, like a dollop of crème fraiche on Bindy's leather sofa. She always called him 'Son'. It was apt. It was personal, since no one else could call him that, and yet had a detached sound that conveyed the feel of their relationship rather succinctly.

'I'm doing my best, Mum,' he replied.

The investigation still mattered greatly to him. But Twyla mattered more. And it was her who was occupying his thoughts the most of late.

'I'm surprised you're not out there yourself, knocking on Collins's door, taking the matter into your own hands,' his mother was saying. 'After what they — '

'Hush, Mum!' he said, flashing her a cautionary look in Charlie's direction. He didn't know what Charlie was feeling, but talking about his abduction in front of him was surely ill advised.

His mother muttered that she was going to the bathroom and left the room, closing the door behind her with a click, like a tutting tongue.

There was a rustle as Bindy lowered her

magazine. 'So, Dills,' she said, raising one eyebrow. 'What are you really doing here?'

★　★　★

Bindy watched her brother's expression change to surprise. He was so easy to wind up, to control.

'What do you mean: 'What am I really doing here?' ' he asked.

Bindy rolled her eyes. 'Come on,' she said. 'Let's go outside for some fresh air.'

'In this weather?' he said.

Their mother returned. 'Could you just watch Charlie, please, Mum?' Bindy said. 'I need Dylan to take a look at the leaky roof in the summer house.'

'Of course,' said their mother. 'But don't be long. I'm meeting Father O'Brien at twelve.'

Bindy pulled open the back door, the rain and wind ruffling her shirt.

'You're mad!' Dylan said, picking up his jacket.

'Probably,' she replied. 'Come on.'

She grabbed his arm and pulled him out into the storm, laughing. It was the sort of thing she would have done to him as a child, had always been doing: pulling him into storms, into trouble that he hadn't courted and didn't welcome.

It couldn't have been raining any harder. They were soaked instantly. They ran as fast as they could to the summer house, throwing themselves inside in a tumble of wet clothes.

Once they had closed the door, barring the

304

storm, things went back to normal. No more laughter or silly behaviour. She plugged the radiator on and sat down on the chaise longue.

'So where's this leak?' he asked, looking upwards.

'There is no leak, you numpty!' she said.

'What?' He looked confused. She could see him standing there, four years old and sweet as pie. *Me not want to set fire to the rubbish bin in the garage, or put salt in Mummy's semolina when she leaves the room. Me good boy. Bindy bad.*

'How else were we going to get away from Mum?' she said. 'You wanted to talk, didn't you?' She pulled a hip flask from behind a cushion and took a swig of Jack Daniel's.

He watched her, a smile flickering on his lips, and shook his head. 'Same old Bindy,' he said. He sat down on a wooden chair near the door and looked out the window, watching the rain.

The radiator began to hum, emitting a burnt smell. It sometimes did that when insects fell down on the grill.

'So spill the beans,' she said.

'There are no beans,' he said.

'Oh, cut the crap!' she said. 'We've only got a few minutes. You heard Mum — Father O'Brien at twelve.' She glanced at her watch. It was half past eleven already.

He shifted as though uncomfortable in his seat. 'Twyla thinks I like a woman at work,' he said, folding his arms.

'I see,' she said, finding the situation faintly funny for some reason. Perhaps it was the idea of

Dylan cheating. Dylan, whose most rebellious act as a teenager was leaving the lid off the jam. 'And do you?'

''Course not,' Dylan said.

'So why might Twyla think differently?' Bindy said.

'I don't know,' he replied, standing up. 'Maybe because she saw me holding her hand.'

Bindy jolted, hip flask mid-air. She tried her best not to snigger. But failed.

'Oh, for God's sake, Bindy,' he said. 'Not everything's a joke.'

'Sorry,' she said, putting the flask down and standing up beside him. 'Look, I know without asking you that there would have been a good reason — a simple explanation . . . Right?'

He nodded.

'Then just explain that to her.'

It was such a rough old day — turbulent, wild. The apples were ripening and rotting, the plums withering on the branches. Trees were shedding leaves as though they were just tossing things down and hang the consequences.

'I tried,' he said. 'But . . . '

'But what?'

'It just seems like . . . well, as though there's something else troubling her.'

Bindy laughed. 'Well, duh! Look what she's just been through!'

'It's not just that.' He turned to look at her. She noticed that his eyes were bloodshot, that he hadn't shaved, that he looked like he hadn't slept in a year. 'I think she thinks that I don't love her any more.'

'And why would she think that?'

'Because . . . well, I told her that if I didn't find out who did this to Charlie, that I would blame her.'

'Oh, Dills,' she said, shaking her head. 'You can't lay something like that on her,' she said, withdrawing to the chaise longue. 'You decided all this together — to go for the operation.'

'I know,' he said. 'And I don't know why I said it. But I did. And I can't take it back. And besides, it's the truth.'

'Oh, to hell with the truth,' Bindy said. 'It's overrated.'

'Easy for you to say,' he said.

'Oh yeah? How so?'

'Because you're not in a relationship. Never will be probably.' He looked her up and down. 'I mean, look at you. Who do you care about, other than yourself?'

She stared at him in surprise, trying to decipher the meaning behind these un-Dylan-like insults. She would chalk it up to emotional distress. After all, there was a woman in one of the magazines at the dentist's who had post-traumatic stress disorder and pulled all her eyelashes out.

So she was thinking, until he overstepped the imaginary mark on the floor — a mark that had been drawn in the dust so many years before that they had forgotten its existence. Yet it was still there and she felt the cracking pain inside as they slammed into it.

'I don't think you ever even really cared about Fee,' he said.

She jumped to her feet and stood with her fists clenched, a hissing sound coming from her mouth in place of words.

'Don't!' she shouted finally. 'Don't you dare say that! You take that back. *Take that back!*'

It was Dylan's turn to stare at her in surprise, to wonder what bomb he had detonated inside her. But before she knew what she was doing, she had run at him and had pushed him with all her strength into the side of the summer house.

'What the hell?' he said, as his shoulders bounced off the wooden walls.

She thought for a moment that the whole thing was going to collapse.

'You were never even there, you moron!' she shouted at him. 'Never there!' And then she backed away, sat down and unscrewed the hip flask with a shaking hand.

After she had drank the flask dry, she spoke, her voice croaky from her outburst.

'You can say anything you like, call me anything you want. I don't care any more. But if you dare say that I didn't care for Fee, that I didn't love her, then I swear . . . ' She shook her head. There was nothing she could say that could describe the intensity of the revenge she would take on him.

Dylan had gone white in the face. Once more she thought of that little boy — of the sweet child who had found her complicated, messy mind so unfathomable.

'I'm sorry,' he said. 'I know it was you who looked after her.' He covered his face with his hands.

The sight of her little brother — her big little brother stood with his face covered like that in shame — made her want to give him a hug. But she didn't because that would have signified forgiveness.

'I think I turned to the girl at work,' Dylan said, his back to her, 'because I was running away. Because that's what I do.'

She wanted to reassure him otherwise, just out of pity's sake. But to do so would have been a lie. And, as he said himself, he rated the truth.

'Just like Dad,' she said.

The slight twitch of his head was the only sign that she had wounded him.

She watched a drop of rain trickling down the leather on her brother's back and thought of the day their father left. He used to have a leather jacket too — a biker's jacket, which was a bit silly because he rode a moped. He zipped about town on his moped, cracking jokes, telling people that the fuel he used was the same one that he filled his lawnmower with.

She had inherited her dry sense of humour from him. It was a way of coping, of self-defence. He had loved comedy shows and liked to perform magic tricks too. Felicity would rock back and forth in her wheelchair, barking appreciatively when he made coins disappear. Bindy preferred the jokes: limericks, knock-knocks, Englishman, Irishman and Scotsman; the more inappropriate the better.

He hadn't taken life too seriously. Nothing bad had probably ever happened to him. So Fee's death had crushed him.

For a while, the only way she could console herself about him leaving was to tell herself jokes about it.

Knock, knock.

Who's there?

Dad.

Dad who?

That was one of the jokes. They weren't very good.

'We should get going,' Dylan said, opening the summer-house door. The wind forced itself through, rattling the windows, lifting the tablecloth. Leaves scuttled forward as though alive.

'Yes,' she said, standing up, shivering.

'Bindy . . .' he said.

'Forget it,' she said.

She told him she would follow him in, and stooped to turn off the heater. She stood for a moment watching him running across the lawn, his head bent against the rain.

She recalled sitting upstairs at the window of her bedroom, her nose pressed against the glass, watching someone else run away. It was raining that day too.

She had watched her father leave, his collar turned up, his head down. A dog was following him. Normally, he stopped for dogs — tickled them, grabbed a stick for them to fetch — but he was ignoring the stray that was jumping around his legs. Bindy had slammed her fists against the window.

'Dad!' she shouted. 'Don't go!'

He turned around by some coincidence. He

couldn't possibly have heard her from that distance, above the rain and the dog yapping.

He waved and blew her a kiss. And that was the last time she ever saw him.

One of their neighbours told her that it was grief that had driven him away.

No, she corrected them. It was a Vespa.

★　★　★

Bindy looked about the kitchen inquisitively, her eye falling on the medication laid out neatly on a tray on the counter. There were goggles in cellophane and tiny sunglasses, gloves, syringes, a thermometer and eye drops.

Her forehead prickled with sudden memory, with the familiarity of such a clinical, highly responsible setting — with the worry of getting the right dose at the right time, day after day, with no respite.

'Here,' said Twyla, handing her a mug of tea. 'Let's go sit down.'

Bindy followed her sister-in-law through to the lounge, noting her diminished form — the frailness at the shoulders and waist. Twyla, in a grey sweater and pyjama bottoms, had just put Charlie to bed. Her hair was fixed up in a ponytail and there were violet shadows under her eyes. And yet still she was gracious, warm. It was a skill of hers, Bindy considered — the ability to welcome people no matter how dire her personal circumstances, how inconvenient the interruption.

'Dylan's at the police station,' Twyla said.

Bindy had hoped as much. 'Good,' she replied. 'Because it's you that I came to see.'

'Oh?' said Twyla.

'Dylan and I had a little chat the other day.'

'You did?' Twyla asked, a trace of colour appearing on her cheeks.

'Yes. He told me about the woman at work.' She put down her mug and fixed her eyes on Twyla. 'And you should know that you have absolutely nothing to worry about.'

There was an awkward pause as Twyla digested the information — that her husband had gone to his sister about such an intimate matter.

'Dylan went through a lot as a child,' Bindy said.

Twyla set down her mug a trifle hastily. Tea slopped over the sides on to the coffee table, but Twyla didn't seem to heed it.

'With all due respect — ' Twyla began.

Bindy held up her hand. 'I know . . . I'm sitting here spouting things that I know nothing about. But I do know that Dylan loves you. And if you're not careful you'll push him away.'

'I see,' said Twyla, stiffening her back. 'So this is all my fault?'

Bindy smiled. 'No one said that.'

'Bindy,' Twyla said, rising, 'I'm not in any fit state to discuss — '

'He'll go,' Bindy said, abruptly. 'He'll run away. D'you understand?'

Twyla opened her mouth to respond, but no words came. She sat back down. 'I practically raised Dylan when Mum hit the ground,' Bindy said. 'I know him like the back of my hand. When things get tough, he goes.'

Twyla looked up angrily. 'You don't think things have been tough already?'

Bindy sighed. 'I know . . . ' She trailed off, looked at her feet.

This was hopeless. She shouldn't have come.

Then she noticed that Twyla was looking at her with a funny expression on her face, as though wanting to ask a question but not daring to.

Bindy would help her out, just this once. 'You want to know when Mum hit the ground?' she suggested.

Twyla nodded.

So many things rushed at Bindy — recollections, injustices. She tried to pick one word to say — one or two to fit the bill, to make her message clear.

'It was when Felicity died,' was the only response she could come up with.

Twyla didn't say anything. There was a silence hanging in the room that went beyond awkward to suffocating. Bindy sensed that whatever it was between the two of them that had always barred their way, forbidden any sort of friendship, it was here with them now, waiting to reveal itself. But she didn't want to know what it was. She just wanted Dylan to be happy. It was too late for herself, but not for him.

She had to try.

'Dad abandoned us,' she said. 'And Mum took to her bed. I tried to keep everything going, but it was all falling apart.' She took a tissue from her handbag and held it not to her eyes but in her hand, scrunching it into a ball. 'I never once saw Dylan cry about Fee. He never mentioned her again. Mind you, I was no better.'

She stopped. Twyla was gazing at her. She couldn't read her expression. There was concern there, but something else too that was just beyond reach.

'Sometimes,' Bindy said, 'it's easier to do nothing. To say nothing. To have nothing. To be nothing.'

Twyla stood then, came towards her, but stopped as Bindy swept her jacket up and hoisted her large handbag on to her shoulder. 'You're going?' Twyla said. 'But you only just got here.'

'You need to rest,' Bindy replied, retreating to the hallway, where she lingered by the front door.

Twyla looked graceful and appealing in the dim light. There was a little alcove by the front door that was painted lagoon green. Some of Twyla's bola charms were displayed there, lit by a tulip-shaped lamp. They were just behind her now, in Bindy's line of vision.

Without thinking, she reached out to touch Twyla's cheek.

'You light Dylan up,' she said. 'You gave him hope when there wasn't any. Don't take that away from him.'

Twyla's mouth was trembling. She looked vulnerable in a way that Bindy hadn't seen her before, hadn't imagined her capable of being. The sight troubled her. She turned away quickly.

As Bindy walked down the front steps, Twyla turned the lamp on above the door. 'Bindy . . . ?'

Bindy stopped. Twyla was stood on the concrete doorstep in bare feet, her hair lit by the lamp. She moved slowly down the steps towards Bindy with ghost-like smoothness, stopping at arm's length from her.

'Thank you,' Twyla said.

'That's OK,' Bindy said. And then she hurried away, her face averted in case Twyla should see what was hidden there.

She fumbled for her keys and jumped into the driver's seat, slamming the car door behind her.

When she got to the outskirts of town, she pulled over. In the solitude of her car, she cried for Felicity. Not for herself, or for Dylan, or her mother or father. But for her sister — for the pain and anguish Felicity had endured, for her life cut off in its prime, for a life unfulfilled.

When she stopped, she felt disorientated. It took her a moment to remember where she was.

There was nothing she could do about Felicity now. She had tried her best, had tried so hard from the moment Fee had arrived, all bungled and misshapen.

She started the car, moved forward slowly.

She knew now what it was that had stood between herself and Twyla.

From the moment she had met her, Bindy realised what Dylan saw in his shiny new girlfriend, Twyla Thibodeaux. It was impossible not to know, the way she lit everything up. She carried him up somewhere high, away from the dustbins of reality and pessimism. He was happy to float up there with her. And the moment that he accepted the offer, soared with her, he left Bindy behind — Bindy with her morbid memories of her little sister anchoring her to the ground, like ankle weights. She'd wanted to go too — had yearned to drift up high like Felicity's red balloon into the summer sky. But there wasn't enough light for her — not enough to lift her as well as her brother.

She couldn't go on blaming Twyla for that. And for the fact that there had been no cure for Fee.

And it was then that she felt a little snip — the faintest snip inside her as the cut was made.

She put her foot down, gathering speed, the branches of the trees flashing above her sunroof as she sped along the country road.

Fee hadn't weighed her down. If it weren't for Fee, she would have responsibilities like everyone else: marriage, children, career, mortgage.

She had no such burdens.

She drove faster still.

She would sell her house and chuck in her job. She would travel the world, would see all the things she had read in the waiting room magazines. And everywhere she went — every temple, plaza, beach, desert — she would thank Fee.

She was completely free!

She switched the radio on as loudly as it would go. Some awful rock song. She wound down the windows. 'Watch me go, Fee!' she shouted, dangling her head out of the window, the wind buffeting in her ears. 'Woo hoo, Fee!'

316

She was taking off into the night; a little bouncing being full of joy and energy, springing off full of hope.

A pea leapt, see?

21

A fortnight after Charlie's return, during the first week of October, as leaves were shed, apples glowed on trees, harvest festival displays appeared on church steps and a chill gripped the air with a force that suggested staying power, things began to settle.

Twyla and Dylan took an out-of-season trip to Weston-super-Mare with Charlie, where they played football on the beach and ate hot doughnuts from a stand. They went on walks to collect leaves for Charlie to paint for a collage. They visited toy stores and fed ducks. They started house-hunting again and took another look at the cottage that Twyla liked, which was still on the market.

Yet Twyla, despite having imagined this point many times — a hazy, idealised picture of the future — sensed a weightiness about their new lives that she had not anticipated. She woke happy each day and then, as she remembered what lay ahead, felt daunted.

She was normally the first up and would set up the syringes and put on medical gloves, at which point Dylan arrived with Charlie. It took two of them to administer the eye drops, since Charlie fought them, shifting his head about, crying. They would sing to distract him or read him a book.

The one o'clock eye drops were the worst

because Dylan was at work. But her father, who had been staying in Bath for the past week, was a decent substitute. The seven o'clock eye drops were the easiest. Dylan was home; Charlie's bath was over. Sleepy, he complied with the eye drops, whilst Dylan read *Room on the Broom*.

Twyla took Charlie's temperature each night. After his bath — during which she stood tensely over him, petrified that water might seep into his eyes and infect him — she sterilised the eye shields and got the equipment ready for the next day.

In the morning, once they had gone through the eye drops rigmarole again, she would set about clearing up the house, before fixing Charlie's eye shields on his face for their morning excursion. They weren't often free to choose their day's activities, but were dictated to by appointments: doctor check for glaucoma, social worker, speech therapist, child psychologist, health visitor — they were all going strong.

And if, Twyla thought — stumbling to bed at night, more mentally tired than she had been when Charlie was a newborn — the operation originally was a quest to make their lives easier and Charlie less of a victim and more normalised, then she wasn't sure that it had done that. For Charlie's eyes still drew attention to him, perhaps more so now that there was something curious there that people couldn't quite work out.

Implants, Twyla wanted to tell them. But she said nothing. She couldn't spend the rest of her life second-guessing the insults or musings from everyone they encountered. At some point in the future, Charlie would have to deal with that himself. Maybe he would get used to it and just shake hands and say, *Hi, I'm Charlie and I've got implants in my eyes because my mother was determined for me to see.*

If she was lucky, that was what he would say.

She hadn't gone back to the support group yet. The group was for blind children and Charlie could see, albeit artificially. Did that count? Were you always blind if born blind, despite medical intervention thereafter? Or were you only blind if you couldn't see?

Ofelia kept telling her she was overthinking it, that she should come back to the group anyway. But Twyla remained unsure. It mattered to her which side of the fence they were on, where they fitted in.

She had discussed the matter with the health visitor and social worker who didn't find her feelings odd in the slightest. There was no easy answer, they both agreed. Twyla could try the support group and see how it worked out, or she could try a standard playgroup.

But, Twyla thought, what about the germs that Charlie could pick up from being amongst free-range toddlers with runny noses and conjunctivitis and impetigo?

'You're worrying far too much,' her father said. 'It'll all get easier. Even in a few months' time, you'll be down to fewer specialist appointments and Charlie won't be wearing his eye shields.'

They were at the park, setting up the

deckchairs underneath the elm. Stephen had just bought some toy skittles, which Charlie was assembling on the grass a few yards from them.

'But he'll always need the antibiotics,' Twyla said.

'Yes,' her father replied, sitting down in his deckchair. 'So long as he can see.'

She fell silent. He had made his point.

Was it a fair trade: lifelong antibiotics for lifelong vision?

Possibly. Probably.

So long as there were no other complications, which so far there had not been. The more time went by, the greater the chance that the operation had been a success. Yet there were many potential disasters lurking on the sidelines. For the rest of their lives, so long as the implants remained in his eyes they would be dealing with unknowns. Would the implants stay in place? Would Charlie's vision deteriorate? Would he one day grow tired of self-administering the eye drops, of the recoiling of potential girlfriends, of the judgement and repulsion that he would not have seen or cared about had he remained blind? Would he one day decide to just stop, to undo his mother's work and reclaim his natural state?

Charlie was rolling the ball towards the skittles. He managed to knock four down and turned to look at them for approval. They both clapped enthusiastically. 'Atta boy, Charlie!' Stephen said. And then he lowered his voice. 'A few weeks ago, he couldn't do that. And now look . . . '

She watched as Charlie knocked down the

remaining two skittles. It was a still afternoon with barely a breeze to stir the treetops, but it was cold. They were wearing winter coats for the first time since summer.

'Do you think he's happy he can see?' she said.

'Impossible to say,' Stephen said. 'Why do you ask?'

'He just seems so indifferent.'

'Indifferent?' he said, tilting his head to one side to consider his grandson. 'No, I wouldn't say so. He simply doesn't know any better.'

'What do you mean?'

'Only that he might think it's a natural progression,' said Stephen. 'He might think that every child is blind until twenty-two months old and then the lights come on. It's what happens with everything else — their ability to walk or talk, for example.'

'I hadn't thought of that,' she said.

Charlie was setting up his game again. Perhaps all this was part of a game too. Lights on, lights off. Peek-a-boo. Now you see me, now you don't.

'Just give it time,' Stephen said, standing up and fixing his plaid scarf around his neck in one suave well-executed gesture.

Was she like that? she thought. Was she someone who was swish and smooth, adjusting things with a flick of her hand?

She thought of her badly sewn swimming badges clogging the drains in the pool, and guessed not.

Maybe she was more like her mother, someone who didn't click a finger to get things done, so much as drag and fight and beg and plead.

Was that what her mother had been like? Twyla shrugged to herself. She couldn't say for sure, although she suspected that her mother had had a lot of off days.

'How's about a coffee and a brownie, huh?' her father said.

'OK,' she said.

She felt cold and miserable. Nothing felt like she had imagined it would.

'It's all right,' he said. 'You're going to get through this.' He smiled, his eyes creasing in the corners. He didn't often smile, ought to more often. 'Someone once told me the exact same thing on the worst day of my life,' he added. 'I didn't believe him either.'

She looked up at him with curiosity. 'When was the worst day of your life?' she asked.

'I'll tell you some other time.'

She watched him walking to the café. There were a few people sitting at the tables and chairs, pigeons pecking at their feet. He joined a queue, gazing up at the sky.

She knew exactly what the worst day of his life had been, who it was that he saw up there in the clouds. But still they couldn't talk about it.

She was sinking deeper into her coat dejectedly, when she felt a small hand on hers and Charlie was stood there holding out a splendidly red leaf to her.

'Is that for me?' she asked.

Charlie placed it delicately on her lap. 'Leaf,' he said.

'Oh, Charlie,' she said, pulling him towards her and cuddling him, his cold cheek pressed against hers. 'I love you.'

What did it matter — whether Charlie was officially still blind? Whether she was good at sewing, or fixing scarves to her neck in one move? Whether she was like her mother or her father?

No one was like anyone. No one was clumsy or suave, unless they told themselves they were.

Everyone was just muddling through each day — picking leaves, sewing badges, fixing scarves, raising children, doing their best.

'We'll get there, Charlie,' she said, pulling his knitted hat down to keep his ears warm.

And then Charlie spotted his grandfather returning with the brownies, and he pulled free of her and sped off through the fallen leaves, his legs going like pistons at a pace that she would scarcely have believed possible.

* * *

Her father fitted in with their routine more than she could have anticipated, ferrying them to appointments, taking them on outings. He had cleared his schedule, consulting with patients by phone when required.

Whenever Charlie took his daytime nap, she ventured out to the workshop. Her father joined her, sat in the wicker chair, typing on his laptop but not seeming very productive. Today, a wet Friday, he was particularly restless. His fingers had stilled on the keyboard. She could

324

feel him looking at her.

'I think I should go home,' he said.

She stopped working, lay the torch down on the kiln shelf and straightened her back, putting her hand to her neck to stretch it.

'Hmm,' she said, absently.

'It's for the best,' he said, closing his laptop with a click. 'My being here makes your situation more abnormal, as though you're convalescing. When in fact you're doing extremely well.'

She picked up the ball and checked the hook's strength. It seemed good. She put the ball to one side and picked up the next one.

'Do you mind if I take off now to avoid the rush?' he asked.

She looked at him surprise. 'Now? Oh . . . I . . . ' He was packing up his laptop and was waiting for her response.

'I'll stay if you want me to,' he said.

'Oh,' she said. 'No. It's OK.'

He was right. She couldn't keep him here indefinitely. 'I'll just make you up some sandwiches for — '

'No need,' he said, opening the door of the workshop. 'I'll be home well in time for supper if I go now.'

She put down her work and followed him into the house.

At the front door, he reached for his Italian wool coat from the peg where it had rested for the past fortnight. She had liked seeing it there, had peeked inside its fine exterior to see its label. It was part cashmere and smelt faintly of cedar wood and of the city.

He pressed a kiss on her forehead, before opening the front door. 'You're going to be fine,' he said. 'You're strong. You've got a system in place and you've got Dylan. And you've got me at the other end of the phone. I can be here in a matter of hours.'

He walked down the steps to his Mercedes.

'I'll call you at eight,' he said, as the car eased away with a crunch of gravel.

She nodded and returned indoors, feeling rather mournful as she headed back out to her workshop.

★　★　★

Dylan had gone to the police station last night as usual, but they had nothing to tell him. Their most recent line of inquiry into an eye surgeon in Newcastle had led nowhere. It was frustrating and disheartening. Life was moving on; the police's attention was being drawn elsewhere. Dylan could feel the case slipping away, becoming less of a priority, yet there was nothing he could do about it.

Twyla seemed happier. The Molly situation had dissipated without further discussion. And Charlie's recent appointment with the specialist eye team had gone well. They were to carry on doing what they were doing.

But there still remained the trauma they had endured during Charlie's absence, and the fact that he had told Twyla he would blame her if he didn't find someone else to blame.

He didn't feel that way now — had told Twyla

many times that it wasn't so. Yet in order to move on, he needed the truth. He couldn't spend the rest of his life wondering who had done this to them and why.

Today, the first of November, was an unproductive day in the office. A few of the staff were going out tonight so were dressed up more than usual and concentrating less. Dylan found himself gazing out the window lethargically, before deciding to give up and take the day off.

He was almost home when he thought of what his mother had said about him taking matters into his own hands and knocking on Collins's door.

Was that so crazy an idea? Surely it was worth a try. So, instead of turning on to Orchard Drive, he went straight ahead to Midsomer Norton.

He stopped outside Collins's house and turned off the car engine. As he did so, he saw a shape at the window, a twitch of the curtains. It made him shudder slightly and he sat for a few moments, gathering his thoughts.

Collins wouldn't want to see him, would be obstructive. He had to find a way around that.

He knocked on the door and waited, setting his face to a peaceful expression, with some effort. *Good morning*, he practised in his mind. But when Collins came to the door in his brown cardigan, with traces of milk at his mouth and a posture that could only be described as wavering, Dylan found himself thrown off course. All pleasantries escaped him. This reptile was somehow involved in the abduction; Dylan just knew it.

As anticipated, Collins didn't invite him in. Instead, he stepped out and closed the door behind him, glancing up at the sky and rubbing his hands as though expecting rain. 'You're the Ridley man,' he said.

'Could I please come in for a minute?' Dylan said.

Collins glanced behind him at the door, as though it were a wife whose feelings he needed to consult. 'I don't think that's a good idea.'

From a distance, the sound of an ambulance siren cut through the air. The vehicle approached, tearing down the hill at the end of the road. It made Dylan feel as though everything was suddenly urgent, of life and death importance.

'I really need your help,' Dylan said.

'Why should I help you?' Collins asked churlishly.

'Because,' Dylan said, 'I need to know why my son was abducted.'

Collins clasped his hands together in a prayer-like fist; a mixed metaphor if ever Dylan saw one.

'I'm tired of this,' Collins said. 'I wish to lead a good life with my Lord. I don't wish to be troubled in this manner.'

'Then help me,' Dylan said. 'You'll never lead a good life with God, if you don't — '

'How dare you talk to me about God?' Collins said. He flicked at Dylan with his hand. 'Get off my property! Now!'

'I didn't mean to offend you,' Dylan said. 'Please help me. You're my only hope. Without you there's — '

But he didn't get the chance to finish his plea because Collins had retreated indoors, slamming the door behind him.

Dylan slumped his shoulders, dejected.

So that was that.

He got into his car and drove back to Bath. On the way, as he passed the signpost to Priston village he recalled that it was where the detective sergeant lived. Last night at the station they had mentioned that the sergeant was out for the rest of the week on leave. Dylan had his address somewhere, had seen it written down. He thought about it. It was on the card the sergeant had given him when they first met; a personal one so that they could contact him at any time. He fished for his wallet now in his jacket and pulled the card out. Then he turned around and went back the way he had come, turning off at the Priston signpost.

He pulled into the overgrown driveway and gazed at the dark-windowed cottage beyond. The sergeant's car was there.

He got out of the Honda and went to the door, wondering only at the last minute what he was going to say, what exactly he was doing there.

The sergeant answered the door politely, but hesitantly. Perhaps he was worried what fresh trouble Dylan was bringing, or that his lunch would go cold. From beyond him came the smell of bacon cooking.

'Come on in,' the sergeant said. He led Dylan through to a study and flicked on a desk lamp, motioning for Dylan to take a seat in an armchair, whilst he sat in a twin one opposite. 'So what's up?'

'I'm sorry to come here like this,' Dylan said. 'But I made a promise to my wife, or at least to myself, that I'd find out what happened to Charlie. And, well . . . ' He held up his hands and dropped them with a dismal slap on to his legs.

'It's all right,' said the sergeant. 'I'm only sorry that we've not been able to resolve things for you. It's an highly unusual case — one that's had us all confounded.'

Dylan nodded, glanced around the room — at the bookcase, photographs, oil paintings of rural scenes. 'Collins was a doctor, wasn't he?' Dylan asked, his eye setting on a portrait of a man in soldier's uniform.

'Yes. At a hospital in Bristol. He had a breakdown apparently and hasn't worked since.'

A door opened out in the hallway. The sergeant's head twitched in that direction, and then the door closed again and he turned back to Dylan.

'Why did he have a breakdown?' Dylan asked.

'Why does anyone ever have one?' the sergeant said. 'Work-related stress, he said.'

'But what if he lost his job because of malpractice,' Dylan said. 'And then he had a breakdown?'

The sergeant sighed. 'There's nothing to that effect on record. He wasn't struck off. Or, if he was, then it was very well hidden. We've got nothing on him.'

Dylan felt his spirits sink again.

So Collins was clean. But there must be something else, something they were all missing. It was impossible to do something like this without a trace. There had to be a trail of some sort, some minuscule error that they were overlooking.

He looked at the reams of paperwork on the sergeant's desk, at the files and books on the shelves beyond. 'Do you have anything here on the case that I could look at?' Dylan asked.

The sergeant glanced at his desk. 'I've got some bits here, but you won't find anything worth knowing, bearing in mind that we've had experts going through it. Plus I'm not allowed to share the information with you.'

'But what if you were to go have your bacon and I was to have a look without your consent?'

The sergeant stared at him so steadfastly that Dylan lost his nerve and looked away. His eye settled on the painting of the soldier again. That was a man who looked as though he knew the importance of integrity, of knowing the truth.

'Three minutes,' the sergeant said, standing up. 'That's all you've got.'

★ ★ ★

She was missing her father.

She had discovered a new side to him during their time together in the workshop — a soothing, nostalgic side. The space was imbued with him now, so much so that she liked to sit there even when she wasn't working, watching the dust swimming in the sunlight.

In the sunbeams, she could see her family in Jefferson — the rope swing in the back garden, the summersweet shrubs in tubs, the neighbour's yellow car that smelt of petrol and coughed its way along the streets in a cloud of dust. Her mother drove with one hand on the wheel and the other on her bola necklace. If they went over a bump or a pothole in the road, the necklace jingled.

Twyla wondered what Stephen's memory of her was, how she appeared to him now.

There were no ghostly chains and white sheets in Twyla's experience. Her father's story might have been different. Maybe her mother moaned and cursed to him. Twyla would never know.

Perhaps that was the best way — for recollections to be personal, undisclosed. You got so little from the deceased, it wasn't fair or practical to spread the meagre memories out amongst others.

Her mother came to her as more of an energy than a being. She appeared in a raindrop wobbling on a leaf, in the gleam of a seagull's wing in sunshine, in the creaking of a tree, in the heat of an old car, in the jingle of a bola charm.

Twyla straightened the cushion in the empty wicker chair. And then she picked up her work and continued where she had left off.

★ ★ ★

When he saw it in the file, he was amazed no one had noticed it. Yet it was at the back, lost amongst pages of evidence and pointless data. It could only have been found by someone obsessed, some-one who couldn't sleep until they found it.

It was a newspaper article that had been photocopied several times, each time losing definition. The photograph was fuzzy and indistinct, but the text was still good. The article was about a leukaemia fund-raising social, at which one of the prominent guests was one Doctor Stanley Collins.

Doctor Collins, wearing a tuxedo, was seated directly in front of the camera. There were twenty or so men and women in evening attire around him, plus a dozen others standing at the back, their faces dots of ink on the page.

So it was a wonder that he noticed. Certainly it was because he was fixated with uncovering the truth, but it was also because he had the first-hand knowledge of knowing someone on personal terms.

He could forgive the experts their oversight.

Perhaps it was the angle of the head, the width of the chest. The hair was different — bushy, instead of sleek.

He didn't really know what it was, how he had known instantly that it was him.

Yet there he was. Standing at the back, with his head above everyone else, was Stephen Thibodeaux.

★ ★ ★

November in Stockholm was almost as cold as last Christmas had been. He had some business to tend to and Juliet couldn't get away from work so he was travelling alone. He was too early for St Lucia's Day. He could scarcely believe that it was almost a year ago that he had beheld that life-changing vision. Yet as he stepped into Sergels torg, into the public square with its floor of black and white triangles, like a distorted chessboard, he could almost see the girls again in their white dresses with their candles in the snow. And now instead of heartburn, he felt happiness.

He had just been to Leksaker, the antique toy shop again. It was the same assistant behind the counter. She rattled off the worn stock phrases that she used to court the tourists. 'It's a beauty,' she said. 'It is for someone special?'

'Yes,' he said, as before. But this time he added, 'It's for my grandson, Charlie Ross.'

She nodded politely, perhaps to cease the conversation, but he was keen to elaborate. 'He'll be two on Christmas Day. I promised him the best train set I could find. He's very bright and curious about everything, you know?'

She smiled. 'Five thousand krona, please,' she said, putting her hand out flat, like feeding a horse.

Carrying the train set carefully through the crowds, he made his way to his favourite spot in Stockholm, the Opera Bar — an aristocratic gentlemen's club of sorts, set in the same building as the Royal Swedish Opera. Manhattan may have left him behind many years ago, but his penchant for the finest things in life had not. Taking a seat beside the window, he admired the view across the water to the Royal Palace.

Could he remember having ever felt so content? The sun was dancing on the water, spotlights were sparkling on the ceiling, setting off the art nouveau canopy.

He would celebrate with his favourite salt-cured salmon, followed by warm cloudberries with ice cream, and a drop of Clos du la Coulée de Serrant 2003.

The waitress was moving to clear the other cutlery at his table. 'Leave them, please,' he said.

'You not alone?' she said in broken English.

'No,' he said. 'Someone's joining me shortly.'

★　★　★

Dylan pushed the press cutting into his pocket and left the sergeant to his bacon with feigned disappointment, saying that he hadn't found anything. And now he was driving home in a hurry.

Twyla was in the workshop when he got back. He could see her through the shed windows. Charlie would be having his afternoon nap. He grabbed Twyla's address book and set off, closing his car door behind him as quietly as possible.

Night was just falling as he turned off past the ponds on Hampstead Heath and came to a sudden halt in front of security gates.

He checked the address book, which was lying flat out on the seat beside him, like an exhausted travel companion.

'Highfields View', said Twyla's neat handwriting.

It was definitely this one.

A sharp rap on the window made him jump. A man in uniform motioned for him to lower the window. 'Evening,' the man said. 'Can I help you?'

'Hopefully,' said Dylan. 'I'm here to see Stephen Thibodeaux.'

'He's expecting you?'

'Not exactly. I'm his son-in-law.'

'One moment.' The man went to his glass cubicle at the side of the gate to make a call.

The gate began to slowly rise.

Dylan drove along the road trying not to feel awestruck. About twenty detached houses were stood in line, watching him. Stephen's was right at the end, overlooking the heath.

He got out of the Honda and stood with his back against it, gazing up at Stephen's impressive house. It was a brown-brick with huge windows. The gardens were vast and landscaped, sloping up to the front door.

Then he saw Juliet coming down the garden steps towards him, calling out to him. Of course — the man had just phoned them. They were expecting him. Stephen was standing in the doorway of his house, stiff and upright, like a Grenadier Guard.

'Park around here, Dylan,' Juliet was shouting, waving her hand.

He got back in the car feeling stupid. There wouldn't be on-road parking in a place like this. He could see the driveway now, behind the house, underneath a line of young oak trees.

Dylan drove round to the back of the house, to

the turning circle and two-door garage.

Juliet came forward to greet him. He had forgotten how small she was. She was dressed all in orange, like a tiny satsuma.

'What a lovely surprise!' she said, holding out her hands. 'And beautifully timed too. Stephen just got back from Stockholm twenty minutes ago. But let's not stand out here in the cold.' She ushered him towards the house with a sweeping motion of her hands.

As Dylan entered the house, Stephen extended his hand in greeting. 'Good to see you,' Stephen said.

'Stephen,' Dylan said, nodding.

It was warm inside the house. Dylan did his best not to gape at the polished floorboards, the bending staircase and crystal chandelier.

He took his boots off dutifully, like a well-trained child and followed his father-in-law into the lounge, whilst Juliet busied herself in the kitchen.

The lounge was predictably immaculate. The only thing awry was a large carrier bag from some place called Leksaker that was standing in the middle of the room and which Stephen promptly removed from sight.

'Do take a seat,' said Stephen.

Dylan sat down on the edge of a grey-blue armchair and looked about him at the gilt-framed paintings of coastlines and the Persian rugs.

It had just started to rain, pattering above him. He looked up to see a large domed skylight in the ceiling.

'Bourbon?' Stephen asked, reaching for a decanter on the side table.

'No, thank you,' said Dylan.

He watched as his father-in-law poured a drink and knocked it back in one before stretching himself to full height in a dignified yet oddly menacing way.

'So to what do we owe the pleasure?' Stephen said.

'I . . . uh . . . '

Juliet came in with a clatter of china on a tray. Dylan looked at her little orange shoes, feeling sorry for her — for driving all the way here to interrupt her peace. 'Shortbread!' Juliet said. 'I forgot shortbread.' And she hurried from the room again.

Dylan took advantage of her absence and pulled the press cutting from his back pocket. 'Here,' he said, unfolding it and handing it to Stephen. 'I found this in the police files.'

Stephen didn't take the paper, merely glanced at it.

'I didn't realise you knew Collins,' Dylan said.

The rain was coming down heavier on the skylight. Juliet had returned and was hovering behind them.

'I don't know him,' Stephen replied, pouring another drink, dropping ice from a pair of silver tongs into his glass.

'Then how do you explain this photograph?'

'It's possible to be in a crowded room without being acquainted with everyone present,' Stephen said.

Juliet stepped forward. 'Wasn't — ?'

'It's all right, Juliet,' said Stephen. 'I've got this.'

But then ever so softly, Stephen's hand began to tremble, clinking the ice in the bourbon. Stephen quickly stilled his hand, but it was too late.

'Oh, Christ,' Dylan said, his heart lurching in realisation. 'It was you, wasn't it? You took Charlie.'

22

Stephen went so grey in the face, Dylan thought he had killed the man — that he was going to have a cardiac arrest and die on the floorboards of his grand living room. But his loss of poise was momentary. Once he had sat down and was sipping bourbon, he soon recovered. But the room was desperately quiet now that the rain had stopped. No one seemed able to break the silence.

It was Juliet who spoke first, her hands lightly pressed together. 'You have to understand the whole story,' she said. 'It's not quite what it seems.'

'Then tell me,' said Dylan, who realised that all the way here in the car he had been hoping for some simple explanation and not this horrible one.

No one was forthcoming.

A gold clock chimed on the mantelpiece — a clock with all its inner workings showing. Dylan watched the pendulum swaying and the highest of four small cogs slowly turning. The cogs with their circular shape and jagged edges reminded him of Charlie's artificial eyes.

He sat down in the nearest chair and held his hand to his head. He was beginning to get a bad headache.

'How do you know Collins?' he asked.

Juliet went to Stephen and stood behind him,

with her hand on the top of his handsome leather armchair. It seemed incongruous — a man of Stephen's stature needing someone as petite as Juliet for security.

'Stephen was briefly affiliated to the hospital where Collins was based some fifteen years ago,' Juliet said. 'It was when Twyla was studying in Bristol. Stephen made some professional connections in the area in case Twyla decided to settle there. But Stephen and Collins didn't ever officially meet.'

Dylan gazed at Stephen who was staring into space as though incapable of speech. It was like an odd reversal, where the puppeteer was seated and the little puppet was standing behind, speaking.

'One of Collins's patients died. Malpractice was suspected, but the hospital was under threat of closure so the matter was dealt with as quietly as possible. Collins retired soon after.'

Juliet paused. She dropped her hand from the top of the armchair to Stephen's shoulder. Stephen, motionless, silent, didn't react.

'There's no other connection between the two men. Just a brief association years ago. A tragic death in a hospital. A sudden retirement.'

Juliet touched her hair as though checking it was still there. She had the sort of hairstyle that suggested her hair was running thin, puffed up by spray. Dylan felt sorry for her once more. He didn't like to upset small people, especially females. And yet was that fair to the big-boned, the tall? Wasn't everyone the same inside — full of the same twisting cogs, like that fancy golden clock? Wasn't Stephen, the giant, suffering too? Looking at him now, it was impossible to say.

'Back in the summer, when Twyla told Stephen about the anonymous hate mail, he set about trying to find out who was bullying her. The Proverbs quotation led him to All Saints and so he visited them with the intention of having a word, and was surprised to discover Collins there, painting the church door.'

Dylan thought of All Saints — of the picturesque building with its iron gate and lamp. How often he had driven past it, walked past whilst Charlie was missing. Quiet, locked up, the church — their only lead — had seemed excruciatingly cryptic.

'They knew each other from photographs, having once worked in the same circles. Collins looked horrified to see him. So Stephen left without saying what he had come to say.'

She squeezed Stephen's shoulder. The action seemed to wake Stephen, stir him. He looked about him as though confused, before finishing his bourbon in one motion. Then he shifted in his seat and looked sternly at Dylan. 'Twyla rang me in a terrible state five days before the operation,' he said.

'She did?' Dylan said, frowning. He tried to think when that was. Five days before the operation . . . It would have been the Saturday night — the night he heard Twyla crying upstairs to someone.

'It was you?' he said, staring at his father-in-law. And then he considered it some more. 'You?'

Stephen nodded. 'I'd never heard my daughter in such a state before.' His voice faltered. There went Juliet's hand on his shoulder again — the squeeze. Dylan watched, intrigued, disconcerted.

'It shocked me,' Stephen said. 'And I realised then just how serious the situation had become, how dangerous.'

'Dangerous?' Dylan asked, feeling his palms dampen, the hairs on his neck rising. He shifted in his seat, prepared himself for what was to come. Why was he suddenly feeling accountable, guilty?

'Because she was the only one who wanted the operation,' Stephen replied.

And there it was.

The rain began to fall again, pattering softly on the skylight, like lost souls knocking to be let in.

Dylan thought of the mental battle he had fought that night — of the indecision and eventual resolution; of how he had told Twyla to go for it, that he was behind her.

Yet had he been too late by that point? What had his indecision already set in motion?

He looked again at the cogs of the clock, at the swinging of the pendulum and wanted to sweep it off the mantelpiece, to stop its incessant movement.

'The operation was going to destroy your marriage,' Stephen said.

'But how?' Dylan said. 'We were all set. I gave Twyla my blessing, was fully committed to it.'

'Yes,' Stephen replied. 'And had it been a disaster, you would have blamed her.'

Dylan stared at Stephen, unable to reply.

He felt his head swell with anguish, his mouth run dry. He sat back heavily in his chair as though winded.

Only a few weeks ago he had told Twyla the same thing — that he would blame her. Wasn't that why he was here now, looking for someone to point at other than his wife?

'I took Charlie,' Stephen said. 'I facilitated the operation, removed Twyla from blame. Had the surgery failed, it would have been on my hands, not hers.'

Once more a silence fell over the room. Juliet dispelled the shadows by flicking on the reading lamp at Stephen's side.

'But how?' Dylan asked. 'Who did the operation?'

'I only had a few days to act,' Stephen said. He stood, went to his decanter again and removed the glass stopper. 'Fortunately, I'd already done some research into eye surgeons — as soon as Twyla mentioned her interest in keratoprosthesis surgery.'

He didn't say this arrogantly, but factually, wearily. He didn't seem quite so big at the moment, Dylan observed, not quite so sure of himself. He was pronging the ice tentatively from the ice bucket, like trying to clasp wet eels.

The idea of a drink suddenly appealed. 'I'll take that bourbon now, if that's all right,' Dylan said.

'Of course,' Stephen said.

'I'll do it,' Juliet said, appearing at Stephen's side. 'You sit down.'

Stephen didn't return to his armchair, but stood in front of the window with his back to them, his frame blocking the little daylight that remained. Lights were coming on in the vast garden along the paths — fairy lights that lit the way, like an airfield runway.

'A friend of mine from Harvard is close friends with Dr Sigbert Ambramsson,' Stephen said. 'Ambramsson's been at the forefront of keratoprosthesis surgery since the seventies. He was more than happy to participate. He was very interested in this particular case, having not operated on someone Charlie's age before. I met with him today in Stockholm so that we could discuss Charlie's progress. Ambramsson's keen to stay in touch, but I'm naturally cautious about doing so.'

Dylan was clutching his bourbon glass. There was a lot of ice. His fingers were growing numb. He took a sip, wincing as the spirit met his empty stomach.

'But how did you do it without a trace?' he asked. 'The police were thorough. They must have contacted this Ambramsson man.'

Stephen turned to face him briefly. 'Money, Dylan,' he said.

'Bribes?' Dylan said, feeling his fringe go back on his forehead.

'No.' Stephen's mouth formed a strained smile. 'I paid an extortionate amount of money to Ambramsson and his staff to buy their discretion — to fake alibis, cover trails. Our security guard registers every visitor to Highlands View. Charlie's arrival in a tinted car with

345

an eye surgeon didn't make the system.'

'You did it here?' said Dylan, looking about him.

'Yes,' said Stephen.

'Oh, God.'

Dylan put his drink down and held his head in his hands. The idea of Charlie being driven here with some Swedish surgeon, of being operated on surrounded by strangers. The general anaesthetic. The fear of not knowing where he was, of not recognising the voices around him. Would he have known Stephen's voice by then? Dylan tried to think. How much time had Charlie spent with his grandfather at that point? Did they reassure him, tell him who they were, why he was there, where his parents were?

'Oh, God,' Dylan said again, rocking himself.

Juliet approached and stood before him, her mouth taut with sympathy. She was wearing orange lipstick — orange like her shoes and clothes.

'The operation was carried out with maximum efficiency and care, Dylan,' she said. 'Dr Ambramsson was the best man in the world for the job. We got him everything he needed including a full medical team to assist him, as well as Charlie during recovery.'

'Were you there?' he asked.

'Yes,' she said. 'I made certain that Charlie was comfortable, that he felt safe. I would never have let anything happen to him. Nor would Stephen.'

She pulled a handkerchief from her pocket and sniffed. Then she turned and began fiddling with a vase of orchids, removing one of the blooms that was past its best. As she did so, pollen sprinkled all over the floor.

Dylan had never liked orchids — found them messy, damp-looking, insipid. The thought of which reminded him of someone.

'What about Collins?' he asked. 'How does he fit in?'

Stephen spoke over his shoulder. 'The man's full of guilt and remorse. All Saints knew nothing of his past. I guessed as much the moment that we met after all those years — the way he recoiled from me on the steps of his church.'

'It didn't take much to persuade him to help,' Juliet said.

'By doing what?' Dylan said.

'By being on your doorstop at the right time,' she replied.

'I phoned the church and spoke to him,' Stephen said. 'I told him that I was concerned about my daughter and the impending operation, that she could use some religious instruction. There were two conditions: to call round at a precise time, and to say nothing of my having asked him to do so.'

'And he did it to protect his secret?' Dylan asked.

'That and to have an opportunity to preach to a sinner, to possibly prevent an operation that he saw as morally reprehensible.'

'And that was it?' asked Dylan. 'He knew nothing about the abduction?'

'No,' Stephen said.

Dylan picked up his bourbon again and took a long drink.

'You had no right,' he said, staring at

Stephen's back. 'No right to operate on our son without our consent, without us being there for him.'

'I know,' Stephen said.

'I know?' Dylan said. 'That's all you can say? I mean, how could you do that to your own daughter?'

The question seemed to tear right through Stephen. He put his hand to his heart, his knees bending.

'Stephen!' Juliet darted forward and helped him to his chair.

Dylan was astounded. It occurred to him that there was more to it than he realised — that maybe the old man was ill or dying.

Juliet grabbed a throw and placed it over Stephen's lap, tucking it either side of him. But Stephen pulled it off in agitation and twisted in his seat to address Dylan.

'I'm terribly sorry, Dylan,' he said.

The apology sounded heartfelt. Dylan wanted to comfort him. It seemed mean, persecuting an old man in his own home. Yet the crime was too personal, too painful. Dylan couldn't let go of his anger, from the deep sense of someone having wronged him. 'Just tell me why you did it,' he said.

Stephen paused, his eyebrows lifting as though it were a silly question. 'For Twyla, of course.'

Dylan gazed at Stephen and Juliet in turn.

It didn't make sense. It felt as though there were bits missing. Why would Stephen have done this? Why would someone of his profession think doing something like this was even remotely sane?

'Stephen wanted to do something for Twyla,' Juliet said.

'And he did,' Dylan said. 'He donated the money.'

'But that wasn't enough,' Juliet said.

'Not enough money?' Dylan said.

'Not enough to compensate — '

'Don't,' Stephen said, holding up his hand.

'Compensate for what?' Dylan asked.

But the subject was closed.

A silence fell.

Dylan turned away, unable to look at either of them any more.

'There's nothing Stephen wouldn't have done for his only child,' Juliet said. 'Surely you can understand that?'

Dylan stood up and made his way to the door, feeling incapable of driving home, of the journey ahead.

'What will you do, Dylan?' she called after him.

He knew what she meant. She was asking if he was going to tell the police. But, in truth, he didn't know what he was going to do.

'She'll never forgive you,' he said instead.

'Then she must never know,' Stephen replied.

Dylan turned to stare at his father-in-law in astonishment. 'You really expect me to keep something like this from her?' he said, angrily. 'I thought this was about protecting our marriage. A secret like this will destroy it.'

'Which is why you weren't supposed to find out,' Stephen said.

Dylan gazed at him, suppressing the perverse

desire to laugh. He thought again of the clown he had pictured on Charlie's return, when his adrenalin and sense of crisis was high.

This didn't feel like crisis, so much as pathos. But the clown with its painted smile and tears still fitted in well.

He shook his head. 'This is so screwed up,' he said.

'It's love,' Stephen said. 'In all its messy glory.'

★   ★   ★

All the way home, Dylan barely saw the catseyes on the tarmac, the rain on the windscreen, the fierce lights of approaching cars. Instead, he thought about the messy glorious love that Stephen had spoken of.

To him, love had always been a simple pleasure, like hot buttered toast, sunshine on a frosty day, skinny-dipping in the sea. His notion of love was rather like those cartoons he had noted in his father's newspaper as a child: *Love Is* . . . a blanket, or a hug.

He didn't see why it had to be either messy or glorious. Perhaps he had rather missed the point — shouldn't have slept through *Romeo and Juliet* in GCSE English.

He gave a long sigh and turned his mobile back on. It beeped with messages. Twyla had been ringing him — was senseless with worry, she said. He rang her now, told her he had been called out urgently to see a client, that he would be home around ten and for her not to wait up if she was tired.

To his dismay, she was waiting up.

He hid the press cutting inside a road map in the glove compartment. The cutting was presumably the one piece of evidence linking Stephen to Collins.

Was his father-in-law right? Should Twyla be protected from this secret? Or would knowing who had abducted Charlie help her sleep at night, ease her mind? Once more, he felt the familiar agony of indecision. He hadn't expected to meet it again so soon, on such outrageous terms.

It all depended on how much she loved her father.

And there was no way of telling that, as he walked into the lounge and beheld his wife waiting for him.

'I'm sorry,' he said, tossing his jacket down. 'My client — '

'I know where you've been,' she said. She looked pretty with her blonde hair hanging around her face in wisps. She was wearing a pink jumper and purple jeans. He thought fleetingly of violet cream chocolates. They were Felicity's favourite.

'Hey?' he said. 'How do you know?'

'My father just rang.'

'Oh, Lord.' He sat down on the sofa, loosened his tie and threw it on the floor. Had he had anything else on his person, he would have thrown it down too, as though disarming himself. He was all out of power, energy, ideas.

'Dylan . . . ' She sat down beside him, her hands clasped on her lap.

'What did he tell you?' he asked.

'Everything,' she said.

'Everything?' he said, looking at her in alarm.

'Yes.'

She looked so controlled, contained. He didn't think he would be the same were it his mother. Although if it were his crazy mother, he would have expected it. But not Stephen . . . who had been a sort of demi-god in Dylan's eyes. Yet perhaps that was why Stephen had done this. People like him thought they could do what they liked.

Dylan's head was so crammed with thoughts, it felt too heavy to remain upright. He put his hand to his neck and rubbed it. His body was stiff from the harrowing journey, having barely moved a muscle the entire time.

'So what are you thinking?' he asked.

She shook her head. 'I don't know.'

'Me neither,' he said. 'But whatever you want to do, however you want to handle this, that's fine by me. I'll support you.'

She turned to him. 'I want to forget about it,' she said.

That wasn't quite what he had expected.

'OK . . . ' he said. 'Maybe that's your initial reaction. But once you've slept on it, you might — '

'No, Dylan,' she said, standing up, moving over to the window. They hadn't pulled the curtains yet. The yellow street light was casting ugly shadows on the walls.

He joined her. The rain was still falling, hadn't stopped the whole way home.

'If it was my family, I'd probably feel the same,' he said. He reached for her hand. 'But look what he did to us. Look what he put us through. Don't we need to address that?'

'You mean, tell the police?' she said.

'Yes . . . No . . . I don't know.'

She eased her hand from him and turned away. 'You don't understand,' she said, her voice small.

'Understand what?' he said, pulling her round to face him again. He brushed her hair from her eyes, tucking it in gently behind each ear.

'I knew,' she said. 'I knew about Charlie.'

★ ★ ★

As soon as she spoke, she felt Dylan backing away at great speed, even though he wasn't moving.

'Say something,' she said.

He was staring at her in horror. 'What do you mean, you knew?' he said.

'Dylan . . . ' she said, moving towards him.

He held up his hand. 'Stop! Don't touch me!'

'Let me explain. It's not what you think.'

'You knew your father was taking Charlie?'

'No,' she said.

'Then what?' he said, the whites of his eyes shining.

She had never seen him so scared, so angry. She thought frantically of how to say this, of how to explain before too much damage was done.

'I didn't know right away,' she said. 'I was as

petrified as you were when Charlie went missing.'

'So when?' Dylan said. 'When did you know?'

'Just before he came back,' she said. 'Literally. An hour or so before his return. My father took me out for the day, remember? The day they found the Jones boy in the river. He told me what he'd done, but he didn't give me any details. He said the less I knew, the less incriminated I'd be.'

She stepped forward to him again, tried to touch him. 'Please, Dylan. You have to believe me. I didn't — '

'I said, don't touch me!' he shouted, yanking his arm away from her. He looked about him wildly, as though searching for facts. 'So you knew an hour before he came back?'

'Yes. But I — '

'But that was — ' he looked about him again ' — a month and a half ago. You let me worry all that time? You let me keep going to the police and going over and over the case, driving myself half mad?'

'It wasn't like that,' she said. 'I couldn't tell you because I was worried you'd tell the police.'

'So you let me suffer instead?' he said.

'Well, what else was I supposed to do?'

'If you'd have told me,' he shouted, 'I could have helped you figure that out!'

'But I *couldn't* tell you!' she shouted back. 'I've already told you that! I couldn't hand my father over to the police! And I was trying to work out how I felt about it myself and what to do about it. Don't you understand? He told me, and then Charlie came back and I had to face the police, and look after Charlie.' She put her hands to her forehead and pressed her temples, reliving the stress that she was recalling. 'It was all too much. And I was livid with my father! When he came down to help afterwards, we had a humongous argument. I told him I never wanted to see him again.'

She sank down on to the sofa, her throat sore from shouting.

'So what changed?' Dylan said quietly.

'What do you mean?' she said, looking up.

'Well, he stayed on in Bath for two weeks. Plus you're obviously talking now.'

She thought about that. 'Because I knew that deep down he was trying to help.'

'By taking our son?'

'By protecting me,' she replied.

There was a pause.

'When I became a mum,' she said, plucking a tissue from the box beside her and shredding it slowly, 'I thought it was about right and wrong. About doing things the right way. But . . . '

'What?'

'It's not about that at all.'

'Well, thanks for the parenting lesson,' he said. 'But what's — ?'

'It wasn't supposed to turn out like this. Dad wasn't thinking about right or wrong. He was just doing the best he could.'

'Dad?' said Dylan. 'So it's 'Dad' now? It was 'Stephen' not so long ago. Do you remember that, Twyla?'

'Yes, I do,' she said. 'But then he started to

355

make a real effort. He's actually been very supportive.'

Dylan's face changed at that — turned from anger to something else that she couldn't decipher.

'You rang him,' he said, resting his hands on the mantelpiece and bowing his head.

'Rang him?' she said.

'That night when you were upset about none of us wanting the operation, the night when you were crying on the phone . . . It was him that you turned to. And not me.'

She paused.

'Well, then I guess we're even,' she said.

'What's that supposed to mean?'

She shrugged. 'Molly?'

She shouldn't have said that. He swung around to face her, angry again. 'So this is how I'm punished?' he said. 'For not being sure about the operation? You go running to Daddy and he fixes it?'

'I wasn't punishing you, Dylan,' she said, standing up. 'And no, I didn't go running to Daddy. I wasn't in control of any of this.'

'But that's just it . . . ' His mouth sounded dry. His lips were cracked, sore-looking. It struck her that he had probably been on the move all day, hadn't rested or eaten. 'You *were* in control,' he said. 'Right from the start. It was you who wanted the operation, you who pushed for it and your father who got it for you. It had nothing to do with what I wanted, with what I was feeling.'

'But I consulted you every step of the way!'

she said. 'I cared so much about your feelings, about what you wanted for Charlie.'

He took a step towards her. 'So would you have cancelled it?' he asked.

'Cancelled what?'

'The operation. If I'd begged you to stop it, would you have?'

She stared at him. He stared back.

And then she moved away from him.

'Thought so,' he said.

She swung round. 'You can't ask me that!' she said. 'It's not fair! You know how much I wanted the operation for Charlie, how much I wanted him to be able to see.'

'Oh yes,' he said, laughing scornfully. 'We all know that.'

She sat down again, feeling suddenly depleted. 'I don't want to do this any more,' she said.

'Well, that makes two of us,' he said, making for the door.

'Where are you going?'

He didn't reply.

'It's all really about my mother,' she called after him.

He stopped, his hand on the door handle. 'What is?' he said.

'All of this,' she said, picking up a cushion and holding it in her arms. 'It's all to do with the fact that she . . . '

Twyla stopped. She had never said the words out loud before, not to herself, not to anyone.

'She what?' he said impatiently.

'She killed herself.'

There was a twang as he let the handle go.

'She drove her car deliberately into the lake,' she said, tossing the cushion aside. 'My father told me it was an accident. But I knew it was a lie. And I hated him for lying to me.'

'Oh, Christ,' Dylan said, sitting down on the arm of the sofa with a heavy sigh.

'I think he was more affected by Charlie's blindness than I realised. I think it set in motion some kind of reaction in him, long before he knew about the operation. It made him think, you know?'

Dylan nodded, but his expression didn't look as though he knew very much at all.

'He said several times that he wanted to help,' she said. 'I think it was because he wanted to make up for lying to me and for the rubbish relationship that we'd had for thirty years because of it. So when I rang him in tears about the operation, he did what he could to help. Did whatever it took.'

She stood up and approached, stopping just short of him. 'Which is what I was trying to say a minute ago — that being a parent isn't about right or wrong,' she said. 'That's why mums harbour their sons even when they're rapists. And my dad — in his own stupid way — was doing the same thing. Bending the law to protect his child . . . ' She trailed off.

Dylan looked lost. He was shaking his head.

'None of this makes sense to you?' she asked.

'God knows,' he said. 'I'm just amazed that you couldn't tell me about your mother before now.'

'It's not that amazing,' she said. 'I was five

when it happened. I buried it and kept it there. It's not so different from what you did with Felicity.'

He stared at her. 'It's totally different,' he said. 'I did tell you what happened with Fee — the basics. I'm not saying you have to spill your guts. It would have just been nice for you to confide in me, as your husband.' He stood up and made for the door again. 'But then after what I've found out tonight, I'm starting to realise that that was never going to happen.'

She followed him. 'Stop walking away from me,' she said. 'I feel as though you're always walking away from me!'

'That's because I need room to think,' he said.

He started up the stairs, three at a time.

She put her foot on the bottom step. 'Where are you going?' she whispered after him, conscious suddenly of Charlie asleep upstairs.

She listened. He was in their bedroom several minutes, moving quietly around so as not to disturb Charlie.

When he reappeared, he was carrying a holdall.

'What?' she said in shock. 'Where are you going?'

When he reached the bottom of the stairs, he brushed past her. 'Like I said — I need to think.'

'About what?' she said.

They were stood by the front door now, their voices rising again. 'About everything, Twyla!' he snapped. 'You don't seriously think I can pretend none of this has happened? Not even you, with your great acting and lying skills could — '

'I haven't lied,' she said. 'Not once have I ever lied to you.'

'Then I guess we need to redefine lies, along with everything else,' he said, reaching for his jacket.

She tugged on his sleeve. 'What about Charlie? What will I tell him when he wakes up tomorrow and you're not here?'

'You'll think of something,' he said.

He picked up the holdall and opened the front door. It was impossibly cold. The trees were bending in the wind, nudging towards the house as though trying to eavesdrop.

'You always said this would never happen,' she said. 'You always said you'd never leave me.'

He turned and looked at her. She sensed that he was about to tuck her hair behind her ears, that he was hesitating.

To her sorrow, he didn't move.

'I'm not definitely leaving, Twyla,' he said, tears appearing in his eyes. 'I just need some time, some space.'

His tears suddenly inflated the enormity of the moment, startled her into fully grasping what was happening.

'No,' she said, beginning to cry. 'You can't go. This was why I was upset that night on the phone to my dad — because I was worried I would lose you if I went ahead with the operation. The whole point of what he did was to stop this from happening. So you can't go. You can't let all this have been for nothing.'

'But it wasn't for nothing,' he said, wiping his eyes brusquely. 'Because Charlie can see. And that was all you really wanted. Right?'

She opened her mouth, which became filled immediately with cold winter air, with no space left for words.

'I'll call you tomorrow,' Dylan said, turning away.

She remained on the doorstep watching him — as he put the holdall into the passenger seat of the Honda, as he started the engine, glanced at her, and drove away.

23

They moved into the cottage that spring. There was no chain so everything moved quickly. They called the cottage Summersweet.

Growing outside the back door were red robin plants with leaves that glowed scarlet at the tips. Twyla recreated the sensory garden on the lawn. When the wind moved the chimes and released the scent of rosemary and thyme, it reminded her of where they had been and where they were now.

In the back garden, between two plum trees, was her workshop. Dylan had insisted on constructing it for her. It was bigger than the old shed, but its interior was replicated painstakingly.

He called round every other day to see Charlie. He was renting an apartment in town for the time being. Sometimes he took Charlie for a walk or for a milkshake. Mostly they just pottered, enjoying each other's company.

Charlie was thriving and far more confident in movement and in speech. He was able to run freely and everything began to flow at once as though oiled, with words coming along by the handful. He no longer needed the eye shields and had made several friends at a playgroup for children with a wide range of special needs.

The long-term prognosis remained unknown — whether the implants would prove durable, whether Charlie would reject them himself in years to come. His eyesight could go suddenly, or deteriorate over a matter of years and they would be back where they had started. And yet it would all be different because no one would be able to retract the visions that he was experiencing on a daily basis — the rainbows and dragonflies and hot air balloons that she had longed for him to see.

Stephen hadn't moved in with them right away. There was a pause as everything was negotiated. He had decided to move closer to them, even though it meant spending less time with Juliet who didn't want to leave London. He was wary of moving in with them, yet Twyla persuaded him.

Everything, from Charlie's eyesight to their living arrangements was tentative, on a temporary basis.

She still hoped that Dylan would come home. She often found herself sitting by the window of an evening, watching for him — not that he would show up like that, by dark, unannounced. Yet still she sat there. And besides, it passed the time. The nights were long, and the bed was achingly lonely.

Moving helped. There were no memories of Dylan here. But each time he visited, she felt herself drawing closer — to catch a part of him, to inhale his scent, to feel the warmth of his skin. But he was too far away, even though he was right beside her. Just like Bindy had warned her.

Bindy was on the other side of the world. Auckland, New Zealand was where her last postcard had arrived from. She had packed up her house in the new year and gone travelling, just like that.

Eileen was equally as distant, although still local. She visited for short periods, looking about the cottage as though trying to find something she recognised. She was put out by the new arrangement, by the fact that her son had been displaced by his father-in-law. It wasn't proper, her lips hinted but daren't say.

There had been no displacement, however. Her father had bought the cottage outright for Twyla and Dylan as a fresh start for them. It was Dylan who declined the offer, who suggested that Stephen move in instead to give Twyla support round the clock.

And it was this that kept Eileen away, Twyla suspected: the notion that Charlie's home wasn't a Ridley home now but a Thibodeaux one.

* * *

They were sitting outside one warm afternoon in April, one month after moving in, when Stephen remarked that he was surprised Twyla could remember the summersweet in Jefferson.

Charlie was playing on the swing that Dylan had built him. He couldn't swing himself yet, but liked to climb on it and wobble the ropes.

'Of course I do,' said Twyla. 'I remember more than you know.'

Stephen was thinner in the face. He slouched in his chair, as though he were less important nowadays. He was doing minimal hours at his practice, treating a handful of patients by webcam and phone.

She wasn't sure how she felt about him. She found herself watching him often. Sometimes their eyes met speculatively, before they both looked away again. But the fact was that they were sitting here now, co-existing, and there was something to be said for that.

'Coffee?' she asked.

'Please,' he said.

It was cool inside the cottage and tranquil. She had felt it the first moment she had stepped inside at the viewing last year with Charlie blind in her arms, holding his hands out around him as though touching ghosts.

There was only one ghost here that she knew of.

She reached forward to push the window open. Charlie was a few yards beyond. A robin was hopping about underneath the plum trees, pecking at the grass. Charlie spotted the bird and pointed at it excitedly.

'Wobbin!' he shouted. 'Wobbin!'

She saw her father jolt in his chair and turn to look for her. She moved away from the window, not wanting him to see her there.

So Charlie had learnt a new word. And it was her mother's name.

She frowned anxiously as she made the coffee.

There were some things that they still couldn't talk about. They couldn't talk about her, and they couldn't talk about that day.

And yet that was when she had become who she was now.

It was a day like any other, was shaping up exactly the same. Her dad had just left. The sun was hot. The next-door neighbours were with them. And her mum had borrowed the yellow car. Except that she didn't ask Twyla to go with her, and she gave Twyla a long hug goodbye. Which was odd, as she was just going on an errand. But her mum was prone to doing funny things, so Twyla got on with mending her doll's arm which was coming loose.

When Twyla heard that her mum wasn't coming back, that the yellow car had taken her off in an accident, that she was somewhere now that wasn't with them, she began to look for her elsewhere.

She didn't have to look far. That night when she peeled back her bed sheets, she saw something shining underneath her pillow.

There was the bola charm; her mother's necklace.

By taking her precious necklace off and leaving it there, her mother had told her that she wasn't coming back, that she had chosen not to come back, that it wasn't an accident at all.

Her father had lied. And her mother had deserted her.

And it was then that Twyla decided to choose something too, just like her mother had. Stood on the precipice of the worst abyss that her five-year-old mind could imagine, she chose not to jump but to have hope.

She had carefully put the necklace around her neck, whispered goodbye to her mother, and didn't tell a soul about what she had found. For she sensed even then that her hope was the most fragile thing possible. It was her secret. And if she told anyone about it then the hope might break.

In the end, it wasn't her optimism that broke when she finally told the secret, but her heart.

★   ★   ★

'Perhaps you could start by telling me how you felt at the beginning, Twyla,' he said.

She smiled.

In some ways, it was easier then, she told him. They were naive, finding things out for the first time.

'Does that mean that you wouldn't do it all again, Twyla? I'm sure everyone's curious to know the answer.'

She opened her mouth to reply. The reporter sat forward, pushing the recording device closer to her. The photographer was waiting in the background, leaning against the bookcase, one leg tucked over the other. From beyond the closed door, came the muffled sound of Charlie Ross laughing, followed by her father's laugh.

She took a deep breath. 'I'd do it all again in a heartbeat,' she said.

The reporter gazed at her for a moment, before turning his recorder off. 'Perfect,' he said, standing up, shaking the creases from his trousers. 'I think that's everything . . . Paul?' He spoke over his shoulder. 'Want to do the honours?'

As the photographer approached, Twyla

flicked her hair from her eyes, adjusted her jumper, sat up straight.

'When do you think the piece will be in the paper?' she asked the reporter.

'Hopefully next week.' He bent to pack up his bag. 'What made you change your mind about doing the article?'

'I'm not sure,' she said.

'Well, whatever it was, our *Herald* readers will be grateful. It's an interesting story.' He smiled at her. 'Thanks for telling it to us.'

He left her alone with the photographer, who was kneeling down, fiddling with a miniature tripod. She looked out of the window. There had been a frost this morning, yet the trees were beginning to flower for spring — governed by forces that were invisible, yet omnipotent.

Just like her.

When they were living at the old house, the *Herald* had asked her several times to do a follow-up article on Charlie Ross, but she refused. Yet on moving here, once everything had settled down, something had dawned on her. And when the *Herald* approached her again, she agreed. For she felt more at ease with her story now that she understood it.

This hadn't been about perfection, she had realised. Perfection was merely what had spilled out, like molten lava. At the core, hidden underneath, lay something far more powerful than her own needs or desires.

She had been ruled by her indomitable love for her child. And to condemn that was to condemn nature for its earthquakes and volcanoes.

'Are you ready?' the photographer asked.

She nodded, tried to smile.

'So how have you been?' she asked.

'Good,' he said. 'This is my last assignment at the *Herald* actually.' He led her to the French windows. 'How about over here with the plum trees in the background. A couple shots of you alone. And then maybe a couple with Charlie, if that's OK?'

'Your last assignment?' she said.

He nodded. 'I'm setting up my own business. My brother makes furniture so I'm starting off by doing the photography for his catalogue. And I'll go from there.'

'Cut-throat media not for you?' she said.

'Something like that. Now . . . ' He motioned for her to move to the left. 'If you could just . . . That's right . . . Great.'

He turned away to grab the tripod. His jacket was slung over a nearby chair. She glimpsed something sticking out of the pocket and reached over to pull it out. '*The Art of Acceptance?*' she said. 'Do you carry this everywhere with you?'

'Not really,' he said, colouring slightly. 'I brought it over for you.'

'Oh,' she said. She looked at the front cover. *How to be happy with your lot, without settling.* 'So did you ever find out what the secret was: the so-called art of acceptance?'

'Yep,' he said, squinting into his camera.

'And?'

'You'll have to read it to find out.'

'But how will I get it back to you if you're leaving the *Herald*?' she asked.

He shrugged. 'Keep it.'

'Oh,' she said.

'And my business card's inside the front cover,' he added.

★ ★ ★

Afterwards, when the reporter and the photographer had gone and *The Art of Acceptance* was lying on the coffee table; when the cottage was quiet and the sky was beginning to darken for nightfall, Twyla sat down to read a picture book with Charlie. Her father was doing a patient consultation by telephone in the study — his study, really. She could hear the rumble of his deep voice. It was comforting — a sound from childhood, like a forgotten radio theme tune.

'And the little boy looked up at the stars in the sky,' Twyla read.

Charlie was motionless in her arms, transfixed by his favourite story.

Before reading the final line, she paused to kiss the top of his head, feeling that insane, muddling, intoxicating swell of love wash over her as she did so.

'And he knew that tomorrow was going to be a beautiful day,' she said.

Charlie gave a little sigh of contentment.

And then she closed the book.

Acknowledgments

I would like to thank the following: Emma Beswetherick for her talented editing and for believing in me; the entire team at Piatkus Fiction for their hard work and support; John Carey, Brenda Corbett, Karis Southall and Anita Rowden for cheering me on; and Mum, Dad, Nick, Wilfie and Alex for all the love and understanding.

Author's note

It was several months after *Blind* was written that I first realised how much I had drawn upon personal experience to create Twyla's story. Sometimes — just like the characters in *Blind* — you are too close to something to see it.

When I was expecting my first child, my hopes were high. If we had a boy, we would name him after the poet Wilfred Owen. I pictured a soulful boy, someone with whom I would share hopes and dreams.

But pregnancy made me ill. At thirty-five weeks I was induced and Wilfred was born. He needed help breathing and was making odd growling noises, but was otherwise perfect. After ten days in hospital, we were allowed home.

At home, the growling intensified. Lying in my arms, Wilfred suddenly went white, red and then lifeless. We rushed him back to hospital where we were pushed aside by a flock of white coats. They didn't know what was wrong, but that it was serious.

That evening, petrified and on my knees in the children's ward bathroom, I prayed for my son's life.

Wilfie had an intestinal disease (necrotising enterocolitis), leading to septicaemia and meningitis. He responded well to the medication and was later transferred to intensive care, where for the next month he was starved in order to heal his bowel. Seeing Wilfie skeletal and covered in wires was grim, but one of the other babies had just had his leg amputated so we couldn't complain.

Six months on, Wilfie had convalesced and we took a breath of relief. But then we were told that his leg muscles were stiff (hypertonic) as a result of the meningitis, and that he might struggle to walk or run.

I remember the shock of this being worse than when he had fallen ill. Why that might be, I couldn't — and still can't — say.

Wilfie had intensive physiotherapy. His legs loosened. And he walked. And he ran.

But something began to happen to me as Wilfie grew. As he started school and sports activities, I felt terribly unhappy.

To the outside world, Wilfie was in great shape. He could walk and run. Moreover — he was alive!

Yet when he ran to me out of the school gates with his awkward gait and toppled over, I wanted to cry. At the toddler rugby class, when he struggled to keep up with the others, I wanted to sob.

If only his legs weren't stiff.

On the few occasions that I dared raise the subject, most people frowned blankly. It couldn't be that serious. Where was Wilfie's wheelchair, or leg braces? They looked at me as though I were making it up.

Then I read that having a child with a mild disability can be very distressing because the support and empathy just aren't there.

And then one day I noticed that somehow, softly, my sorrow and anger had slipped away.

Today Wilf still has physiotherapy and he wears leg casts at night, but I look at him differently. I don't see the intensive care baby. I don't see stiff legs.

I see a handsome strong boy called Wilfred, with whom I share hopes and dreams.

It took me a while to realise and acknowledge that Twyla was born of my own frustration and isolation during those early years.

But Twyla, like every woman worth her salt, had to tell it her way, in her own words.

Blind is her story.